Hell Is Naked

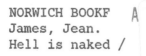

Jean James
and
Mary James

Hell Is Naked

Book designer Karen Polka

Inquiries should be addressed to:
Woodrock House
13097 Hwy. 45 N.
Finger, TN 38334
ISBN- 978-0-9848605-6-2
Printed in the United States of America

We would like to express
our appreciation to

Robert James
Karen Polka

Other Books:

Sparrow Alone on the Housetop

God Knew There Would Be a Today

Wherefore Art Thou, Jane?
*(Readers Favorite International Awards-
First place mystery)*

Methinks I See Thee, Jane

Sea Red, Sea Blue

Hell is naked before him,
and destruction hath no covering.
Job 26:6

Chapter 1

A friend once told me a woman would run naked into the street to save her baby, but a man would stop to put on his pants first. I didn't buy it—until now.

For ten minutes, I had watched this gal, dressed somewhat like an alien kangaroo, bounce giddily across the floor in front of two cameras, a production crew, and a few hundred paid extras. If she forced herself to such extremes for the insignificant pay she earned, no doubt she would march through hell without hesitation if some important matter faced her. No way could I expose myself to such embarrassment, not for fifty dollars, not for a million. When I undertook this job, I never imagined it would lead me to a crowded movie set where I would attempt to behave like an experienced extra. All day I had tried to melt into the masses, but six-foot-six of quaking flesh didn't conceal easily.

No need to look again at the picture in my inner jacket pocket to know for sure I had found my missing girl. I located her three friends too, all altered versions of the pictures I carried, but after a few mental adjustments, I could see they matched. My third day of humiliation and the job neared completion. If she would give me her address, I could leave this land of shorter people and go back to Chicago, but until that happened, fear would reign.

No one who had witnessed my terrorized bearing the past few days would have seen in me a police officer of twenty years, nine of them SWAT—a man trained to intimidate. Some high-risk, tactical, counter sniper, search and rescue, undercover operation involving weapons of mass destruction would feel cozy next to the present situation. Sadly, I left those days behind me two years ago when I turned forty-two, not because forty-two disqualifies one for police work, but because I relentlessly abused my body for too long, and it insisted on a break. Even when I politely asked it to perform some strenuous task, it answered back sarcastically or utterly refused.

Now I had to be satisfied with any job my detective friend, Bob Caine, threw my way. Today I found a missing person for him; tomorrow I might perform boring security work for a big corporation. My wallet approved of the work, it paid better than retirement, but I missed the action.

No feeling of satisfaction accompanied this newest conquest. I guess I could call it a noble cause, a father paying a detective to locate his too-long-gone grown daughter, but a twenty-nine-year-old runaway was pushing it a little far. Evidently, remorse or love or some other redeeming reason drove him to find her. Heck, the man had money, so motives didn't count. The girl probably got too busy living her life and forgot about Mom and Dad the last time she changed her address. I couldn't explain the changed identity. She and her three friends in no way resembled the pictures Bob had given me, but maybe that was just Hollywood and the movie industry. The client had insisted on haste since the girl's mother suffered health problems. Bob and I both knew that a client often buried the truth under a pile of lies, but it was a job.

"You haven't done this kind of work before, have you?" my missing person said as she stopped at the clothes rack that I gripped for moral support.

I liked the laughter in her green eyes and the friendly smile on her perky face. I hadn't expected it to be this easy. They never, ever, came to me.

"My third day. Someone told me I could earn a quick paycheck this way. I believe I'd rather starve."

"It must not have been that bad."

Either my acting had improved or else she was used to liars. While I tried to think of something witty to say, a real girl, dressed in white shorts and a California suntan, stepped out of that ridiculous costume and smiled at me again.

"You survived the first two days and came back for more punishment."

"I barely survived. I hid in the bathroom most of the time."

"You're the one who shouted after they signaled for silence, aren't you?"

"Yep. I'd finally grasped that extras were supposed to shout, and then everyone shut up. . . . I was the one who left their cell phone on during that bedroom scene too."

"Stay with me, and I'll steer you through the rest of the day. Extras return to holding now. We'll have time to get something to eat at craft services."

"Not me. They ran me off—rudely."

"We can't prevent the rudeness. It thrives here. But you are allowed to eat. Take all you want—I'll protect you."

With her confident backing, I headed for the table I had eyed all morning. She immediately grabbed my arm.

"Wrong table. That's for crew and SAG actors—members of the Screen Actors Guild. Our table's over here."

"But their table has meat . . . and candy bars."

"Ours isn't so bad." She led me through the milling crowds. "Hurry, before all the good stuff disappears."

Now I felt much wiser and understood why I went hungry my first two days. I wondered why she didn't use the SAG table. According to Bob, she joined SAG when she turned eighteen and had worked at such ever since. That added up to eleven years of extra work, and that was why he believed she would still be here, even though her father thought she had changed her name and moved away. Bob knew people and knew I was strong on identifying them, so he sent me to where I should find her.

He told me I would be hitting a slow season of filming and could look at most of the full-time LA extras in two weeks if I registered for extra work—the only sure way to get on the film and TV sets where extras worked. That part proved relatively painless. I flew to LA, rented a cheap car, and drove straight to the large casting agency he had recommended. I filled out a few papers and used my own information except for a fictitious LA address. The agency took my picture—unflattering. It made me look like I had accumulated excess poundage. When I suggested they try again and use a different camera angle, they just stared at me and sent me on to a person who finished the registration process.

Another efficient person gave me phone numbers to call for upcoming extra jobs, and before the end of the day I had a comfortable motel room and a booking for a shoot on the morrow—a TV show. I had brought only one suitcase. Luckily, I found clothes in it that met their specifications.

There followed two terrifying days where I made every mistake imaginable and didn't find anyone who even remotely matched my pictures—not even when I snooped around on other nearby shoots. I did see repeats of many faces, though. Today ranked as mega terrifying, but I had found the prize, and Bob's hunch had been a good one. His shrewdness rarely made a mistake.

"I'm SAG," she volunteered as we pillaged the correct table, "but I'm working nonunion today. Most everyone here is nonunion, so you don't need to feel uncomfortable."

I wasn't uncomfortable—now. I held food in my hands and had filled my pants and jacket pockets with bags of chips and canned drinks. She laughed at my pile of food, a good laugh, low, with a warm, happy sound to it. While she fixed herself a cup of hot chocolate, I studied her more closely. Her face had a childlike innocence that made her seem younger than twenty-nine. My picture showed her with long, straight, red hair, but today she wore short, light-brown curls. They looked like they belonged. Her height matched the five-foot-eight figure her father had supplied, but where he had described her as thin—I would have called her about perfect, with a straighter, more muscular body that most of those around us.

"Come on. There's room at that table over there."

I followed dutifully and noted the voucher in her hip pocket. Her name, or the name she used now, should be on that slip of paper. Bob said her actual name was Lorraine Wray—Rainy Wray with the actor's union. I would have to play helpless, something I excelled at lately.

"Do you have a minute to help me with my paperwork? I've done it wrong both days. . . . Maybe I could copy yours."

She hesitated while a look of uncertainty passed over her face.

It lasted only a second.

"Your voucher? Yes, you have to fill it out correctly if you expect pay, but you can't copy mine, or they'd send me your check." A glib smile followed. "You can use it as a model, though." She handed it to me and glanced over at a dark-skinned girl in jeans who had motioned to her. "I'll be back in a minute. Holler if you need help."

There it was, Rainy Wray, along with driver's license number, address, and everything else. The address was a post office box, so more work awaited me. When she turned her back to me, I copied her info, stuffed it away in my pocket, and filled out my own voucher. Meanwhile, the two women drifted closer, and I caught the end of their conversation.

"You did right. Forget what your father said. He loves you and thinks he's helping. You'll find work, and if you need help, call me. You have my new cell phone number."

She hugged the girl goodbye and headed my way. I hadn't meant to eavesdrop, so I turned away, but Rainy read the guilt on my face.

"This business is hard," she said and sat down beside me. "It's especially tough for those who still own a conscience or morals. They come out here with dreams of stardom, but soon they can't pay their rent or afford food, and they can't find any jobs on the casting lines. While they desperately look for a way to survive, new jobs come on the lines that call for partial nudity or full nudity or simulated sex or poll dancers or . . . or something of that sort. Those jobs usually offer five times as much pay as regular extra jobs or more at times. That's the point where many of them compromise."

"Was her father telling her to give it up and come back home?"

"Her father lives out here too and works in this industry. He reprimanded her for being prudish and for not taking a naked job. He asked her how else she expected to earn her rent money or get anywhere."

"Dear old Dad. . . . Do you run into that same problem, or is it strictly a nonunion matter?"

"It's much worse with union work. It seems like eighty or ninety percent of female, union jobs have to do with sex or exposing the body. It's rather discouraging."

She checked my voucher to see if I filled it out correctly.

"That's a nice area. Rent must be high. Or do you own?"

Now I had to act. "It's a friend's address that I borrowed while I find a new place. You know, not enough work, too many truck repairs, and it still doesn't run. It's back in the shop waiting on parts I can't afford."

"I've been there a few times. It doesn't matter what your vehicle needs, a fan belt or a new radiator hose, the bill always starts at $600. Car repairs and rent are the two killers around here. That's why I share a . . . a place with other extras, those three over there." She pointed in the direction of the three friends I had already identified. "Cost of living runs high in LA. . . . If your truck's broken, how'd you get here today?"

"A rental. I'll keep it till I land a check or two. Don't want to kill my credit card or take a job as a poll dancer."

She didn't laugh but instead appeared thoughtful.

"What's your regular occupation? You're not trying to break into the movies."

She said it with complete certainty, and that hurt my feelings. Now I had to jump into the part Bob had prepared for me.

"A carpenter for Frye Construction, but they haven't had any startups lately, and I couldn't find anything else. Someone I once thought of as a friend put me onto this extra work. I figured I could stand it until something else came along or Frye started a new job. Now I know I can't."

She looked down at my voucher. "Well, Warren Roberts, time to go back to work. The second AD just called for all background."

"Second AD? Background?"

"You are new at this, aren't you? The second assistant director wants all the background actors—extras—to come at once."

"Your name's Rainy?"

Silence reigned for almost a minute while she studied me with intense, clear eyes.

"Call me Karen, Karen Sharpe—or nothing," she said, almost in a whisper. "That's my name on this shoot's list of extras, but I still have to fill out and sign the voucher in my own name. It's complicated but . . . a temporary problem. Ordinarily I get the voucher signed with no trouble because they don't pay much attention on these big shoots."

"Oh." I was burning to ask more but knew enough to keep my mouth shut. Either I had just passed her scrutiny test, or this girl's trusting nature had no limits.

"We're supposed to fill those bleachers. Let's sit up at the top since you're tall. They'd probably put you there anyway."

When we passed by the craft service's table, I grabbed another cola and stuffed some more fodder into my bulging pockets. This strange, extra work had suddenly changed its demeanor, and I didn't mind it anymore. I could sit back with this easy-to-look-at, easy-to-talk-with, unpretentious woman and eat. I wondered how she could act so warm and trusting if she had worked for eleven years around this unholy mob of humanity. My police acquaintances weren't exactly a mild bunch, and in my line of work I had heard just about everything or at least thought I had, but some of the conversations I overheard the last three days genuinely shocked me.

I also noticed how Rainy drew people to her, even while trying to go incognito. I hoped she wanted her parents to find her. The father paid Bob a hefty sum to locate her, and I would get a good portion of it. Still, I couldn't help but wonder what kind of change I might bring into her life. Was she in some kind of trouble?

Later, during a bathroom break, I called Bob and left a message that I had found the girl and her friends. I gave him her new name and told him I might have to follow her home to get her address. When I returned to the bleachers, she was trying to line up a job for the next day.

"Thank you, anyway." She soberly put her phone away. "So far I've found no big shoots for tomorrow except one that's already filled."

"Don't the small ones pay as well?"

"They do, but I've worked around here a long time and most everyone knows me. I'd prefer anonymity, and it's easier to keep your distance in a crowd like this one. If it weren't for the others, I'd move away for a while."

"You mean your three friends?" They had moved closer and now sent furtive glances her way.

"Yes, they depend on me. I'm Mother Hen. We have only two cars between us and one's mine. Luckily, I managed to get us all on the same shoot today."

One of her friends motioned for her to come over. I knew they didn't want me to hear, so I held my phone at my ear to give a preoccupied appearance and listened closely.

"Rainy, for heaven's sake don't make new friends or help anyone—please. Do you know that man?" the girl said in a high voice that carried in spite of its softness.

"Don't worry about him, Tia. The poor fellow doesn't know what to do. He's botched things all day, and they were about to send him home. That's why I scraped his acquaintance. And he needs the money . . ."

Botched things? I didn't think I did that horribly. Was that the only reason she came to me—not because of my charm or good looks? Her words shook me up so much I missed part of what they said. At least they talked in normal tones now.

"Rainy, they just put that job on the line, the one we wanted. Tim and I booked it, and Grady's talking to them now. Do you want him to pass the phone to you when he's through?"

"Yes, and I want to get Warren on the shoot too." She turned my way and motioned me to come over. "Warren, you haven't booked tomorrow yet, have you?"

"No, I . . ."

I didn't get a chance to say more. She took the phone and gave the casting agent her social security number. Before I realized what was happening, she had booked the shoot and had told the agent they had one more person to go. I reached for the phone like for a poisonous snake, but managed to stumble through the requirements and get booked.

"Great, Warren. Now all of us can work tomorrow. Any special wardrobe required, Tia?"

"Any shade of green, orange, or brown—casual. And tennis shoes."

"Warren, meet my friends—Tia, her brother Tim, and Grady here, who just turned twenty four but can book as a teenager. His youthful appearance gets him more work than any of us get. And please don't call us by name. We have all become someone else for a while."

"Is that a normal practice in this business?"

I saw right away that her friends strongly disapproved of her openness with a stranger. Three sets of suspicious eyes glared at me. They had fallen into some kind of trouble, all right.

"Not normal and not long-term, we hope."

"Don't worry. I'm not a blabbermouth—Karen."

I wanted them to know I could keep a secret. Tim and Tia still looked at me like they wished I would disappear. They were both about Rainy's age and both on the slim side, an unhealthy sort of slim. I got the impression that their arms barely held up their hands and that they had never heard of the word posture. In spite of that, Tia was decidedly cute. The Tia in my picture had medium-length blond hair. This Tia had the same length hair, dark brown, and arranged differently. Tim possessed a nice face too, which looked better in the picture where he sported hair. His new bald look didn't go well with his face, and the earring in his left ear didn't help.

Grady, the shortest one of the group, no longer seemed bothered by my presence. A couple of female extras who chatted nearby had caught his attention. He was thin but looked wiry. Neither his thick mat of black hair nor his black, bushy eyebrows grew there naturally. Still I might have been fooled if I hadn't seen his before picture of light brown hair tied back in a ponytail.

Bob said I would receive a bonus if I located the three friends and got information on them. I guessed the father anticipated loosing Rainy again and wanted contacts so he wouldn't have to pay a detective agency next time. I felt rather pleased with myself, but the second AD came and ruined it.

"All extras, between row eight and the top of the bleachers, come down. You'll do crosses in this next scene."

I had just enough experience with crosses to want to find the bathroom again, but this time they had caught me.

"Everyone gather round. You'll line up here. When I nudge you, walk around the camera and cut as close as you can to this screen. When the first team comes out, I'll show you whether to cut in front of them or behind them. Normal walking speed everyone.

When you reach the other side, keep walking until you're out of camera range. Then get back here and be ready to go again. We need constant movement, so don't dawdle."

Somehow I had lost Rainy and had been placed third in the line. I didn't know what first team meant, where I was to walk, or when I would be out of camera range. He shoved the first extra off, and the guy had to lean half over to get around the screen and not bump the camera. I didn't think I would fit. I watched the second person and knew I wouldn't fit.

I had reached a sad state of wretchedness when he shoved me off to never-never land. He actually pulled the screen back a few inches to help me get through. I turned to nod my thanks, and the coke can in my pocket grazed a piece of equipment. It made an embarrassingly audible clunk. Blindly, I kept moving. Directly in front of me, two people walked past. I didn't know where to go. Finally, I dove between them and heard a loud, exasperated cut. I had heard that tone before.

"Who sent King Kong in there? He's half a foot taller than Vince, and he almost trampled Marti. Lose him quick. Reset the scene."

I didn't turn around and go back, but walked until I guessed I had left the reach of the camera. From my new, distant location, I heard them call action, and I dared to turn and look. I then realized that I had cut between the two stars of the film. How could I know that? I had never seen them before, and it wasn't my fault that I was taller than the hero. I sat down behind a building and drank my three cans of soda and ate all my chips, pretzels, and peanut butter crackers to console myself. That's where Rainy found me thirty minutes later.

"I'm sorry, Warren. Don't let it bother you. It happens all the time on set."

"Yeah, but not always with the same person."

She laughed, long and hard.

"Really, Warren," she said, still unable to conquer her mirth, "it was the second AD's fault. He shouldn't have sent out someone taller than the male star."

When she saw my pile of empty cans and bags, she laughed again.

"A soda can! I wondered what banged . . ."

"You deserted me," I accused before she could remind me again of my latest blunder.

"But I'm here now." She smiled innocently.

Chapter 2

She stood beside me like something real in the middle of an artificial world and graciously steered me through the rest of the day. In return, I carried her satchel and garment bag to her car. That worked for someone like me, deficient of verbal dexterity around the opposite sex. I could show my appreciation and finish my job at the same time. Her three friends got into a van parked next door to her car. That gave me two vehicles to follow in case I lost one. I memorized both license plates.

"Warren, I forgot to ask if you have wardrobe for tomorrow. Those pants will work, but you'll need a brown, green, or orange shirt and tennis shoes."

"I'll pick up a shirt and shoes at the store," I said too quickly and not at all like a poor, jobless person.

"You'll never raise money for your truck's repair at that rate. Extra work doesn't pay like carpenter work. We may have something at our place that you can use if you don't mind driving to Long Beach. Our little group of extras used to number five, but one . . . had an accident a short while back. He was tall, but thin. You might fit some of his clothes, and you're welcome to anything you can use. Extra work requires an ample wardrobe. Most males don't have enough variety to fit the different jobs. If his clothes don't work, there are thrift stores nearby."

"A fatal accident?" The cop inside me couldn't help but ask.

"Totally. He fell off a cliff at a shoot."

"Understandable. I contemplated jumping off a cliff all three days. . . . Sorry, didn't mean to sound irreverent."

"We didn't know what to do with his stuff. Why don't you follow me to our place and see if anything fits?"

She had said the magic words that simplified the last portion of my job. I hurried to my rental and parked it beside her car while she arranged her trunk.

"How can you afford a place to stay and a rental car too? Or do you live in it?"

She had asked matter-of-factly, as if she saw no shame in being homeless and sleeping in your auto. I decided to investigate the limits of her sympathy to see where more lies might take me. Bob wanted information on the friends, and she might furnish an opportunity. I checked out of my motel that morning, so my suitcase on the backseat gave credence to my poverty.

"I had a room last night but figured the car would do for tonight. I'm not strapped yet, but I'm not sure I can keep on with this extra work."

"Considering your size, I think it would be impossible."

"You mean they don't want big extras?"

"Big extras? I mean you'd have to bend your legs double to sleep in that car."

"Oh, the front seat tips back. And car rentals come cheaper over the internet."

"Warren, why not stay with us for a few nights? Don't consider it charity. We live in less than a barn, and it sits in less than a barnyard, but there's an empty, uncomfortable sofa available. The others will resent it, but you can ignore them. They don't trust anyone right now. I paid for this temporary abode, so they can't say anything."

I couldn't believe this woman's trusting nature. She hardly knew me yet had taken me under her wing—a possible rapist, murderer, or both. I wondered how she had survived her years out here. Maybe my face looked honest, even if I didn't look like I belonged in movies. But still—this was a strange woman.

"I'll stay tonight if you let me pay."

"No pay. Save your money to get your truck out of hock. And why not take back your rental car? You can ride with me for a few days and save a little more. We could return it right now. Even fifteen or twenty dollars a day can add up."

My mouth must have hung open for at least a minute. At forty-two dollars a day, I thought I had negotiated a good deal. I amiably submitted to her suggestion and let her follow me to the rental office. Upon completion of my assignment, I could call a taxi to take me to the airport. It felt strange to leave the rental place with no wheels and at the mercy of this determined woman, but I saw a few nice things about it too.

On the ride back, I tried to get her to talk about herself. If she asked me any more questions, I would for sure give myself away. I knew nothing about the LA area, and I had seriously depleted my store of memorized lies.

"I take it you've worked around the movie scene for a while."

"Eleven years now."

"Can you make a living at it, or do you supplement it with other jobs?

"I've never worked another job. I don't get rich, but I survive. Where else could I work at a new job on a new set in a new location almost every day? Of course, there's always a chance to land a speaking role, which lends more excitement to it."

"Have you done any speaking rolls?"

"Small parts in TV shows and SAG experimental films that never went anywhere. Soon I plan to produce my own movies and documentaries. I've learned a great deal in the years I've worked here."

"Considering how you feel about the morals of the industry, it surprises me you stayed with it."

"Sometimes it surprises me too, but I think the moral issues actually attract me. Every day new people arrive, some of them come with wide-open eyes and wide-open morals. They step right into the raunchier side of the industry and have no qualms about it. However, many newcomers are decent and some are totally naïve. Those people generally meet that crossroads of compromise before they half unpack. It's funny, you know, because I don't go out and look for people in distress, but somehow they find me. Rarely a day goes by when I don't get a chance to do something worthwhile."

"Thank you for making Warren Roberts your worthwhile

project of the day."

"You looked so utterly helpless."

"One more insult would have blown me away."

"I doubt that. You look too big and solid to blow away that easily. I guess construction work does that."

Wow! She said solid, not fat. My ego must have swelled visibly. I felt like saying, Try four hundred pushups a day, lady, and a ten-mile run. Instead, I opted for something that sounded less cop-like.

"Yeah, I guess moving all that plywood and lumber will do it, all right."

We abruptly arrived at our destination, which stifled further opportunities to sound stupid. We followed a weedy drive around behind a shabby house. The yard, enclosed by a scraggily, overgrown hedge, echoed the look of the entire neighborhood. I carried Rainy's tote and my suitcase into what looked like a freestanding garage behind the house.

Someone had cheaply divided the building into three rooms and partitioned off a small alcove that pretended to be a bathroom. The bare, oil-spotted concrete floor confirmed that it was a garage on the inside too. The garage door, apparently jimmied shut, had no windows. I saw a couple of windows through the open doorways of the two back rooms, but the main room's only window was the upper glass of its entry door. They evidently came in desperation and hadn't resided here long. There were stacks of unpacked boxes and almost no furniture, but I did find the old sofa Rainy mentioned.

"You see now why you can't pay? We lived in a nice apartment not long ago. Circumstances put us here. It's only slightly better than sleeping in a car, but at least you can stand upright to change clothes and there is a bathroom of sorts. . . . I've got to run to the store for a second and get some cat food. I adopted this adorable stray. He was almost starved to death when I found him, but I'm bringing him back to life. He's a voracious eater. If the others come before I get back, don't let them bother you. I'll call them right now and warn them you're here."

Panic hit me for a second when she drove out the drive. She had escaped, and I wouldn't find her again. When I saw her tote lying on the table, I relaxed somewhat. I made a quick walk to the street and jotted down the house number. The house looked empty. Maybe its occupants were at work and kept everything closed up tight because of the neighborhood. I called Bob with the address as I headed back.

With nothing else to do, I checked out Rainy's new, temporary home and wondered what mystery now enveloped their lives. My investigation of the first bedroom showed more unpacked boxes and a pile of sports equipment—probably for the extra work. There were ski suits, wet suits, rollerblades, surfboards, baseball bats, golf bags, basketballs, skateboards, even a bicycle. Bedroom two also contained boxes and a stack of pictures on top of one. I leafed through them and found a snapshot of extra number five who had gone off the cliff. He smiled at me and held what looked like a small movie camera. An actual camera, matching the one in the picture, sat on a nearby box. That box probably contained what remained of his personal effects.

Before I had finished my study of the camera, Bob called back.

"Warren, her dad wants you to get the names of her friends, the names they use now if they're different from the names I gave you. He said he'd feel better if he had the additional information in case his daughter ever disappeared again. Since you said they all live at the same address, those names will complete our assignment. The father booked a flight and said he'd be at her place before morning. He'll stop by my office and drop off the check on route to the airport, so try to get me that information right away if you can. Oh, and he's paying extra for you to stay there until he arrives."

I grumbled but agreed.

"Bob, it would be better if you didn't call me again tonight," I suggested when Rainy drove in with the van in her wake. "I'll call you if I get the names, and I'll let you know when Daddy arrives. Expect me back tomorrow."

The father wouldn't get the other's new names from me, extra pay or not. Let him ask them himself if he felt it mattered. The situation felt uncomfortable. If Rainy's life had taken a serious blow, her father would have to mend it. I hoped he possessed the capabilities. Maybe they all faced real trouble, or maybe they had fallen victim to their own over-active imaginations from working in the imagination industry too long. Disguises and changed names sounded rather theatrical, but when I looked around their new premises, something didn't jell. They might be actors, but their fear rang true, and no one could enjoy living in this hole.

I rose lazily from the dilapidated couch to meet three suspicious faces and one apologetic one. She gave no one a chance to say anything but immediately motioned to me.

"Come in here, Warren. You need wardrobe for tomorrow. Let's see if Calvin's shirts or shoes fit you."

I took off my jacket and shoes and put them neatly on my suitcase by the sofa—my claim to that piece of furniture regardless of hostilities. In the bedroom, she dug through Calvin's box and came out with a green shirt, a light brown one, and a pair of tennis shoes.

"See if any of these fit. It doesn't bother you, does it, that he's . . ."

"Not at all."

A wayward part of me wanted to say, "Of course not. We construction workers deal in death every day."

"Cal was a nice person—so ambitious to produce his own independent movie. He took his camera everywhere, always with the hope he'd get some useable footage. He cast all of us in his movie, and it was almost finished. His dream died with him."

"Was it . . . a good film?" I asked in an attempt to make conversation about something I knew nothing about.

"Mediocre. It probably wouldn't have helped him or us. But he should have had his chance."

"Death happens."

"Sometimes it doesn't have to. . . . Sometimes it's helped to happen."

"You mean murder?" I mentally kicked myself for acting like a cop. "You think his movie threatened someone?" Guess I should have kicked myself harder.

"Not the movie itself, but we all witnessed something, all five of us, in an offhand sort of way. We feared that someone knew about it. We hoped not, but . . . but two days later Cal falls off a cliff."

When Tia called Rainy to the other room, my thought processes jumped into high gear. Rainy's information set off an alarm in my cop brain that wouldn't stop ringing. Was I as loco as these four? I couldn't stop the flood of questions that poured over me. Had Bob seen his client in person or just made telephone contact? The father could have emailed the pictures. There must have been a deposit made, but Bob hadn't mentioned it. In either case, Bob wouldn't have any reason to be suspicious of a father looking for his daughter. Now the man was on his way to Bob's office with a check, probably for the balance. It sounded normal, but I needed to call Bob and see how much he knew for sure about the situation. I needed a description of his client, and I needed Rainy to show me a picture of her dad.

The tennis shoes would never work—much too narrow. I bent double in an effort to pull one on, but failed.

"Rainy, the brown shirt works, the shoes don't."

I was close to losing my balance, half in the shoe and half out, when I glimpsed a long object heading for my skull and . . .

When I regained consciousness, a pale light shining through the window told me that only the dregs of daylight still lingered. Other than lying prone on the floor, I hadn't moved far from my original position. Everyone else had, though. I couldn't have been out long, but it was long enough for all four of them to disappear, along with most of their belongings. A few items remained, but the boxes had all disappeared. A baseball bat lay on the floor beside me, and I guessed that object had collided with my skull. Someone had tied my ankles, legs, and wrists poorly but thoroughly.

If my hunch proved correct, sometime before morning a person I didn't want to meet would show up here. This person wouldn't use a baseball bat and would never take time to tie a victim. I studied my immediate situation. The lump on my head didn't require my touch to confirm its presence. The comfortable lump on my calf, my thirty-eight, had been missed in their hurry to tie me. My bindings looked like shoelaces and a robe belt, four separate knots and none within reach of my fingers or teeth.

A simple assignment like this one usually doesn't have a potential for violence, so I hadn't come heavily equipped or armed on this trip. However, force of habit always kept me moderately ready for anything. The knife and Glock in my suitcase would have served me well if my suitcase hadn't disappeared. They must have taken it with them. That left the penknife in my shirt and the razor blade in my boot. The penknife would be the most accessible, so I rolled across the floor to where my shirt lay in a heap. Using my teeth and finally my fingers, I accomplished freedom in less than five minutes.

It took only a minute to scramble into my boots and jacket. I watched out the window of the only working door while I checked to see what Rainy and her friends had left me. They had taken the pictures from my jacket pocket. That confirmed my suspicions about my bruised head and their quick exit. My pants pockets no longer housed a wallet or cell phone. A few coins clunked in the depths of one. I couldn't call a taxi, and I couldn't pay for it if I did locate one.

All at once, my inner alarm went off again, either from instinct or from some tiny bit of tangible evidence. Had my eyes caught a glimpse of something that didn't belong, or had the sudden stillness spooked me? I was barely ready when visitors entered through the hedge—four of them. They were easily identifiable as gang members, a white gang, and not the professional hit man I had expected. It didn't really matter. These louts understood the words ruthless and deadly, and it took just five seconds of observation to convince me they knew their business. Someone had arranged a low profile hit and an effective one in most cases.

I ran to the back window on the off side of the building, broke out its glass thoroughly, and rushed back to the main room. It took two more seconds to push the sofa out a ways from the wall and squeeze behind it. In the total silence, my thirty-eight and I waited. At least Rainy and her friends had left me something for defense. The gang fell for the bait. When they burst through the door and saw the broken window, they rushed back out and around the garage to see where their victims had fled. I ran back to the door and located two more members outside. Naturally there would be more—there were five of us to kill.

For a long minute I held back and watched for more trouble to materialize. The two showed signs that they would soon bolt from their waiting posture and follow the rest. That would be my chance to vacate. I had already gripped the doorknob when their attention turned elsewhere. A familiar car coasted into the drive. The two latecomers slunk back under the hedge, not twenty feet from me, and I now saw the Uzi hidden at the one's side. I watched Rainy, and they did too. That intense quietness had returned. She had no idea anyone was here, that is, anyone besides comatose, tied Warren Roberts.

She got out of the car, and her gentle call, "Kitty," barely reached me. She had drawn close to the two in the bushes when a long, gaunt, gray flash bounded toward her. She stooped and gathered it into her arms, hugging it close. The two in the bushes hesitated. Her boldness had made them unsure whether she was one of their intended victims. Now they knew, but their hesitation had cost them the prize. My piece spoke three times as I dove out the door. I literally dragged Rainy and cat toward the garage. The other four had circled back. Two came around the building behind us and two crossed between her car and us. She fought me, unsure who to befriend.

"Rainy, these guys came to kill you. I didn't," I hollered in her ear.

When we entered the garage, I literally threw her behind the sofa. At once, the first two bolted through the door. With no time for anything fancy, I fired while plunging left to keep Rainy out of return fire. The shell didn't do any damage, and I lost my thirty-eight to a club I hadn't seen. While I grappled with the one on the left, the one with the piece tried to get off a killing shot without harm to his buddy.

My piece still lay out of reach, but my steel toed lace-ups had substituted for a weapon more than once in my line of work. A boot to the side of his head took out the one fumbling with his gun even as I fell to the floor with the other one straddling me. I installed my fist in his open mouth, painful for both of us, and scrambled to my feet while he lay stunned. Rainy ran toward us with the baseball bat.

I thought I would be pounded on the head again, but she went to work on the one I had sent sprawling with my boot. She didn't see his knife, and I leaped ten feet to get between them. I took out the knife as I landed on him and banged his head hard against the concrete floor three times before he went limp.

With Rainy's bat, I swung hard at the other one's neck before he reached us. A second swing eliminated him and cracked the bat. My gun rested firmly back in my hand when the last two came through the door. I fired as I dove into their fire and brought them both down with my bulk. A hit stung me, but there was no time to baby myself—not if I intended to stay alive. My left hand took away the one's gun while my right squeezed off a round directly into the other man's knee as it crushed down on my windpipe. That caused him to give up his gun too. When Rainy rushed back brandishing a golf club, I borrowed it from her. I never cared for golf, but it had a nice feel to it, and I did my best.

I risked a second or two to search the pockets of the one who led the first charge. I found the pictures, identical to mine, of Rainy and her three friends. That proof seemed unnecessary at this point, and Cal's death wasn't an accident or his picture would have been there too. I kept the pictures and with the course temporarily clear, we dashed for the door. The cat ran out ahead of us and disappeared under the hedge. At once I noticed the empty spot that should still be occupied by the two I shot earlier. That was bad news. The worst news was that they had fled in Rainy's car. She conveniently left the door wide open and the key in the ignition. That meant one of them, for sure, stayed alive and now drove the car. He would know where to find more friends.

Rainy started to run after the cat, but I pulled her with me down an alley.

"Not now, Rainy. There'll be more."

"I don't want more. I want that cat."

"I meant there'll be more of them coming—with guns and knives. I don't know my way around here. Point me in the direction of some populated area, preferably upper-middle class."

"I don't know this area well either. We've only lived here a couple of days. If we head that way, we'll hit the beach. I know my way around there. You're bleeding . . . and limping."

"My head hurts too."

We must have gone miles when we saw a bus. I guessed that Rainy probably put my wallet in her purse, but since she carried no purse, that wouldn't help. Her purse would be in her car—wherever that was now. The change in my pocket wouldn't buy us a ride. Rainy must have had the same thought because she pointed at the leaving bus.

"We're not far from the Passport Shuttle's line. It's free. We can take it partway."

Four more blocks took us to one of the Passport's stops where we finally rode. I had hardly gotten comfortable when Rainy signaled it was time to leave the bus.

"After Atlantic it's not free anymore. I know a reasonably safe place about three miles from here—Alamitos Bay, across from Naples Island. I used to swim there."

My leg immediately complained about the distance, but it still carried me to the bay at the far end of Long Beach. Darkness had set in, but there were a few scattered lights at the beach. We found a rise of sand near the water's edge, and I plopped down behind it. It felt good to stretch out and be immobile for a minute. It felt good to be alive.

"There's enough light here to check your wounds, Warren."

"Just the one in my side."

Rainy knelt above me and undid my shirt. A sharp pain directly below my rib cage told me when she found the spot.

"The bullet cut through an inch of your flesh, directly above your belt. I can see where it went in and came out."

"If I hadn't put on thirty pounds of extra padding it might have missed me altogether."

"Or you might have been too light to knock them both down when you plowed into them."

"Thanks for the excuse. I do like to eat."

"Wait here. There's a restroom over there. They may not have locked it for the night yet."

"I can walk, Rainy. This injury is nothing. My knuckles hurt worse—and my leg."

"Did they shoot you in the leg?"

"Just an old injury, the one that retired me from SWAT. It hurts all the time, but worse when I work it like I did a while ago."

"SWAT? Not a carpenter then."

Her droll speech and comical expression left me uncertain.

She took my shirt and tee shirt in to wash the blood from them. After fifteen minutes I grew worried.

"You still in there?"

"I'm drying your shirts on the hand dryer. They're almost done. I have some tissue to put on your wound but nothing to hold it in place."

"A city vehicle pulled up, Rainy. Let's go. Time to lock up I guess."

With possible gang members on the lookout for us, we couldn't safely move about. We slid into the darkness and circled back to our sand mound. I pressed the tissue hard against the wound, pulled on my tee shirt, and tucked it under my belt. After a quick study of all the nearby shadows, I decided our spot would do for a while. We both leaned back against our sand mound like a couple of moon bathers.

"I sure need my suitcase, wallet, and phone right now. I guess you put them in your car, right?"

"The others have them. We thought they'd show us who hired you to kill us."

"I hope you realize now that I wasn't hired to kill anyone. I'm an ex-cop doing a job for a detective agency. I'm supposed to locate a missing daughter, Loraine Wray, for an anxious dad and mom. Do you have parents in Chicago?"

"Ohio. I call them almost every day. They're never anxious."

"Is your mother in frail health?"

"Perfectly healthy. Dad has rheumatism. He still farms though."

"Whoever is behind this must have some kind of clout with that gang. It could be strictly a money arrangement, but I'm guessing he knew someone and knew how to contact them. I recognized the tattoos on the one who carried the pictures. He belongs to a gang out here called the Nivs. They're not a large or well known gang, but they do have a small branch in Chicago, and that could have some bearing on why this new father of yours chose a detective agency in Chicago. On the other hand, maybe the detective agency's location didn't matter as long as it wasn't from around here. I take it you've offended someone?"

"Must have. . . . So not only are you not a carpenter, you're not from this area either?"

"Never been in California."

"And you don't have a truck in a repair shop?"

"Yes, I do. I left mine to get four new tires and a front-end alignment while I flew out here for this job. And I told the truth when I said I'd never done extra work before."

"I didn't need your enlightenment about that. Do you . . . have a family back in Chicago?"

"No family. My wife died nine years ago, no children, and my parents retired to Florida last year. Enough about me. If I'm to help, I need to know more about you and this situation. After that, we should go directly to the police."

"That might not work well for you. I told the others to give me an hour to find my cat before they reported you to the police as the person who murdered Cal and who attempted to murder us. We figured they'd go to the house, find you tied up, and take you off our hands for a while, at least long enough for us to find a new place to hide."

"You really expected me to stay tied long enough to be caught by the police?"

"I thought we tied you rather well."

"Well, now you have anyway. If your friends have reported me, that ties my hands about getting any quick police help, especially since I have no credentials. I don't even have a cell phone to call my agency and have them identify me to the police. And I'm hungry. I haven't had anything to eat since craft services. Pretzels don't stay with you forever."

"I'm sorry. I did have some money. You can use my cell phone anyway."

"Wasn't it in your car?"

"It's in my pocket. Extras put on their phones before they put on their shoes. We can call to our heart's content. I probably should report my car stolen, but there won't be anything left in it when they recover it. Let me call about my bankcard and credit card right now before someone uses them. After that, you can use the phone all you want. . . . I need to go back and get my cat too, before he thinks I've deserted him. He had just begun to trust me and to put a little flesh on his boney body."

"You can't go back to that neighborhood, Rainy. The cat will hang around there. You've fed him at that house."

"We've only lived there two days. He's not used to the place, and he won't be able to find his way back to our old place. He'll run off, and I'll never find him again. He'll . . . starve to death."

For the first time, she sounded discouraged, not at all like the optimistic, light hearted person I thought I knew. Her shoulders shook, and I guessed she was crying—not over her desperate plight but over a ridiculously ugly cat that might be lost and hungry in a bad neighborhood.

She walked a few steps away, and a short while later I could tell she was on the phone to her bank, canceling her old card number. That raised the question of how safe my cards were with her friends. I realized I didn't much care right then, but would sell my soul for a hamburger if the opportunity presented itself. I considered again about involving the police. If it weren't for the added complication of Rainy's friends reporting me, the cops would have been my first information source. For now, I would have to do my best without their aid. They could fingerprint me and find out I was telling the truth, but still they didn't know me. The process might tie me up for too long—long enough for four little nonentities to become nonexistent. I couldn't risk it—not this night anyway.

"Warren, if you didn't cause this situation, how did they find us?"

"I'm responsible. I made the phone call to Bob at his detective agency. I gave him your new name and address, which he gave to your pretend father. Bob told me your daddy would fly here and see you before morning, and that he insisted I wait with you until he arrived. I should call Bob right now and warn him about what's happened. Maybe he can enlighten us more."

Bob didn't answer his cell phone or his home phone, but I left a message for him to call me, and I gave him Rainy's cell phone number. An uncomfortable feeling crept into the pit of my empty stomach. I needed a large dose of facts—the sooner the better.

"All right, Rainy, you see my side of the story. Bob, my boss, sent me out here to locate you. He gave me a picture of you and some of your close friends. He figured you'd stick with the extra work, so he told me to sign on as the same and study faces."

"Didn't our disguises fool you? Even our closest friends didn't recognize us."

"Knew you the second I saw you. Knew your friends too, but that's something I'm good at, so don't feel bad. You did a satisfactory job."

"I've noticed you're good at a few other things too."

"Better call your friends now. See if they're safe, if they're close, if they've got my stuff, if they could bring us a pizza."

She started laughing again.

"I've tried their number a couple of times. I'll try again."

I rested there on the sand and reviewed my list of friends who might wire money or who might have influence with the police department. It wasn't a long list. I didn't keep in touch with the guys on the force after I retired. It hurt to see them still involved in the action I loved. If I had stayed, they would have considered my leg a handicap. I gave myself that excuse anyway, but maybe it went deeper than that. Maybe I wasn't ready to step down from being the biggest, most intimidating one on my team and watch someone take my place. I knew for sure I couldn't face a desk job. Maybe if I had been older . . .

Since going the freelance route, my only close friend, other than my Glock, had been Bob. He got me enough work to keep me going, and he would have helped me out of this dilemma—if I could have reached him. I couldn't call my parents in Florida. It might shock them too much if I called and asked them to wire money. Heck, it would shock them if I called at all. Actually, I wasn't familiar with their financial situation. Maybe they didn't have any money to wire. Now Rainy obviously knew her parent's financial situation perfectly. I began to see how much I had lived to myself lately. I couldn't ask a favor of anyone but Bob—because this time I wasn't sure I would be around to pay it back. I faced either quick death at the hands of the gang or slow death by starvation if I had to wait for new bankcards like poor Rainy.

Such deep morbidness rarely overwhelmed me as it was doing

this time. I never realized that the loss of a wallet and a few cards could cause a man to feel so naked. Without my master police officer retirement badge, my lifetime concealed weapons permit, my credit cards, and my driver's license, I was just an overweight, six-foot-six target with the only thing going for him strapped to his leg. I would sort all of this mess out later when I had more time and less hunger.

Chapter 3

"I can't reach them, Warren. Either they drove out of reception or their phones died."

"We have to contact them or they could die. Where did you arrange to meet them?

"At tomorrow's shoot—up by the desert. You booked it too, remember?"

"I can't go. I don't have tennis shoes."

The silence lasted at least a minute before we both laughed so hard we feared we would give away the location of our hiding place.

"On the set there'll be a meal, Warren, maybe two meals, and craft services too."

"Do you want me to look in that dumpster for some old tennis shoes, or should I take them off the next tall guy who walks his dog in this direction?"

"Don't worry. I'll think of something."

"Aren't you starved?"

"I'm used to hunger. Besides, we ate on set not that long ago. I've gone foodless for a day many times.

"I don't believe I have—ever."

"I'm sorry."

"I can't understand why the four of you still intended to risk showing up on a movie set after finding me with your pictures? Surely you realized that more than one person could be a threat."

"We planned to meet there and decide. Cal had his accident on this film and location, and tomorrow might be our only chance to investigate it further. Usually they use the same crew all the way through a film. That means we can talk with those who worked there the day Cal died. We could also see if we recognized anyone from . . . from the set of the movie where all this trouble started."

"Rainy, the man who wants to kill you knows the name you're using now. I gave it to Bob. I didn't give him any new names for your friends, so they're probably still unknown—for a while anyway. But you've also been seen by those gang members in your new identity. I've been seen too. They could describe either of us adequately."

"No one would risk murdering us on this shoot, would they? It would look too suspicious after Cal going off a cliff on the same set."

"Well, that's something. At least we know none of us will die falling off a cliff." I gave her my best long-suffering look. "Don't you think it would help if I knew a tiny bit more about what's going on? I've had a few years of experience in this line, you know."

"Give me a minute to check something first. Wait here."

"Hey, someone could see you."

"I'll be over at that short pier. You can see me from here so don't get up. I don't want to wash blood out of your shirt again."

She walked out on the wooden dock and bent low over the edge. In a few seconds, she rose and walked further out, repeating the same. The third time she repeated the act, I heard her gasp. She rose so startlingly quick I knew the gang had returned. I was running toward her, gun in hand, when I saw what had caused her excitement. She held a length of line with a large flat moving object at the end. When I got closer, I saw the flounder clearly.

"Look, Warren. Dinner! People set lines from this pier at night and check them in the morning. I used to swim here and saw people pull in lines with fish on them. I hope you didn't hurt yourself. Do you have a knife? I need a fire. There should be something in one of these dumpsters I can burn."

She talked so fast, so excitedly, I hardly kept up with her.

"Give me the fish, and I'll filet it."

"Save the carcass for Kitty. May I borrow your shirt since you're not using it? It's so windy here that I'm chilled. Aren't you cold in just a tee shirt?"

"No—I'm hungry. Just hungry."

After digging a deep hole in the soft sand, she rushed off to the dumpster. When she returned, she carried an armload of old newspapers and pieces of wooden furniture. Before I could say anything, she dropped them by the hole and went back for more. I watched her in amazement as I finished cleaning the fish with my penknife. To humor her, I wrapped the fish remains in a piece of the newspaper. Soon she came back with more wood and a stack of real estate magazines from one of those free racks.

"Do you have a cigarette lighter or matches?"

"Nope—didn't expect this kind of major operation over one missing girl, but I can get you a flame. You wait here this time."

"If you're going far, I'd rather go with you."

"Not far . . . but come on."

"I'm sorry, but I believe I'm nervous, and it's safer for both of us if we stay together I think."

It surprised me to hear her admit to any weakness. She hadn't acted nervous or scared for even a minute. A brief search around some outside picnic benches turned up a moderately long cigarette butt. Popping it between my lips, I took her hand and headed down the beach sidewalk. The first three groups of walkers couldn't oblige me, but number four gave me a light.

Rainy laughed that happy laugh again when we rushed back to our hideout. I was too busy keeping the damp cigarette alive to express any joy.

"I'm sorry you had to put that nasty trash in your mouth."

"It's worth it if we get to eat."

I scientifically built up a pile of paper and wood while Rainy cut a few green sticks to hold the meat above the fire. I ignited a piece of paper with the cigarette butt and in less than a minute had a fire. The fuel wasn't ideal or plentiful, but as soon as the varnish burnt off, it smelled like wood.

Rainy found some plastic containers in the dumpster, which she washed with sand at the water's edge and set them on our sandy dinner table. Between those, she stuck the stem of a rose into the sand—a slightly tired looking rose. It probably lived in the dumpster too. I didn't ask. The meat came out singed and sandy—but good. A cup of coffee would have gone nicely with it, but I didn't dare say it out loud or Rainy would probably have gone off and begged at the back door of a restaurant.

After we devoured all of the fish, we both tried to call our friends again, but still no luck. I greedily took a lighted stick out to the dock to see if any other lines had caught a fish—but no luck there either.

When I returned, I decided it was time for Rainy to tell me about their trouble. We stretched full length on the sand with sand for pillows. The dark sky hovered silently above us, and it felt good to be here. This type of satisfaction usually came after an aggressive SWAT operation, only tonight felt fuller. Rainy lay silent beside me, and I felt the warmth of her arm through the shirt's cloth.

"Tell me about this movie that caused all your troubles. Did they shoot it on the desert too?"

"They shot it here in Long Beach—at the other end by the city boat docks. It's a spooky thriller called "Torment Reef." We were booked for a 2:00 AM shoot the day this all started. They planned to shoot two boat scenes, a night scene and an early morning scene, back to back."

"On a docked boat?"

"No, they anchored a yacht a good distance from land and used it for the actual movie scenes. A smaller cruiser housed the main actors and most of the crew. The production tents and trailers were on shore, close to the docks, and we waited in the extras holding tent after we arrived."

"All five of you came for this shoot, correct?"

"Yes, and Cal brought his movie camera. After we sat around for a while, we went outside with him and clowned while he videoed us and adjusted the camera. He planned to attach the camera somewhere inconspicuous on the yacht and set it to record the ocean at night. Even if the camera didn't pick up anything interesting, it might capture some ambience scenes for his film."

"How could he find a place on the yacht that would work without someone noticing him? Wasn't he leaving a lot to chance?"

"He'd recently worked two boat shoots for the same film and knew the yacht well. He'd already picked out a place to hide his camera. Cal did that sort of thing all the time."

"I guess the production wouldn't take kindly to someone doing that."

"Absolutely not.

A few stars had come out, and I could see their reflection in her eyes. She rolled to her side and studied me for a moment.

"Cal's intentions were harmless and honest." She looked at me apologetically, as if embarrassed by Cal's lawlessness. "But the producers would never have allowed it."

"I saw the camera. It didn't look like the cameras I see on set."

"No, but a lot of independent film makers like that model since it's inexpensive and small. Cal wore a loose fitting jacket and slid the camera up his sleeve while they boated us out to the yacht in the transpo boat."

"What breed of boat is a transpo boat?"

"Transportation's pontoon boat, in this case."

"How many extras did they use?" I knew I was sounding like a cop. Maybe that was a good thing. But good or not, I couldn't help myself. I needed information if I expected to be of any help.

"I think about three dozen of us worked on the yacht that night. They took us out twelve at a time. Once onboard the yacht, Cal slipped away and set the camera."

"All of the crew were on the yacht with you?"

"For the night scene. For the daylight scene, the crew moved back to the cruiser so they could shoot the yacht from across the water. That's when Cal retrieved his camera and kept it up his sleeve until we left." She sat upright and hugged her knees. I could see her eyes staring past me. "It was bright daylight when the transpo boat brought new extras to the yacht and boated all five of us and some other extras back to holding so we could eat. After they set us ashore, they loaded up with more extras and headed back out. The transpo boat was still in sight when we heard there'd been an accident on board the yacht—an explosion and fire."

"Could you see anything? Smoke?" Now she had my complete attention, but I stayed on my back and looked up at her. The wound in my side was throbbing, my leg was throbbing, and that sand felt so comfortable.

"All we could see was the transpo boat. It turned and sped back to the dock. They hollered at the extras to get out of the boat so they could return and help in the rescue. Apparently the yacht sank quickly and dumped a lot of people into the water, mostly extras."

"Casualties?"

"People said there were some, but at that point we didn't know much of anything except that none of the main actors had been hurt. No one came to take our vouchers and check us out, so we waited in holding. Later someone announced that an explosion in the engine compartment blew a hole in the bottom of the yacht and caused the fire. The film's star, Britt Turner, became the star of the day because of all the people he rescued."

"I think I've heard of him—a swimming champ?"

"Yes, from a family of swimmers. He won some national competitions. That got him his first big role, the one that made him famous. Evidently, he used his aquatic abilities that morning to swim people to the boats. We still waited in holding when the transpo boat brought back its first load of people, all of them wet and miserable. There were ambulances all over the place and people rushed here and there, but no one told us anything—except to stay away from the rescue operation. Eventually they brought in everyone, either on the cruiser, the transpo boat, or on another boat that answered their distress call."

"So the explosion didn't damage the cruiser?"

"It wasn't anchored that close to the yacht. It was the last boat to return and brought in as many people as it could hold. Not long after its return, Cal called us over to see something on his recording." She looked straight at me now. Her eyes were big and full of trouble. "He said he'd caught nothing but ocean except for two places he wanted us to view. The first one showed a man dressed in the pants half of a wet suit. He walked quickly and somewhat stealthily across the bow of the yacht. He carried a dark bag under one arm and had a small white towel that he dropped on the deck before he went over the side—obviously into the water. Cal fast-forwarded about twenty minutes, and we saw the same person climb aboard in the same spot, only without the bag. He picked up the towel, rubbed it a quick pass through his hair and stooped to mop water from the deck. That part of the recording was very dark and the man was only visible for a few seconds before he stepped out of camera range."

"I want to see that recording!" I was sitting beside her now. I don't remember rising but my pain, all at once, seemed unimportant.

"You can't. The extras wrangler saw us and took the camera away. Cal was upset, terribly upset. He feared that the production would keep it. When they finally checked us out, the same person handed back Cal's camera, but without the memory card."

"You have no idea who might have seen it and kept the card?"

I must have sounded a little harsh because she winced at my words. I tried to put on my friendly cop look and even managed a half smile—I think.

"None whatsoever. We didn't know if anyone had bothered to view it. They could have tossed the card away for all we knew. But if anyone had looked at it, they would have seen all four of us at the beginning of the recording. Actually, they would have seen all five of us, because we recorded Cal for a few seconds too. The incident left us feeling uneasy but not actually scared until Cal's accident two days later. When that happened, we guessed that the man in the wet suit saw the recording, and that he probably orchestrated both the boat accident and Cal's disaster. He must have been the only one who saw it, since no one questioned us about it."

"Could you ask the extras wrangler what he did with the camera?"

"I did yesterday. He said he took it to the director and producer and told them he got it from an extra, but with so much confusion over the accident, no one paid any attention. He left it on a table and went about his business. It still sat in the same place when they told him to send us home, so he brought it back to Cal. He didn't know anything about the missing card."

"Who would be allowed in the area where he left it?"

"Anyone could wander over there. Even an extra could have taken it, and no one would have noticed. You know how it is on set."

Yes, I knew how it was on set. I didn't know much about the beach area where we were hiding out, but I was hearing a lot of motorcycle movement, too much. I was sure I had just heard the same cycle for the third time. I didn't mention it to Rainy, but I realized I couldn't let my guard down for even a second. I stood and looked around for a long minute before seating myself on the sand again.

"Rainy, could you make out anything special about the man on the recording? Have you tried to identify him?"

"We've tried. We watched the scenes half a dozen times before the wrangler took the camera. The wet suit man must be someone involved with that movie. That's how he found Cal so quickly and got rid of him so easily. And that's why he was aboard the yacht that night."

"I'd guess you're right about that. You have suspects, then?"

"Too many, and absolutely no proof. The director and producer act openly antagonistic toward each other. The director wanted off the film, and the producer wouldn't release him. They mutually hate the writer, and I think he hates them. Both lead stars were unhappy with the production. Neither one's career can afford a flop right now. The boat captain would receive insurance money. We made a list of lesser suspects too, but we have no solid theories whatsoever—nothing to take to the police. And if the police investigated on the strength of our statement, the wet suit man would want to get rid of us right away. Wouldn't he?"

"He already intends to get rid of us right away. He would be the man who hired Bob to locate you. I hope you realize what this means. We injured those gang members, maybe killed some, and that gives them a few more reasons to get rid of us besides just filling their original contract."

She looked at me gravely. "Tomorrow, on the shoot, we'll get any information we can without arousing suspicion."

"Your friends might not want to risk another shoot after they hear what happened with us."

"Maybe not, but I'm sure they want to stay alive. If we ran away and never came back, could the guilty person risk letting us live? He proved that he's desperate enough to commit murder. The recording may have looked more damaging to him than it did to us."

"If he recognized himself in the footage, you should be able to do the same. He would have destroyed the card, but you have your memories. You, all of you, need to write down everything you saw before you forget something."

"I remember his athletic physique, though it's difficult to be sure about his height with just water in the background. I'd guess he's six foot plus."

"When we find the others, we'll document everything and see if we can cut down your list of suspects. Give me your phone. I'll try Bob again."

I dialed his cell phone and heard a deep male voice, not Bob's. The man didn't identify himself, and he wanted to know my identity and why I called. I knew that kind of arrogance. I'd been a cop. A deep sinking feeling attacked my stomach, and this time it wasn't hunger.

"I'm Warren Roberts, retired Chicago police officer. I'm in Los Angeles, handling a missing person job for Bob. What precinct is this?"

I could be arrogant too. I gave him my badge number and told him I was using a friend's phone. The silence on his end told me he was checking my story. I waited for what I already knew would come.

"Roberts, your boss, Bob Caine, had a break-in at his office, probably late afternoon or early evening. When he never came home, his wife drove to his office and found him there—dead. Looks like robbery."

"Is Lauri there now? Can I talk with her?"

"She went home—been here all evening. I wouldn't bother her tonight."

"How was he killed?"

"Two shots to the head. Don't have anything more on that yet."

"He had a safe. Did they break into that or just steal his wallet?"

"Safe was open and empty of cash. No damage to it. The person or persons probably forced him to open it at gunpoint or else found the combination after they shot him. We found his wallet on the floor, empty of cash, but all his cards were there. His wife confirmed that nothing was taken but cash."

Bob would never leave a combination around. I pictured a

lone male arriving late in the day with a cash payment. Bob wouldn't worry about robbery because he almost never put any cash in his safe. He promptly took all large, cash payments to the bank. In this case, the bank would be closed, so he might have put it in his safe. He might even have done so while he talked with his client since the safe sat close beside his desk. Either the wet suit man handled the job himself or hired gang members, as he did here. They could have caught Bob unprepared, forced him to open the safe, and killed him.

I couldn't investigate Bob's death unless I went back home, and I couldn't get a list of people who flew between LA and Chicago unless I placed the matter in the hands of the police, who probably wouldn't want to share the information with me even then. If I tried to tie the Chicago problem to the LA one, that would put Lauri at risk, and I couldn't protect her and still lookout for these four who courted worse danger. I genuinely hoped Rainy's friends hadn't talked to the police here yet.

"Prints tell you anything?" I finally asked.

"There checking those now."

"If you talk to Lauri, would you give her my sympathy?"

"I'll see her tomorrow and tell her. I may need to ask you more questions, later. Sorry about your friend."

I was sorry too. My list of friends had just shrunk, and I couldn't afford to lose any more. We said goodbye without my divulgence of any information or suspicions. Let them think robbery for now. At least Lauri would stay safer if I didn't throw in any new angles. If the murderer had tried to make it look like a burglary, he wouldn't be rash enough to kill Bob's wife and make it look otherwise—unless it became necessary to conceal his identity. If I gave out any information, it could put Lauri at risk.

Any papers in Bob's office that concerned my missing person job probably traveled out the door in his murderer's pocket—probably, but not for sure. I needed to search his place in Chicago, and I needed to throw this whole, gruesome case in the lap of the police, but I couldn't yet. I had work to do. The police needed more to go on than a well-built shadow walking into a nonexistent video recording. If I gave it to them now, it would only make the killer more cautious and more dangerous. Like Rainy said, he would desperately get rid of witnesses the quickest way possible.

That left it in my lap for the time being. I had lagged and consequently failed to save Bob. A second failure was unthinkable. I must have looked my sadness because Rainy patted me on the shoulder.

"I heard most of the conversation. I'm sorry, Warren."

"Call your friends again, now."

I couldn't help the sharpness in my voice and didn't apologize. She reached them this time, and when I learned that all three were still with us, I walked away to let her tell our story her way. Not many minutes later Rainy came beside me.

"They know everything now, Warren. They want to know what they should do."

"Where are they?"

"They had no cell phone reception up at the shoot, so they came back down to an all-night IHOP in Pasadena."

I knew it was irreverent, even letting it into my mind, but for a minute my thoughts where filled with bacon and waffles with maple syrup. My first words obviously echoed my thoughts:

"Do they have my wallet?"

"They have everything, and they didn't report you to the police. They found your badge and firearms permit and were afraid to do anything."

"Can they meet us here?"

I waited impatiently while she talked with them.

"They're out of gas and don't have enough money."

"Tell them to use mine."

"They said your cash would be gone when they pay their bill at the restaurant."

"So they're at least not afraid to spend my money. Okay, tell them to use one of my credit cards. Tell them to act confident—pretend they're me. Can they do that?"

"We're actors, Warren. I'll convince them it's all right to use your cards."

"I don't think they need much convincing on that score. Tell them to hurry. We need to get out of here pronto."

With a chance for more food in sight, I didn't mind leaving

my sandy bed. Gritty from head to foot, I shook the sand from my clothes and hair. Rainy returned and announced it would take them about an hour to fill up with gas and get down to Long Beach.

"That means it will probably take us an hour to get back up there and an hour or two to eat. That won't leave us time to get a motel room before the shoot. Have to wash the sand out of my hair in cold salt water, I guess."

"I've waited eagerly for you to say you wanted a hot shower. Come with me. I have a surprise."

She led me to a small building that stood alone on the sand, not far from our hiding place. From one side of it protruded an ancient shower nozzle. She adjusted the spray until a hard blast of hot water pounded the sand and steam rose invitingly.

"Keep guard, Rainy. This vision can't be true, but I intend to jump in before it disappears."

"I discovered this spot long ago and would warm up here after a cold swim. I guess the lifeguards forget to turn the water heater off when they leave for the day. I checked its temperature a while ago while I looked for wood. Hang your clothes on this chain link fence."

I stood dumfounded for just a second. I had intended to step under the water with my clothes on, but she had her back to me and . . .

"I'll keep watch, Warren—in this direction at least."

I heard her stifle what sounded like a giggle. I promptly peeled and slung my clothes over the allotted fence. It felt strange to stand naked on the beach and take a hot shower with only the stars for light and this blithe hippy nearby to keep watch for gang members who would murder us on sight. My gun lay within reach, but I never had to use it.

While I put my clothes back on, I wondered if Rainy would avail herself of the hot water to wash the sand out of her hair.

"It's all yours, Rainy. I'll keep watch now." I turned to find her already unfastening her shirt. Her shoes and cell phone lay neatly on the sand. I was wishing then I had taken a cold shower.

She took her turn at the shower, but I was a poor watchman. I wasn't listening for motorcycles or cruising cars. All I heard was the splashing of hot water. All I saw were wafts of steam drifting by. A dozen gang members could have attacked, and I would never have heard or seen them.

We still had time to spare before her friends arrived, so we walked along the water's edge while the wind finished drying us. When Rainy's phone rang, announcing their arrival, I was almost disappointed.

Chapter 4

Tia drove the van, and her brother had settled on the other front seat. No other seating presented itself, so Rainy and I joined Grady in the cargo area and made ourselves comfortable on the boxes of their belongings. Right away, I sensed that their animosity toward me had fled. A new expression radiated from their faces now, its unspoken message being, "We're scared and helpless and expect you to save us from this situation." That was okay, because I expected the same from myself. I knew my job, and it had just begun.

Only Rainy wore an inscrutable look. Though I couldn't read its message, it definitely spoke nothing about fear. I tried to analyze it as a look of camaraderie, like she intended to do her part and more if necessary. When she crept forward and knelt beside Tia's seat, I realized her mind held more than camaraderie.

"Tia, I need you to drive within a safe distance of our place. I have to pick up something . . . if it's still there."

We brave men immediately opposed the idea and called it insane. Rainy ignored us and whispered something in Tia's ear.

"You shouldn't, Rainy. Not because of us, we can keep watch and drive away if necessary, but because someone may wait there."

"I won't make the same mistake again. I'll be incredibly careful."

When she said that, I began to understand. That was when I noticed those newspaper-wrapped fish remains on the floor beside the box where Rainy had sat."

"Rainy, we can't," I pleaded, but when I looked at her eyes, I recanted. "I'll go."

"He would run away the second he saw you. He'd only come to me."

By then Tim and Grady had caught onto what she intended. They expected me to dissuade her from her wild quest, but they hadn't seen the silent sobs I witnessed earlier. She didn't bind up their wounds, prepare them dinner out of nothing, and find them a fountain of hot water on the cold, sandy beach. In the end, Tia took her defense.

"You're a bunch of big bullies. Think of all Rainy has done for us."

"You're right, Tia," I seconded. "Drive where I tell you. I'll find a safe spot where you can wait, and Rainy and I will try to find the cat. Keep watch. If something worries you, drive away to a populated area. We have Rainy's cell phone and can meet you somewhere else if necessary. Don't expect us back soon."

Rainy and I climbed out of the van six blocks from their dwelling. I took a route that, hopefully, would let us see before being seen. Nearing the house, I dropped flat to the ground and Rainy did the same. From that point on, I crept so slowly that no one would see our movement in the dark. It took the better part of half an hour to reach their hedge.

In spite of my well-developed powers of observation, Rainy saw the two eyes peering out from under the branches of the hedge. The cat had waited there for her, but it also looked ready to bolt. I stayed dead still while she called it with a soft voice almost as quiet as a whisper. Another second of hesitation and it leaped into her arms. I knew she couldn't crawl flat and still carry the cat, so I rose and led the way as quietly and hastily as possible. Rescuing that cat was, by far, the most foolish gamble I had ever attempted, but I couldn't suppress a smile when I saw her happy face.

When we entered the van, Tia greeted us with, "We need to buy a litter box."

That told me the van probably belonged to Tia. The female mind baffled me. I thought that our only important consideration was to vacate this area while we were still alive enough to do so. Rainy agreed with Tia about the litter box and added that we needed to buy a food and water dish for the cat. Rainy looked lovingly down at him as he clawed her arm to get further away from me.

"Doesn't he have beautiful eyes? The poor baby's suffered hell. He's scared to death of everything."

When I watched him go to work on that fish carcass, I decided his hunger outweighed his fear. He seemed contented with eating and licking his paws, so I insisted we put a good distance between Long Beach and us before we stopped at a supply store. It felt good to own my wallet again. When we eventually found a store, I gave Rainy a credit card to use for whatever we needed.

They all went into the store while I stayed in the van and kept watch. The cat had finished grooming himself and surprised me half to death when he leaped onto my lap. This ragged, emaciated, rat-like creature that must have measured over two feet long could never be described as a beautiful cat. He made me think of a villain cat I once saw in a cartoon—big and gray with long whiskers and the ability to devour half the mice in Long Beach. Now he purred and rubbed his head against me.

I felt rather pleased with myself when the four of them came out with armloads of bags. When Rainy showed me their purchases, I knew they had spent my money frugally. They bought some cheap cat supplies and a pair of sneakers for me to use for the shoot.

"I guessed at your size and bought the largest pair they had in stock. Try them. I'll take them back in if they don't work."

They actually fit. I hated them—big, white, slabs of rubber that looked like they belonged on a clown. I managed to smile gratefully.

They brought out a few other timid expenditures for which they said they would pay me back when they got their checks. I told them to forget it. It felt so good to have money again. A man should never be broke. That is not his best state. Maybe I possessed an expert's knowledge of survival and a few exemplary police-type talents, but this gypsy and her pet wharf rat deserved the true-survivors award. That fish served as a banquet for both of them, and I was hungry already.

We drove to the all night IHOP where they ate earlier that evening with my cash. While still in Tia's van, I found out that all three of them had shared one order of pancakes. My hard feelings toward their culinary indulgence faded into oblivion. I had pictured a hot pot of coffee sitting on the table and waiters bringing them platter after platter of hotcakes. Instead, they had shared a dinner of water and three pancakes. I invited them all to eat. They insisted that wasn't necessary since they could eat on set in about six hours, but I told them we needed to discuss our investigation so that we could make the most of the day. They gave in quickly and we all rushed inside.

Those four hungry people refused to order anything more exotic than pancakes and eggs while I had a T-bone steak, three eggs, three pancakes, and hash browns. I felt true happiness when they placed my platter in front of me. Though I immediately got down to the business of eating, I wasn't too busy to observe that their food vanished almost as quickly as mine. When we had devoured everything but the coffee, I brought up our investigation.

"Fill me in about these suspects. Rainy's told me the basics and about the heavy hostility on set."

"The director and producer finally agreed on something—that the boat captain should take blame for the accident," Tim said. "Of course, they don't either one want to take responsibility."

"Could the director be liable? Did he hire the yacht, Tim?"

"The producer hired it, but talk went around that maybe the pyrotechnicians left explosives in an unsafe spot. That could cause an explosion, and they could blame the director. But usually the director wouldn't be held liable unless he did something illegal."

"But what did he have to gain by the explosion?"

"He wanted off the film. I heard he had an offer of another film and couldn't take it because he'd committed to this one. But he wouldn't want to soil his reputation either."

"Couldn't the same be said for the lead male actor? Rainy told me he was unhappy with the production."

"Only big stars can afford to throw away a role and expect to find another one," Tim explained. He had obviously thought about it a great deal. "I don't think he wanted out of the film, no matter how unhappy he felt. Maybe someone staged a harmless stunt for more publicity, a stunt that backfired."

I considered that possibility for a minute while I drank my coffee. Almost anyone in the production could benefit from publicity, but it seemed farfetched.

"Rainy, you told me the boat captain might benefit from an insurance payoff."

"Just a guess. We don't know if such a matter would help him or not. It looks like it would only hurt him and make him liable for lost lives and injuries. We didn't want to rule out any possibility."

"Maybe his wife blew it up to kill her husband and to get his life insurance and the boat insurance too. She could have a boyfriend that planned it all," Grady piped in and reminded me this was Hollywood.

For another hour, I listened to the opinions of four actors, all steeped in melodrama and mega drama. Still, years of working with criminals reminded me any motive was possible.

"We've gone around in circles trying to figure it out before it figures us out," Rainy said wearily. "We knew Cal's recording could cause enormous trouble for the perpetrator of the accident. We considered running away to the ends of the earth—until you showed up. Now we know for sure we should have run."

"I'm sorry, Rainy. If I hadn't located you, someone else would have, someone who might not want to help you or might not know how to help. You'd have been found, even at the ends of the earth."

"Will you stay . . . to help?" Tia asked.

"Even if I didn't want to. I'm a target now too. Rainy's fictitious father gave orders I should hang around with all of you until he arrived. He needed to get rid of me, and it was more convenient to kill us all at the same time. He also told my boss that he wanted me to get the new names of Rainy's friends. I never gave out that information, but you can see he wouldn't hesitate at anything if he would go so far as to have my boss in Chicago killed."

Their expressions plainly told me that Rainy hadn't enlightened them about that. Tia gave Rainy a meaningful look.

"I guess Tim and I won't go home after all. It would put our family in danger and wouldn't protect us."

"I decided the same," Rainy added. "If this man would go all the way to Chicago to kill someone, he wouldn't mind a side trip to Ohio. Grady doesn't have any family to visit, but I wouldn't leave him here to face things alone anyway."

"Is your family in Ohio too, Tia?"

"North California—much too close."

When she shivered, I changed the subject quick. Such rank fear would ruin their investigative skills on the set that day.

"Maybe someone can explain to me how you can change your identities and keep on working the way you have. What about social security numbers and that sort of thing? And how will you work today, Rainy, if they ask to see your social security card or your driver's license?"

Tia pulled out a pile of cards and slid them across to me. She had two driver's licenses on Rainy. One was a good copy of Rainy's actual license, with the correct name. The other also looked believable, with Karen Sharpe as the name and a few other minor changes.

"We always kept copies of each other's stuff—even before we created new identities to protect ourselves," she explained.

"Why would you need copies of each other's identities? Is theft that common out here?"

"If Rainy got booked on a job, but later a great-paying union job came on the line, she could try for it, knowing I could replace her on the other job. She's not supposed to work nonunion, but when you're desperate for money, it's sometimes the only way. Now when I need ID to get on set, I use hers because I have a copy. Usually it's not needed anyway. If the person who checks us in or out notices we're not the person listed, we just explain that the other person was sick or accidentally got double booked or had some kind of last-minute emergency. That's usually adequate. But we always fill out our correct information on the voucher when we leave. It has to be legal." I don't know what Tia read into my expression, but she had the look of someone who thought I might arrest them. "I know. It sounds confusing, and sometimes it is. We're only trying to survive."

"But what if everyone was already booked except Tim? He couldn't fill in for Rainy?"

"I have!" Tim laughed. "I looked them in the eye and said, 'I'm Rainy Wray.' I've never had anyone question me, though I've gotten some strange looks. By the way, I'm the one who made copies of their social security cards and drivers licenses. I didn't feel bad about making duplicate copies of our legal documents. I felt we had a right to have spares. But I hated to change our identities in this manner."

"How did you do it? At the casting agency, I mean?"

"We changed our looks as drastically as possible, picked new names, and picked new social security numbers," Tia explained. "Tim scanned our old ID cards into his computer and changed what was necessary to print new cards. We each one went into the casting office, did the paper work, and had our pictures taken. We had our cell phone numbers changed too."

"But what happens to the person whose social security number you stole? They'll have to pay taxes on the money you earned."

"That can't happen. Like we said, we always fill out the vouchers with the correct legal information. The false social security number is solely for identification at the agency. We thought we'd only have to use them for a week or two. None of us had money enough to run away and hide. If this threat is ever over, we'll cancel those false IDs and go back to being us."

"I see. So Rainy doesn't need to worry about her stolen purse?"

"We're extras," Rainy reminded me. "We have spare purses, and I'll use Tia's copies of my stolen cards until I can replace them."

"If we're ever at a police station, please don't give them this information. Please." I must have sighed too loudly because Rainy gave me her reprimanding look.

"We didn't plan this deception for the fun of it. It took all the money we could dig up to get a new place to live, change our identities, change our looks, and reregister. And we can't afford to do it again. Don't you bend rules too? You're not a cop anymore, and you shot those . . . those Nivs. One of them could have died. "

"Hopefully the one with the Uzi pointed at you. You know the saying, 'It's better to be judged by twelve than carried by six.'" Somehow, Rainy had turned the tables and put me on the defensive. "I know you did what you had to do, but I don't want any of you to get into trouble for it. Let's get your true identities back. . . . Could we have some more coffee, please?"

When I turned away from the waiter, three cops walked into the restaurant for coffee. Jealousy instantly ate at me. I should be at their table, not babysitting these four, star-struck infants. Finally, I decided it was their uniforms that made them look so impressive. Not a one of them had my height or girth—and they looked soft. I could probably take them all out with a good dive. I could knock over the one on the right with my forearm while I turned the table over on the other two. Then I would . . ."

Rainy shook my shoulder and ruined my mental SWAT operation.

"Warren, we should sleep a couple of hours. We have an early call time."

"Okay, give us a few more minutes to wade through the rest of this information so we won't waste the risk we'll be taking. We have suspects in mind, and there could be others. Rainy told me about your experiences the night of the accident. Can someone rehash the accident itself, as close as possible? I know you were all on shore, but you no doubt heard plenty about what happened on board."

"I talked to a friend who was on the yacht when it happened," Tim said. "They were preparing the next scene and had placed all the actors and extras. When the captain started the yacht's engine, the male lead would pretend to see something in the distance off the boat's stern and draw everyone's attention to it. They never got that far because when the yacht's engine started, a puff of gray smoke appeared, followed by an explosion and flames. He said the flames engulfed most of the yacht. Everyone rushed to the stern because of the fire, and though the rupture was midship, the weight of all those people sent it down stern first."

"And they'd just replaced a dozen of us with the same amount of elderly and child extras," Rainy said.

"Yeah, that made the rescue effort worse," Tim explained. "All of the yacht's lifesaving equipment sank with it, so those who could swim headed toward the crew's boat. The transpo boat hadn't arrived yet. Britt and a couple of other good swimmers rescued people and brought them to the crew's boat. They helped the children and elderly to board the boat, but everyone else had to hold onto lines or flotation until the transpo boat got there. Even the cruiser and transpo boat weren't big enough to pick up everyone. Some had to stay in the water until another boat showed up to help in the rescue."

"Was Britt the only swimmer in the movie's cast, Tim?"

"Only Britt and his leading lady, Jana, came on that day's shoot. Jana wasn't in the next scene, so they had boated her back to the crew's boat before the explosion happened. That's why Rainy came ashore with us. She was Jana's stand-in. The camera naturally turned on Britt when he brought people in one by one. The news portrayed him as quite the super hero. The incident no doubt helped the film and his career."

"I take it the cameraman who filmed these scenes couldn't swim."

"I heard an angry female extra ask him that question—a wet, angry extra," Grady said as he drew his interest away from the two girls seated on the other side of the restaurant. "The cameraman told her that someone ordered him to keep the camera rolling because the film might help them locate missing people. From what I heard, only one or two from the crew's boat actually got in the water. The others helped people to board the boat and handed out flotation. The crew's boat couldn't move in close until the flames died down. By then, the yacht had sunk."

"Did the captain live?" I asked Grady as his gaze began drifting back to its former targets.

"Yes, he had burns though. Four people died that day and another died the next day in the hospital—four extras and one of the captain's crew. There were plenty of injuries too—an expensive lawsuit for someone."

"Have any of you tried to remember body or facial features, anything, about the man on the recording? Do you remember anything distinguishing about him or the wet suit? About the way he walked or moved? Think sizes, colors, movements, marks, jewelry, tattoos, the line of his hair in back, any excess weight around his waist, hip bones, neck bones, shoulder bones, everything. Think about what you saw and don't overlook anything."

"We've compared notes," Tim said, "but we didn't think about the way he moved or some of those other things you mentioned."

"We probably won't find a big piece of evidence pointing to

the guilty person, so we need to accumulate every tiny piece we can find. Each of you make your own list about what you saw. If you already did that, do it again. We don't want someone else's memories to flavor yours. And please make me a copy because I'm flying blind right now. I need to see the man in the recording through your eyes."

"Time to get some sleep," Rainy announced before I could solicit more information.

"Is there a motel near here?" I looked at Rainy hopefully.

"We're due on set in three and a half hours. We'd better get what sleep we can in the van. We'd lose too much time checking into a motel and it wouldn't be worth the expense."

I thought it might be, but obeyed Rainy, and rode with them to the extras' parking lot for the shoot. We rearranged a few boxes and all stretched out on our hard, uneven beds. One of my boxes crushed down to half its height, which didn't heighten my relaxation, and the cat's tail kept brushing my face. That didn't help either. Finally, I took my aching leg and throbbing side to the vacant driver's seat and slept endurably, if not comfortably, in the upright position.

Chapter 5

It seemed only minutes before the outside world lit up and extras began to arrive at the parking lot. We stacked the boxes to one side and each of us took our turn in the van to dress. It felt good to get alone with my suitcase again. Fortunately, I had packed a light, tactical vest with its pistol holster. It held my Glock and a knife comfortably and still fit nicely under the loose shirt I wore. With the thirty-eight strapped on my leg and the Glock within easy reach, I felt much better. I stepped into my new clown shoes and went out to meet the day. This acting torture should have ended when I found Rainy, but here I stood, ready to commit humiliation in the first degree again.

"Don't hang together except when necessary," I advised when we headed toward the set.

"Rainy, it's the same PA they used on the Torment shoot. Isn't he a friend of yours?" Tia asked.

"Oh, it's Jeff, isn't it? That's helpful."

She left before I could say anything and looked much too pleased with the situation to please me. I started to follow and take a good look at this guy, but just then a breakfast line began to form at the catering trailer. I hurried over to sign in only to find that this Jeff fellow manned the check-in table. He let all of us lowly extras wait impatiently in line while he welcomed Rainy. He recognized her the minute he saw her. Evidently, her disguise didn't fool everyone. He asked her to keep him company, and she accepted much too readily and affectionately. Anyone could see he was enamored with her, and she actually flirted with him. I decided right then to add him to my list of suspects.

I had never seen this side of Rainy, and my appetite suffered a harsh blow. Oh well, I could still keep an eye on her from the food line. I might as well console myself.

Catering's generous supply cheered me somewhat. After I'd thoroughly abused their bounty, I cruised past craft services. Rainy and her friend slid totally off my brain waves when I saw the many boxes of donuts set out—endless donuts and endless coffee to wash them down. The scene looked like heaven—pure heaven. One could really get into this extra business! Now I could sit back and keep track of my four charges while they collected information.

Grady stood nearby with a small group of girls. I doubted he would collect much usable information. He didn't exactly emanate astuteness, but he had a likeable personality. Tim, the most analytical of the four, had wandered away from the set and now studied a sign that read, "Warning: No one allowed in this area." I wondered if that sign had anything to do with Cal's final goodbye. Tia was bright enough, and I approved of her loyalty to Rainy. She sat by herself with a cup of coffee and wrote in a notepad, no doubt listing her observations about the man in the recording. Rainy carried coffee and breakfast plates to the PA's table, so she and Jeff dined together. I had accounted for all four of them when the second AD interrupted my work.

"We need fifteen background over here right away. If you've checked in and finished breakfast, follow me."

I tried to ignore him, but he came around and pointed at people when enough didn't come readily. He led us into a nearby building set up like a restaurant and seated us four to a table. They picked out a woman about sixty to sit beside me as my wife. That hurt somewhat, but she looked attractive in a powdered-perfumed sort of way and acted friendly. Two extras, twentyish, sat at our table—supposedly our son and daughter.

The three apparently knew each other. I listened to their chatter, half disinterested, until the girl asked the older woman if she had totally dried out yet from the Torment Reef shoot. Now they had my attention.

"Dry, yes. Warm, no. I call it the Torment Shoot. I was never so cold in my life. I could hardly move when they pulled me onto that boat. I'll be one of Britt's fans till the day I die, and I hope to God my end doesn't come in a cold ocean."

"You didn't lose anything when the boat sank, did you?"

"My shoes and my hairdo. They didn't let us carry anything on board, so our belongings stayed on shore in holding."

Conversation ended when someone brought us meals.

"When the camera rolls, pretend to eat," the fake waiter instructed. "Don't actually taste anything because the meals are props and may be two days old. Converse like you would in a nice restaurant."

I hated that part of extra work. I had to converse with this fluffy, pink lady while they shot the scene. I could never think of anything to say. Maybe the three would take over the conversation again, and I could just listen and pretend to chew.

When I heard "background action," I plastered a smile on my face and stared at her.

"Were you on that dreadful shoot?" she asked me.

"No, but I heard about it. Where were you when the explosion happened?"

"About the middle of the boat, with extras on each side of me, but when the boat tipped, we all fell on top of each other. I would have been crushed if the boat hadn't sunk so quickly. But then I was sucked under for what seemed like forever."

"Can you swim?"

"I can tread water, but not very well in such a cold ocean."

"How long did you tread water before someone helped you?"

"It felt like a long time but it must have been only a few minutes. The star, Britt Turner, helped me to the boat, and other people pulled me on board. I believe I was the third one rescued."

"Who rescued the two before you?"

"One of them swam to the boat by himself. I believe a stand-in, or . . . or maybe one of the photo doubles rescued the other person."

"Did the fire start with the explosion or after it?"

"I saw fire with the explosion, but then the fire ballooned

down the boat toward us, like it was alive. Terrible! I . . .

"Cut. . . . Checking the gate."

In my pursuit of information, I forgot about the movie scene. My temporary wife smiled at me.

"I guess they got their scene. I enjoyed it, didn't you? You're quite good at this, aren't you? I can never think of anything to say. You made it so easy with all your questions. I bet you could play a cop convincingly."

"Listen up, background," the AD's voice announced. "We want the same again—this time no sound."

I hated these scenes more than the talking ones. I absolutely couldn't move my mouth like a dummy and not make any sound. When I heard them say action, I picked up my empty coffee cup and kept it to my lips until they said cut. When they redid the scene four times, I did the same each time. When they finally released us, I bolted out to check on the others. I found them all together, positioned for a street scene. All at once, those boxes of donuts called me. I had almost made good my escape when someone from the wardrobe department stopped me.

"We need someone who can wear a size thirteen shoe."

"That's my size," I foolishly affirmed. If it had been a man instead of an attractive female, I might have been smart enough to keep my big mouth shut.

"Try these on. Some of the background who were supposed to bring inline skates didn't show up. We need to fill up the scene, and this size is all we have left."

"I can't skate, not on those things."

"Just stand and hold onto something. That should be enough. Try them on so I can see if they'll work."

I struggled and tried to make it look like they wouldn't fit, but she got down on her knees to help, and I gave up.

"Those will be good. Put on these knee and wrist guards too."

I struggled into them and got her approval.

"You'll be in this street scene so hurry down to props. They'll fit you out."

"Where do I find props?"

"Follow the others." She pointed and left.

About ten people rolled down the sidewalk of a side street. Not one of them carried their blades, and there wasn't time to take mine off anyway. In one rash move, I pulled myself erect with the help of a lamp pole. I had always liked being six-foot-six, but now I felt, well, too tall. I took a few timid steps and actually made it to the next pole by inventing my own skating walk. Before attempting any more reckless moves, I looked around to see if anyone watched. There stood Rainy with a horrified expression on her face. That didn't help my confidence. She couldn't abandon the scene to come help me, and the other rollerbladers were rapidly leaving me behind. The loud speakers bellowed that they were ready for the rollerbladers.

It was now necessary to speed my progress. That wasn't difficult since the sidewalk sloped downhill. I saw the prop trailer a couple of blocks ahead, but only a few blade people still waited in line. I tried to slow my speed but didn't know how. Fifteen feet in front of me loomed another lamppost, which I aimed toward and tried to grab. The wrist guard hampered my grip and made it almost impossible to hold onto anything. The top part of my body stopped, but my feet and legs kept going till my hands lost adhesion and held only air. It didn't feel like a pretty fall, and I could affirm it wasn't painless. Why hadn't she given me a tailbone guard?

I didn't know if anyone had seen my mishap, but when I took birdie steps the rest of the distance down to the prop man, he actually laughed. Instead of giving me a backpack or a water bottle to carry, like most of the others received, he searched a back shelf and came out with a neck brace for me to wear. He helped me put it on and then laughed again. I guess I looked funnier to him than I felt right then. Luckily, the movie was a comedy. When I made it back to the street scene, Rainy walked over to stand beside me.

"Well, Warren, I guess no one will have to kill you. You're obviously capable of doing the job all by yourself."

"Get me out of here, Rainy. I'm dying slowly. This work is so not me."

"What is you, Warren?"

"If you don't know now, you'll never know. You've been with me when I was myself."

"The gang?"

"I'm just a bruiser, Rainy."

"Don't be so melodramatic. You do what you have to do . . . like I do. I don't like to hit people over the head with baseball bats but . . ."

"I love it."

"Warren! Today may be our last chance to learn anything, and we'll never figure this out without your help."

"I didn't mean I'd desert you, but do I have to keep up this acting con? That fall hurt worse than the hole in my side, but I'd suffer both incidents all over again rather than step in front of those cameras."

"Maybe all cops should be required to do extra work as part of their training. It would not only give them more finesse, it might tone down their arrogance."

"Speaking of arrogance, who is that stuffed shirt you've been hanging with?"

"He's the PA."

"Pansy . . . "

"Production Assistant—Jeff. He's very important to us because he worked on Torment Reef the day of the accident, and he was the PA on this film the day Cal died. He knows everyone who was here that day. It will take time and delicacy to get that information from him.

"I'll get it for you. Let me question him."

"Warren! I know how you'd question him."

"I can question people. I've spent my life investigating and interrogating people."

"Terrorizing people. You always come on like a cop. You don't have any light touch or acting ability. We don't need to make anyone suspicious at this point."

"I don't mean to scare you, Rainy, but now isn't the time for delicacy. By sheer good luck, we survived that last onslaught."

"By the grace of God."

"Well then God probably considers the first warning adequate. He would expect us to realize the next charge will be more substantial—and soon."

She finally looked concerned.

"I thought we could safely make it through today, at least. We badly need information. Should I send the others away from this shoot, hide them in a motel room?"

"They're safer than we are. Their identities haven't been exposed yet. If they all left the shoot at once, it might awake the suspicions of the wrong person. Someone might follow them, and I wouldn't be there to help. We'll ride this through, get what we can, and get out of here. Better go tell the others they have no time to dawdle – but act casual."

"Okay, you woke me. Since the murderer and all those gang members already know both my identities, I'll forego personal caution for now. I'll make up some ridiculous story and shamelessly ask Jeff what I need to know. I'm a good actor. I'll pull it off. I only hope I don't get him involved. Enough people have died."

"Look further than him, Rainy. Anyone could know something, even the caterer or craft services or transportation or makeup. Talk to anyone who came that day. The least important person on the set may have valuable information."

"I realize that, of course. I just talked with the writer."

"Did he know anything?"

"Yes, he said that craft services put out a lousy selection and the pretzels were stale. I'll casually tell the others to get busy. In the meantime, please don't volunteer for any more stunts like this skating fiasco. We may need you."

Eventually the scene ended, and I was able to dump my blades and props. Having learned my lesson, I strictly watched the four of them and managed to elude the extras' coordinator and the second AD. After a while, I missed Grady. He worked in the last shoot, but now I couldn't locate him. I didn't find him in the restroom or extras' holding, so I circled the parking lot to see if he had gone to the van.

The taped off area with the warning sign sat adjacent to the parking lot, so I visited that spot to reconstruct Cal's accident. The steep, rocky hill had almost no plant growth. Using the terrain to my advantage, I dashed from rock to rock, staying out of sight of the production until hidden by the upward slope of the land. A hasty study of the hillside revealed the only probable location of the deed—one dangerously steep place with a deep enough drop-off to insure accomplishing the deed. The rise of the ground right before it would block any sound or sight. That meant it could have happened any time, even in the middle of a shoot or preferably in the middle of a shoot.

A slight movement caught my attention, and I soon made out someone inching along the slope in the direction of the drop off. It didn't take long to identify the crawler as Grady. He had pluck, anyway. I scooted in his direction and quickly outstripped him. Rather than startle him and maybe cause a second disaster, I sent a tiny pebble in his direction. The sound stopped him, and he looked up the slope.

"Grady, hold up."

His startled expression turned to one of relief, actual pleasure, when he recognized me. He waited while I crept over to him.

"That's where it happened." He pointed to the spot I had already chosen.

"Did he have his camera with him?"

"No, he never took it on set unless either Tia's or Rainy's vehicle was available to stash it if necessary. That camera was his life."

"It was his death. . . . How did he get to the shoot?"

"Tia and I dropped him on the way to our shoot. Rainy had a photo-doubling job on another film, but she went to pick him up at the end of the shoot and found out about his accident. She came back and gave us two hours to pack everything we owned into the vehicles. We lost half a month's rent on our apartment and had to live in our vehicles until we rented that pigpen."

That explained why Rainy wouldn't think anything of my living in a rental car. She did what had to be done. Grady and the other two probably were alive now because of Rainy—dependable Rainy—who at least hadn't been too trusting when it counted most.

"What reason did they give for his presence on that cliff?"

"They didn't. Someone spotted his body at the bottom. He'd already been carried away when Rainy got there. She saw a sheriff's deputy investigating it, but she didn't wait to talk with him."

"Do you know if the area was taped off that day like it is now?"

"I didn't think to ask."

"Do you know who saw his body and reported it?"

"Don't know that either."

"See how the ground slopes down to that drop-off point? Calvin could have slipped, slid down the incline, and rolled off the edge accidentally. You all said he constantly looked for a place to record scenes for his own movie. Probably others knew that about him too."

"Sure—common knowledge, at least with the extras."

"Although we have to consider every angle, I'm betting it wasn't an accident. I'm also betting that the person behind this puzzle didn't use a gang this time but took care of Cal personally. With the drop-off point hidden from sight of the shoot, anyone could stand down there unnoticed. I think we could climb around to the point from here. His murderer could have killed him elsewhere and dragged him over to that point in broad daylight. That wouldn't work so well if he was alive, screaming and kicking.

"He could have walked out there, like you said, in search of a move site."

"If our man needed to do away with him, he couldn't gamble on Cal walking out onto that point at exactly the perfect time. And it's not easy to shove a live person off the edge of a cliff. The shove administrator could end up taking the plunge. Did they perform an autopsy on his body?"

"We don't even know when or where they buried him. We steered clear of the situation. I think his mother resides in a nursing home in Louisiana. He never mentioned a father or any other relatives."

"The murderer could get to that rock point from the top of the hill or from this side, and could push Calvin's body off from almost any spot. He could also climb down and drag Cal wherever he wanted him, but that would take time and involve too much chance of error or of leaving evidence. Cal's body might hang up on a rock half way down. I'm guessing he killed him elsewhere, maybe in the parking lot, then dragged him over to that drop-off point on the same route we're taking. Because of the downhill grade, anyone in reasonably good physical shape could handle the job and easily roll him off the edge.

"How would he kill Cal?"

"Probably whacked him in the head with a hard object. Did you know that a simple baseball bat can kill someone?"

Grady turned white, then bright red. He looked down at his toes for at least a minute.

"I figured you'd find out that I hit you. Sorry. I didn't want to kill you, but we had to get away. All we had was the baseball bat."

"You acted wisely considering the circumstances. Some people would have hesitated—and hesitation kills people. . . . It was smart to investigate this cliff, too."

His face beamed so much I feared he would float off the side of the slope.

"I'll edge over to the drop-off point and then climb down to the bottom. Can you keep watch? If someone comes, send a few small pebbles down to warn me and flatten yourself behind these rocks. You can't be seen from either side if you stay put here."

Considering my bad leg, he should make this climb. But considering my experience, I elected myself. I studied the slope for a good five minutes in search of any irregularity or evidence of recent travel. When I found nothing noteworthy, I returned to the parking lot and followed the route I would have chosen if I had done the job. Even if it had rained since the accident, the rock surfaces should show some sign. That was one of my specialties, but it would require slow careful work.

Twenty yards from the point, I found slight scuff marks. It took me ten minutes to get that far, but I had traveled leisurely and searched for marks. I could have dragged a sizable corpse and easily made the distance in the same time. If the murderer possessed a normal physique, he could have made the entire trip in at least fifteen minutes. He could get away from the set for that long and not cause notice—if he actually worked on the set. Grady and I had hid here for half an hour and no one had missed us.

I soon came upon definite scrape marks along the rocks. The terrain had also become steeper and smoother, which presented a different type of challenge to the murderer. Eight feet further on, I confirmed the soundness of my theory. The killer had left obvious signs that he had returned on the same route and had even tried to wipe out evidence—irrefutable proof that some sightseer hadn't made the marks by an accidental slip.

Right then I would have given anything to have the authority of an active duty cop. I could examine Calvin's clothes, especially his shoes, and order an autopsy. I guessed that any medical exam would disclose a killing blow to his head, and I doubted it would have rock particles in it. It was much easier to swing a longer, thinner object.

I saw no need to climb all the way onto the ledge. The killer wouldn't have left any evidence there. Instead, I traveled to where a down-mountain trek would be less steep and worked my way toward the bottom. I slid and crawled as fast as possible and tried not to think about the uphill climb that awaited me later.

With about two thirds of the descent behind me, I felt cocky, that is, until pebbles rained over me. I turned and saw no one up there but Grady. A second look told me someone crouched beside him—Rainy. All at once, he stood and heaved something out above me that resembled a boomerang. Didn't he realize his first signal did the trick? Then I saw the object where it landed thirty feet below me—saw it at the same instant I head the dirt bikes approaching around the bottom of the mountain.

With no time to consider the odds of breaking my neck, I dove down the mountain in the least graceful, least safe way available. I had to get my hands on that missile. While I bruised the heck out of my already abused body, I told myself I could have come in from below—in an auto probably.

When the bikers pulled to a stop below me, they witnessed a large, limping man innocently climbing down the hill with a wooden cross in his hands. Its diminutive size made it less than impressive, but it would do the trick. I blessed Rainy for knowing what I needed. I held my hand over its splintered base—evidence it had been ripped loose from something in great haste. All at once, my cell phone rang.

"Warren, tell them we promised to mark the spot for Calvin's mother in Louisiana."

Three construction type men glowered at me as I held the phone to my ear. I knew Rainy would be game for anything, so I made my best shot.

"I'm here now, but I'm not sure where to put it," I called

into the phone with a reasonably loud voice. I turned to the stern witnesses. "I wish I'd known there was an easier way down. We promised Cal's mother in Louisiana that we'd mark the spot with a cross. If anyone here knows where they found him, I'd appreciate the information."

I waited for the explosion—ready for a fight. I held a good position.

"I'm Kevin, the key grip. It happened over here." He pointed to a place I had already pegged as the landing field. "Please don't ever do anything like this on one of my shoots again," he said as he walked toward the place. "I'm in charge of safety on this set. We don't need someone else going off that ledge."

"Did you view him here . . . before they took him away?"

"It wasn't a picture you'd want to describe to his mother."

"She'll want to know anything we can tell her. How'd you ever find him? Who thought to look here? Or was it by chance?"

"Some extras saw him go to the parking lot but never saw him return. Then someone evidently saw him in the taped area and told some other extras about it. They went over there and looked down. Simple as that."

At least now I knew that the area had already been taped off, but what I really wanted to know was who told those extras that Cal had gone into the forbidden zone. That person was likely the murderer. Since Cal didn't have a car in the parking lot, the murderer must have asked him to meet him there—someone he knew, someone who struck him dead. I kept my phone to one ear as I followed Kevin to the exact spot. Rainy told me the shoot ended ten minutes ago, so I wasn't AWOL. She also told me that a kneeling mourner saw more clues and should say some words when he placed the cross.

Now I was dead in the water. I stumbled forward and dropped to one knee on the rocky ground. My knee was uncomfortable and I was uncomfortable. I leaned the cross against a rock and felt panic rush through me. Rainy must have sensed my agitation because she quietly recited a couple of lines, which I did my best to stumble through.

"Dear Lord, we thank you for the years we shared with Calvin. . . . Give us the strength and courage to leave him with . . . in your care. Amen"

The silence was embarrassing as I rose ungracefully from my knee. Kevin acted as self-conscious as I felt. I glanced up the hill at my return route, and Kevin gave a quick tug on my sleeve.

"I'd rather you didn't go back the way you came. Hop on, and I'll give you a lift."

"Thanks."

"You're lucky my friends wanted to see the place where it happened. You'd still be climbing if we hadn't come along."

"Sorry to cause you trouble."

"It's all right. We know that Rainy asked you to do it. The PA called and told us about you just as we pulled up."

Rainy and the others greeted me when Kevin dropped me at the set. I began to understand what drew these three under Rainy's protective presence. Here stood a girl everyone knew and trusted. Grady wore a big grin, and we both headed for the tent to turn in our vouchers. The PA looked at me with an odd expression but didn't say anything.

When I got to Tia's van, I saw half the story. Someone, probably Rainy, had unceremoniously dumped a box of her belongings onto the floor of the van and had ripped the cross from what looked like a fine wooden Bible stand upholstered in red velvet. The cat sat placidly in the empty box.

"It's all I could think of to do when I discovered where you were. I knew those men were headed that way. I gave Grady the cross because he pitches more accurately than I do. He actually practices that kind of stuff. After he sent it sailing, I called Jeff and told him I sent you down there. I asked him to keep you out of trouble for my sake."

"I'm sorry about your Bible stand." What else could I say? As usual, she amazed me.

"I didn't think you wanted a big scene where everyone would hear about it and about all of us. We have to stay low key if we want to stay alive, right?"

"Right, Rainy, but I think we deserve a high-key motel room tonight. You earned us that luxury with your quick thinking."

We didn't accomplish the quick getaway I desired. Along

with my wounded side, my almost-broken tailbone, and my newest bruises, I had to endure Rainy's long, affectionate goodbye to this PA, Jeff. I watched patiently through two hugs, five pats, and a kiss. After all, it was my job to keep an eye out for their safety. Granted, the kiss wasn't much to write home about, but it was closer than I had been.

When we finally escaped the set, I instructed Tia to make enough turns and short cuts to lose anyone who might try to follow. In a completely different area, I secured a motel room and ordered four large pizzas. I would probably eat two of them. How could anyone live on extras fare? I sat at the foot of one of the beds, afraid to get too comfortable. I didn't want to fall asleep and miss our pizza party. Anyway, it was still early, and we had much to do.

"We have time to get our facts together and make a plan. Did you get any worthwhile information from your boyfriend today?" I couldn't keep all the sarcasm out of my voice.

"He gave me a list of everyone who worked on the shoot the day Calvin died—even the extras."

She said it smugly and waited for my praise, which she knew she deserved. I knew it too, but memory of this Jeff guy brought out my obstinacy.

"What about the Torment Reef shoot? Tia said he worked on that one too. Did he give you a list of who worked that shoot the day of the boat accident?"

"We'll have to use our memories for that one. I didn't want to make Jeff overly suspicious. I told him I wanted to talk with a few people who may have seen Calvin on his last day so that we could give a report to his mother. Jeff doesn't know anything about Cal or Cal's family. I also learned two very interesting facts from him. The executive producer of Torment, Don Denlin, is one of the four producers on the film we worked today. And he and Britt Turner visited the set for a short while the day Calvin died. They came in the same car, maybe to discuss the other film or maybe just for company. They were there during the time the accident took place. I couldn't learn any more about that."

"Darn good job, Rainy." I felt ashamed of myself for my jealousy. "All of you look at her list and put a mark beside anyone who worked on the Torment set the day of the accident. On the bottom of that same sheet, start a list of suspects. Begin it with this Denlin, and put Britt Turner down too."

"Does this rule out the director?" Tim asked.

"It doesn't rule out anyone. What's his name?"

"Allen Ertsly"

"Put Ertsly down too. Just remember that the person behind these incidents may not be the one who killed Cal. He could have hired his killer. He wouldn't even need to be present to oversee it. If I could fly here from across the country and become an extra as easily as I did, think how easily someone could get registered and get on a set."

"Easier than those who've been around for a while. Productions always want new faces," Tim said.

"Speaking of faces, I'd like to see what the main actors look like, and the director and producer too. Since you four saw the recording of the man in the wet suit, maybe we could remove some suspects right away. If we could get pictures of . . ."

"There's Wi-Fi here. I'll bring in my computer. We can find some photos online," Tim interrupted.

"I'll go with you. I need something from the van too." Rainy hurried after him.

Although I felt certain we could hide out here safely for at least a day or two, I went with them. No matter how many precautions we took, there was always the element of chance. It had killed more than one good cop. I kept watch while they dug through their boxes.

"Bring his camera in too. I'd like to look it over."

We got to the room at the same time the pizza arrived, and I saw right away I should have ordered five—or six. I also saw Rainy furtively take the lid off the box she had brought in and slip a large slice of pizza into it. The purring that resulted sounded louder than the rumblings from my stomach. Luckily the motel had an attached restaurant.

While Tim set up his computer, the others gave me their notes on what our mystery villain looked like. Their information lacked detail, but it gave me something to go on.

"Everyone listen to this description of your wet suit man and stop me if something doesn't sound right to you. We have a man about six feet tall, muscled—though not heavy muscles. He has dark, medium-short hair. Both Grady and Rainy remember a brief side view that revealed hair on his chest and arms. Was it heavy hair or sparse and was there any on his upper arms?

"I couldn't tell for sure," Grady said. "I guess I'd call it light growth, sparse on his upper arms, but still visible. I don't remember any on his back, do you Rainy?"

"No, just his arm, and sparse like you said. I'm not even sure about the chest hair. It could have been a shadow."

"All of you seem to agree he was lightly tanned with no suntan lines, his wet suit pants looked ordinary and black, and he wore a two or three inch wide utility belt. There's no mention here of jewelry, a watch, or a tattoo, so I'll assume there were none. How about his feet? Did anyone notice anything noteworthy?"

"The camera didn't pick up his lower legs and feet," Grady said. "But I did notice the man moved with ease, took long steps, and when he climbed back aboard the yacht, he did it quickly and with no trouble."

They all nodded their agreement, so I added that to the description.

"The object he carried under his arm could be important. All of you described it as a black, duffle type bag about two or two-and-a-half feet in length and half as broad. That bag could have contained any number of things—a diving tank and gear, tools, explosives—or all of those items. We at least know for sure he didn't bring anything back on board with him. He may have used an oxygen cylinder or diving gear belonging to the yacht. He could have attached the bag to any below-water part of the hull when he'd finished his job. That way it would appear to be part of the wreckage after the explosion."

"Would there have been time for him to set up an explosion like that in just twenty minutes?" Grady asked.

"Depending on this man's relationship to the film's production, he may have had other opportunities to rig the yacht for an explosion. The explosives may have been placed a good while before the camera caught his night trip into the water. If Calvin worked only as an extra and yet knew the yacht well enough to attach his camera where no one would see it, it's obvious we can't discount any possibility."

"I've found some internet pictures of the lead and secondary actors if you want to look at them," Tim said.

"Good. If you each have your picture of the wet suit man clearly in your head, we should be ready to compare our suspects."

Tim found quite a few pictures of the lead and secondary actors. Of that group, only Turner fit the description adequately. With most of his pictures showing him in swimming trunks and even one in a wet suit, that possibly swayed our opinions, though he looked like such a boyish, harmless soul that even my hardened cop eyes couldn't picture him as a murderer.

We found a few party and award shots of the producer. He wore evening clothes in all of them, so it was difficult to picture him as the wet suit man, but we couldn't eliminate him. His height, build, and hair all matched our description.

"The director fits too. I came up behind him once and mistook him for Britt," Grady said. "He's tall, got dark hair, and a regular build. I've never seen him in swimming trunks, but he wore shorts on set once and had hairy legs. He'd probably have arm and chest hair too."

"We have three suspects listed—Ertsly, Denlin, and this Britt Turner. Someone mentioned the boat captain as a suspect. If he owns the yacht, he's a possibility, but I doubt he'd blow up his boat. If he wanted insurance, he'd more likely sink it when no one was aboard. Why risk a bunch of lawsuits? Put him down anyway."

"Maybe the wet suit man wanted to kill someone on the yacht for revenge or insurance or . . . whatever."

"I'd consider that, Grady, except it's too unsure and risky. Even if someone intended to destroy the yacht along with everyone on it, it would be difficult to assure such results. Any explosion would likely have survivors, and help waited only twenty yards across the water. I doubt anyone would attempt such a complex maneuver just to murder someone. Still we won't rule it out. Would anyone else gain by the yacht sinking? Is the movie political? Controversial?"

They all laughed.

"It's a horror story, supposed to come out before Halloween and about as controversial as a pumpkin," Rainy explained. "It's rather corny too. I'm sure no competing movie would feel threatened enough for sabotage."

"That gives us four suspects. Try to come up with other possible motives. You know this business better than I do. I might have overlooked something. If not, then we've got the job of eliminating three of these names. That's where we'll use the list of names Rainy got us. Someone on her list may have information, especially someone listed on both shoots."

"If we expect to question any of those people, we'll need to work on set again." Rainy wore her best here-in-the-real-world look. "I do have some of their phone numbers, but if I call someone and ask a direct question, they'll know I'm investigating something. On the other hand, if we chance upon someone on set, we can always work our way around to the subject and get the information without drawing too much attention."

"I understand, but we can't risk any more shoots. Put down whatever contact phone numbers you know, and we'll try to find a way to use those. . . . Who knows how to operate Calvin's camera?"

"Any of us. We all helped Calvin with his productions. He played a part in his movie too, so whoever wasn't in a scene would operate the camera. Would you like to see some of the movie—and see what Calvin looked like?" Rainy asked.

"It was a SAG experimental film and not far from completion." Tia's eyes sparkled with anticipation. "Calvin was a SAG actor like Rainy."

I sat back and watched a scene that began with Rainy and Tim in a tough situation. To my unprofessional eyes, it looked pretty cool. Rainy played someone called Laura, but I never caught Tim's name in the scene.

"Are we just going to sit here and see nothing, say nothing . . . do nothing? What will happen when the sun sets?"

"It will be twilight, Laura."

"I mean what about after that?"

"Night . . . just night"

As soon as Tim said the "night" line, Tia's character appeared in the scene and rushed up to Rainy and Tim with a frightened look on her face.

"I-I think they're c-coming back . . . Do you hear voices?"

"I hear more than voices." Tim paused to look behind him. "They're coming like a flood. Find a place to hide . . ."

Grady's character entered into the picture at that point, and he led the others up a narrow, rough flight of stairs into a small crumbling tower.

"We've already played hide-and-seek. Let's try king-of-the-mountain." Grady played his part well and seemed like a different person from the Grady I knew.

"There's no place to stand." Tia clung to Grady and looked down.

"Have you noticed there's no place to fall?" He pushed her behind him.

"Okay, I'll stand." Tia's look of fear and determination were perfect to my eyes.

All of the action and acting amazed me. I glanced around at them and saw that I had viewed the scene alone. Four sets of eyes watched me and waited for my reaction. They weren't thinking about murderers. They wanted to know what I thought of the film and of their performances. These were actors. If they stood at death's door, they would still want to do their crosses believably and use perfect facial expressions.

"I'm sorry the film can't be completed. I'd like to see the finished product. I'm . . . amazed."

"We all put a lot of work into it," Rainy said. "Cal even paid other extras and actors to do small parts in it whenever he had a few dollars to spare. We didn't charge him for our parts. I know we should try to contact a relative and give them the recordings we have and his camera, but we've been so much on the run since his death that we haven't risked anything."

They showed me another segment with just Calvin and Tia. Calvin looked thinner than I expected, and I pictured someone dragging his body across that hillside.

"I'm glad you put a cross to mark the spot." Rainy sighed and put the camera away.

"Let me see if I can scare up some coffee at the restaurant here. Be back in a minute."

"I'll come along and help carry," Rainy volunteered and followed me out the door.

Along with the coffee, I ordered half a dozen hamburgers—the extra one being for me. While waiting on the order, I called the airport. A flight to Chicago with only one stop would leave in an hour and a half. It would get me there about five in the morning, considering that I would lose two hours to time zones. That would give me part of a day to investigate, pay my respects to Lauri, and still get back before evening tomorrow. I called a taxi so none of them would have to leave the safety of the motel.

When we got to the room with our eats, I grabbed my coffee and two burgers before Rainy got any ideas. The cat still had half a bag of dry food. That should be a feast for its scrawny hide.

"A taxi will be here shortly to take me to the airport. I'll return tomorrow afternoon or evening. That van can't be seen again until this is over, so stay put here and rest. We'll find some place to store it when I get back. While I'm gone, Tim, would you try to find a way I can reach the captain of that yacht? Get his name and phone number—an address too if you can find it. I'm gambling he's not a suspect, but just the same I'd like to meet him and talk with him."

Within minutes Tim handed me two phone numbers and an address for a Captain John Nobel. He even found a picture on the internet of the captain standing aboard his yacht—a short man with a beard and mustache. He could have hired someone to blow up his yacht, but since one of his crew died in the accident, I considered it unlikely.

The taxi arrived, so I swallowed my last bite of hamburger with the rest of my coffee, gave Rainy a credit card to use until I returned, and hurried out. I got to the LAX with time to spare, so I ordered another burger, fries, and coffee to comfort me during the wait. I needed sleep, but I could squeeze in maybe five hours on the way to Chicago.

Chapter 6

Early the next morning I pulled into Lauri's drive in my rental. I hadn't called ahead but had gambled on her being there. Groggy with sleep but glad to see me, she rushed into my arms and stayed there a long minute. Her body trembled, but she didn't cry. When she recovered her composure, she stood back and looked at me. Lauri had always been an attractive woman, but now her eyes looked tired and sad. Her usually neat, tight hairdo resembled a rumpled mist of black around a pale, pale face.

"The funeral is tomorrow. . . . Can I fix you some eggs, Warren? And coffee?"

For once I wasn't hungry, but the look on her face told me she craved some kind of natural employment. Bob wasn't there for her to feed anymore, so I said I was starved.

While she worked at the range with her back to me, I decided to tell her what I thought she should know.

"I believe Bob's death resulted from the missing person assignment he accepted and hired me to solve, not from a robbery. I withstood an attack about the same time Bob was killed. It would put you in danger if I told you more. . . . I can't stay long, only a few hours, so I won't be able to attend the funeral. The person responsible for all of this must eliminate me too, so if I hang around here, I put you in danger. I would like to investigate Bob's office, though, to see if the killer removed the information about this case or if the police missed any clues."

She didn't respond, and I wondered if she had heard me.

Absentmindedly, she broke more eggs into her pan than even I could eat. When they were cooked, she turned to me with a different look on her face.

"I wondered." Her voice shook but she worked to regain her poise, and her eyes turned cloudy with anger. "I'd be glad to help, Warren. Do you think I'd worry about danger . . . after . . . after this? The police report sounded strange to me too. With so many richer type businesses available for a burglary, a private investigator's tiny office shouldn't appear lucrative enough to merit the effort."

She turned to dish the scrambled eggs onto a waiting plate but stopped abruptly. As if she had made a decision, she brought out a second plate and filled both plates generously. She intended to eat too. I had been afraid my coming would make things harder for her. Maybe it had helped her just a little. I hoped so, anyway.

After pouring two cups of coffee, she sat down at the counter with me and ate. I got the feeling it was the first food she had eaten since finding Bob dead.

"I'll go to the office with you. I do Bob's bookkeeping and might find something you wouldn't see."

"You're probably right. Just remember that someone still needs to kill me. I want to slip into the office unseen, and slip back out the same way. If two of us . . ."

"You're right. Maybe I should go to the office and bring things here for you to look over."

"I need to examine the entire room. It's possible someone would keep watch there. It wouldn't look normal for his widow to come by and pick up his books so soon after the . . . happening."

"After his death, you mean. It's okay to say it, Warren. I'm all right now. You'll be paid for the missing person job, and I'll pay you additional to investigate Bob's murder. I know this job has cost you money, and I can afford to help. At least you'll have a legitimate excuse to snoop. I'm one of the licensed owners of the agency."

"I won't accept pay, Lauri, but I'll do what I can. I'd like to check into a few matters, but the police probably won't give me the information I need. . . . Maybe you could get his phone calls over the last few days. That might turn up something. Just don't give a hint about any suspicions beyond what would be normal for a robbery."

"I'll do that. Here's a spare key to the office. Will you come back here when you're through?"

"I'd like to but shouldn't."

"Here, take this—my personal cell phone number. Use it instead of the home phone and call if you have any information . . . or need help. If information comes my way, I'll call. . . . Be careful, Warren."

I studied the outside world carefully before I left her home and used equal caution approaching Bob's office. I doubted that anyone would watch either place. Almost certainly, Bob's murderer returned to LA immediately after he achieved his purpose. Still, I couldn't take the smallest gamble with Lauri's safety at stake. With my car parked two blocks away, I entered the small office and tried to piece together the crime. I had wanted to ask Lauri where Bob fell and get details about the bullets and wounds, but when I saw the grief on her face, I decided those facts could wait.

The blood on the floor told me Bob stood or squatted in front of the safe when it happened. I couldn't find the usual job file on this case nor Bob's appointment book. I searched the bin where he kept his recent papers, mostly receipts, reminders, and phone calls, but found nothing relevant. Someone had rifled the bin's contents before I got there—probably either the killer or the police. Finally, I checked his accounting records and discovered that the last page was gone.

With no place left to investigate, I investigated anyway. I studied every square inch of the office. On the wood of his desktop, I found a small Niv insignia—carved there to be found. I wondered if the police had seen it. I wasn't sure why the mark was placed there since I already knew that Bob wasn't killed by gang members. A person this thorough to remove evidence wouldn't trust someone else with the job. I could rely on that one fact anyway—that the killer visited Bob's office that day. It would help if I proved that someone from LA came here to Chicago the day of Bob's murder, but such circumstantial evidence wouldn't convict anyone.

I called Lauri to let her know about the missing books and page.

"I'll see if recent bank deposits tell us anything. You and I both know Bob didn't do that much business. I'll also try to remember any entries I made on that missing page—though I only updated his books once a week. I wouldn't know about those last two days."

"Be careful, Lauri. I can't stay here to watch out for you. This whole mess started in California and will have to be finished there."

"I'll fly out if you need my help. Watch your back, Warren."

On my way to the airport, I remembered Lauri's phrase, watch your back, and wondered why it gave me an unpleasant feeling. Finally, I remembered how many times in the last few days the production crews had used those same words whenever they moved equipment. I didn't mind facing guns or knives, but I hoped I would never again have to face another extras coordinator or assistant director.

My flight got me to LA in the early evening, and I rented a car for all of us to use. Tia's van would have to stay parked. On the way to the motel, I called Captain Nobel. He wanted to talk about the wreck with anyone who would listen, but I put him off and arranged a meeting for seven o'clock the next morning.

Tia opened the motel door and looked surprised to see me.

"You startled me. I expected Rainy. She just left for the grocery. You told us not to use the van while you were gone, so she walked."

"Where's she headed?"

"Go left on the highway out front. The grocery is a mile down on the right side. She won't be there yet."

I caught up with her about half a mile from the motel, walking fast. Her face showed genuine welcome and somehow lifted my spirits.

"Get anything we might need for the next few days," I said when we reached the store.

I stopped at the deli and picked up a basket of fried chicken and quite a few of the sides that went with it. Rainy bought only a small bag of cat food. It was a wonder that she hadn't moved them all into the van to save one day's expense of a motel room while I was gone.

Three excited faces greeted us when we arrived at the room.

"A big shoot came on the lines a few minutes ago. It's out

at Big Bear and, believe it or not, it's the Torment production." Tia bubbled over with enthusiasm. "We're all booked on it."

"How'd you book Rainy . . . and me?"

"I booked myself, gave it to Tim to book himself, he gave it back to me, and I pretended to be Rainy's alias, Karen. Tim took the phone again and pretended to be you—simple as that. Now we can finish investigating."

You mean now we can all die, I wanted to say, but they looked so happy and pleased with themselves. They felt brave, but I knew they had contracted a case of false courage, brought on by soft beds, full stomachs, and the presence of an armed, former cop—none of which could save them if prospects turned further downhill.

"Where is this Big Bear?"

"About 100 miles from here in the San Bernardino National Forest. It's a big shoot, and they hadn't filled the call yet because not all extras want to drive that distance. Also, quite a few extras already booked a big, downtown shoot. They gave us a ten o'clock call time tomorrow morning and asked for casual wardrobe, dark colors, and medium-weight jackets because it's supposed to take place in the fall—on Halloween."

I didn't intend to let them go. Maybe I would go by myself and look over the suspects, but I would keep them in a motel for another day—a different one in a new location.

"At seven in the morning I meet with Captain Nobel. It shouldn't take long. I'll be back in time to drive us to the shoot," I lied. "We'll check out of this motel in the morning and find a new spot for tomorrow night."

I had started on another piece of chicken when Grady stood before me with his arms full of cords and shoelaces.

"That day when we tied you, I thought you couldn't possibly free yourself from our work. Rainy said you escaped right away. I-I . . ."

"I'd be dead and so would Rainy if I hadn't. I had about three minutes to spare."

"How'd you untie the knots? Or did you do it some other way?"

"I used the penknife hidden in the shirt I'd taken off. You'd left it behind. I rolled over to it, opened the knife with my mouth, and cut myself free."

"What would you have done if we'd taken the penknife?"

"I keep a razor blade in my boot. Sometimes I carry one in the band of my shorts, but this job shouldn't have involved any trouble or violence. I came here to locate a missing person, so I left my more extreme equipment back in Chicago."

"How long did it take you to get free?"

He still held all those silly strings.

"I'll be glad to tie you so you can see what you can do."

"Sure, go ahead. . . . Also, I've got some w-weapons I've collected. I'd like to show them to you . . . sometime."

When I tied his wrists behind his back and tied his ankles, I used kindness no enemy would have used. I left the knots and bindings loose enough to allow several avenues of escape.

"When you get free, you can show me the weapons—if I'm still up."

"Rainy said you brought another gun."

I slapped my leg to show him where I carried it.

"Okay, Grady, go to it."

The others watched television, so I joined them while Grady struggled with the shoelaces. I actually forgot him for a while. At the end of the program, Rainy suggested we all get some sleep. Grady remained in about the same state I had left him in earlier. I stepped over him and improvised a bed on the floor, close by the door. It felt good to have the Glock back in my vest where it belonged—a nice lump to sleep with. The thirty-eight and its leg holster reposed under my pillow. Compared with the last two nights, I was living in luxury. I must have fallen asleep before anyone.

Sometime later, a thumping sound woke me—Grady. The others had gone to bed and turned out the lights, but I could make out his location. I found the penknife in my pocket and tossed it in his direction. The thumping grew louder and more violent. I doubted anyone slept at that point. Suddenly the thumping stopped and a gasp of pain filled the silence. I smiled to myself. In the dimness, I saw Rainy rise from bed and go cut him loose.

"It's just a scratch, Grady. Wash it and wrap some tissues

around it. It should be fine."

I saw her outline as she came close to me. I held up my hand, and she put the penknife in it. After depositing it in its customary place, I fell asleep again. It must have been much later when something woke me again. I don't usually make a sound when danger threatens or startles me. Girls might scream—I don't, ever. But when my eyes made out this giant gray cobra head with long gray whiskers perched above my face, I leaped awake and had my gun in my hand. I must have made some kind of sound because the room light came on and everyone was awake.

I rubbed away the wet spot on my lip. It wasn't a dream that a wet nose had touched me, but I could see now that the nose belonged to Rainy's cat. My gun didn't intimidate him in the least. He purred. I quickly hid my gun.

"Everyone can go back to bed," I said in my best grumpy police voice.

"He must like you," Rainy offered.

Mortified, I rolled over on my side and tried to sleep. The cat crawled up close against my back and did the same.

In the morning, Rainy offered to go with me to see the captain. She reminded me she was on the shoot the day of the accident and could help. I doubted it, but knew the others wouldn't leave for Big Bear without her, so I agreed to take her along. To humor her, I dressed in my clothes for the shoot, even though I didn't intend to go near any movie sets. The dark jacket adequately hid the vest containing my gun, and finally I discarded the tennis shoes and wore my boots. At various places on my clothes and body, I had secreted the few weapons I had brought to California. That gave me a comfortable feeling.

"I'll put my bags in your car now," Rainy said. "It will save time when we come back. They can pack theirs while were gone."

"Pack anything you may need for the next few days. The rest of your stuff put in the van. We'll leave it at a parking garage."

She immediately headed toward the door with two bags. A head stuck out of the partly unzipped top of one. She looked at me apologetically.

"I thought I'd better bring him along. I might find someone

who will keep him for a few days."

I nodded resignedly, and we drove on to our meeting with the boat captain.

If ever there was an enraged, wronged victim, I stood before him. Captain Nobel, a short, stocky man who could probably punch a man out with one good blow, looked about ripe for murder. He spoke with a slightly foreign accent, but I couldn't identify its origin.

"The yacht never had problems. The engines were new, everything new condition. These movie people have ruined me financially. The insurance won't begin to cover what I lost. And now they say I'm responsible for the accident—and those deaths. They've destroyed my yacht, my finances, and my reputation."

"Do you have any ideas about what went wrong?" I wanted his story before I fed him ideas.

"I think that those men who make things explode . . . the . . ."

"Pyrotechnicians," Rainy supplied.

"Yes, something like that. I believe they caused it. I watched them explode a small barge one day. I saw how it looked and how it smelled at the beginning. I notice things like that. A few days later, when they shoot film on my yacht, a tiny puff of smoke came from my engine compartment. It had the same smell—faint, almost not there. I checked my engines and found nothing wrong. Even the smell was gone. But everyone on board grew nervous after that."

"How soon after that incident did the accident occur?"

"Just two days later. And when my yacht exploded, it looked and smelled the same as the barge explosion and the puff from my engine—only enormous, so terrible it blew a large hole in the hull. It killed one of my men—my friend. The engines couldn't cause that. They tried to say fuel leaked and ignited when I started the engines. I don't believe that. Not for a minute. Yes, after it exploded I smelled fuel, but not at the beginning."

"Where were you when the explosion came?"

"At the wheel. I started the engines when they signaled me. It exploded that very second, knocked me down, and I was sucked under the water. It all happened so fast."

"Did you keep any diving gear on board?"

"Positively. The yacht has . . . had everything. She . . . had three staterooms, a computer station, and a projection TV, a hot tub on the upper deck, and a full outdoor gas galley. We had a garage for water toys and dive tanks, and the dive platform was . . . was one of a kind."

It was painful to hear him, to watch the tears stream down his face. This man loved his yacht. No, he hadn't perpetrated any foul plots or murders, but he looked capable of such now.

"What size diving tanks did you keep on board? I mean the length of the cylinders, not the capacity."

"I believe we kept twenty-four-inch and twenty-six-inch tanks. I can find out for sure later. The man who took care of them would know. He wasn't aboard the day of the accident."

"Were there wet suits on board?"

"All sizes, kept with the other diving equipment."

Rainy touched my arm.

"Remember the shoot. We can barely get there now."

I nodded to her and turned to the Captain.

"You've helped. I'll probably need to ask you more questions later. Please keep quiet about this visit. Otherwise, it might ruin our investigation. Your help will be needed shortly, so expect my call."

"You may call or come in the middle of the night if you like. Only please hurry. Find proof I didn't cause this."

"That's what we're after. One thing more—do you know anyone with a boat similar to yours? It especially needs to resemble your boat in the upper bow area. It doesn't have to be exact. We may need someone who'd be willing to take a party out for a few hours at night. I'm working on an idea in case everything else fails."

"I have friends who will help, yes. Tell me when you need the boat."

"I'll call you. Don't mention that to anyone either. I'll let you know when to contact them. Stay aware that someone desperate orchestrated this entire situation and anything we try will involve danger."

"Then you have suspicions already?"

"Definite suspicions, but no names. For safety's sake, don't call me. I'll probably contact you in the next few days. If anyone finds out about our meeting today, give any story that sounds reasonable. Maybe I'm an attorney who offered to take your case."

"I need a team of attorneys to take my case—but I don't think I can afford them now."

Rainy showed her agitation when we got to the car.

"We won't make the shoot on time. I hated to interrupt you. I'm aware of how terribly important this meeting was, but we don't want to arrive late and draw everyone's notice. Besides, I've never been late for work."

"I never intended to let any of you go to that shoot. Have you forgotten what happened that day at your house? Just because we have a meal under our belts and a good night's sleep behind us, that doesn't mean the danger is over. We'll face worse the next time. They'll be better prepared, and there will be more of them."

"I'm not a child. Naturally I'm aware of the danger. But the quicker we face it the quicker we can be through with it all."

"You'll be through with it all—most certainly. Look, Rainy, you're not half as desperate as the person who wants to destroy you. Your attitude shows that plainly. That means he'll win. He'll stay one step ahead of you. He'll move faster. He'll already have a plan—and probably more than one. He won't worry about being late for work. He probably hates cats. He won't worry about being nice or appropriate or religious or polite. His only interest will be to destroy you quickly, any way he can, and not get caught. Until you get in the same frame of mind, you haven't a chance of being alive two days from now."

I had to act tough to discourage her. Her friends would scare easily, but it would require sterner measures to curb Rainy's involvement. As usual, I miscalculated. I hadn't prepared for the avenging angel who faced me.

"You have no idea how desperate I am. I can be desperate and still be a decent human being, but if I don't learn the identity of my enemy, I'll for sure be dead two days from now. Thank you for the room and the meal. They didn't fill me with complacency as you suggest. They reminded me I might want to live long enough to have a few more meals and a few more soft beds under me. I refuse to cower in fear, and I refuse to become as vile as the person who wants to destroy me. I'll be nice or religious or anything else I want to be. If I let him take those things away from me, he's already won the first round."

"This isn't the first round, you little fool. The first round ended when someone took Calvin's camera. We've entered the last round, and I know for sure that two of us will go for a knockout. I only wish you and the others would leave the ring. It's darn difficult to step around you."

I couldn't out argue her. I knew that for sure. But if I made her angry enough, maybe she would stay away from the shoot, which was all I hoped to accomplish. When she brought out her cell phone, I congratulated myself for a hard won victory.

"I'll call and tell them to stay put today, but if you go to the shoot, I go. I know you have big feet and a tendency toward clumsiness, but I believe I can stay out of your way and not cause you to stumble."

She controlled her anger well. At least I accomplished half my mission. I was still pondering how to keep her away from the shoot when she reached Tia on the phone.

"Tia, I know we're late, but none of you will attend the shoot today. Call and make some excuse for the three of you—van trouble would be honest since Warren doesn't think it should be seen anymore."

"Too late, Rainy. We're here and signed in. We discussed the situation while you were gone and decided that you and Warren shouldn't risk the danger this time. Those gang members saw you both and know your names. Your pretend father knows your new name too. No one has discovered our disguises yet. We left a note for you in the motel room telling you not to come. Except for the note, the room's empty. We put everything in the van. Just call us when you get another room so we know where to go when finished here. Don't worry. We can investigate this."

"I heard that, Rainy. Give me the phone. . . . Tia, get the others and leave right now before someone sees you. You're an hour early, so I know you haven't registered yet. We don't need any more information. I have a plan."

"I-I can't leave. I don't know where Grady or Tim went. They both headed off in different directions, each set on seeing someone. That's why they wanted to come early."

"As soon as you find them, leave the shoot, but don't wander into any unpopulated areas. Rainy and I will drive your way. Call us before you leave the shoot, and we'll plan where to meet. And Tia, if you sense any danger whatsoever, stay near registration until I get there. . . . Rainy, show me the quickest route to Big Bear."

I watched close for cops and sped the entire distance. Tia didn't call again, so we guessed they hadn't left. We arrived twenty minutes late for the shoot, but there was still a long line at the check-in table. I located Tia's van and parked a couple of spaces over from it. Tia and Tim waited by craft services.

"I found Tim but haven't located Grady yet."

"Where did you last see him?"

"With one of the pyrotechnic crew, over by a supply trailer. I don't know where he went from there. They're calling for extras to sign in now."

"Here he comes. He must have been at the van."

The scared look on his face changed abruptly when he saw Rainy and me.

"I'm glad you came, but you shouldn't have come. I don't think any of us should have come. I was inside the van when two men walked over and looked it over—you know, in the wrong sort of way. They didn't know that I was inside. One of them said something, I couldn't make it out, and then they both laughed. I figured it's something to do with our trouble since Tia's van isn't unusual enough to get anyone's attention. It's just old and boring."

"Thanks, Grady. I didn't know you minded riding in it," Tia said.

"I didn't mean it that way, Tia. Anyway, as soon as they left, I came straight here."

"Can you point out the guys? Look around but don't act obvious." I figured that Grady was just overreacting, but I couldn't take any chances.

Grady found his men, and I walked close enough to hear their conversation. Neither that nor their looks fit the gang mold. I sauntered over to the parking lot and studied the van as I approached.

It had a flat tire on the front. Careful study revealed a screw imbedded in it that could possibly have caused the problem. Tia could have run over a screw, or someone could have flattened the tire to prevent their departure when the others left for the day. Rainy met me half way back.

"They aren't gang members, Rainy, only harmless extras that noticed the van had a flat tire on the front. We have to consider the possibility that her tire didn't flatten by itself. Maybe someone wanted to delay the van's leaving at day's end. In any case, it needs to be pumped or changed while no one's over here. Does Tia have a spare?"

"A spare and a foot pump. By the way, we all checked in for work. It seemed like the best way to avoid attention. Tim checked in for you and got your voucher. He got his voucher first, then went back and got in the line of another PA who helped with check in. We have to work now."

"I need to fix her tire first."

"Don't show up till they finish the scene. It's only a partial call. They don't need everyone and probably won't miss you. Here, I have keys to her van. Be careful."

When Rainy left, I got out my knife and pried loose the screw. It hadn't caused the leak. It was too short, imbedded slantwise, and wouldn't have made it through the rubber. With Tia's cheesy air pump, I manually pumped the tire. I heard no sound of escaping air—good news and bad news. It meant that I wouldn't have to change the tire and that someone had probably let the air out. With a slow leak, the tire would have been low when they left the motel, and the van would have maneuvered poorly, especially on turns.

When they finished their scene, I asked if any of them had noticed its flatness or had felt anything different on the way to the shoot.

"It steered fine coming here. That tire's almost new and has never leaked," Tia assured me. "Did you change it?"

"Pumped it full. I'll check it again later. If it flattens again, I'll put on your spare."

"I have an auto club card. I could call for someone to come and change it."

"And draw the attention of half the people here."

"I was trying to be helpful. By the way, you said on the phone that you had a plan. Will you tell us about it?"

"I planned to carry out its first stage by myself and didn't intend for any of you to come here. Now I'm afraid to send you away, so you might as well help with the work. I need one of you to take as many pictures of our suspects as possible, secretly, of course. You can take still shots or moving shots. "

"I wore the bulkiest jacket." Grady patted his well-concealed chest. "I'm sure I could video most of our suspects. All but the boat captain are here. I can get the camera from the van and start now before one of them leaves."

"I'll use my cellphone," Rainy added. "I can get some shots with that, and Tia can help me. Grady, you keep Tim with you so he can help hide the camera and keep you from looking suspicious. What will we do after we get these pictures—study them to figure out who Cal videoed that night?"

"We'll try for that, but if the pictures don't tell us anything, we'll actually record a scene of Calvin's movie. We'll have to write the scene—a boat scene—and we'll shoot it at night on the bow of a boat. During one short portion of the scene, a man wearing the lower half of a wet suit will do exactly what the man on Calvin's recording did."

"Who will play the man?" Rainy asked.

"It would be better if one of us did the part, but no one fits the man's description. We need someone who looks exactly like the man on the recording, and at the same time he must look like the director, the producer, the lead actor, and any other suspects we might add to our list."

"You should use an actor. Britt's stand-in or his photo double would either one fit the bill. I know both of them, and I'm sure either one would welcome the work. Actors who take background or stand-in jobs generally love to get an actual part in a movie, even in a low-budget independent film. I'm in that category and would jump at the opportunity. We'd have to offer them a day's pay though," Rainy explained.

"What's the difference between a stand-in and a photo double?

Which one would look more like the person?"

"Usually the photo double. They actually replace the actor in parts of a movie. The stand-in replaces the actor while they fix lighting, adjust the camera, and all that, but they step away when the real actor comes for the actual scene. Both have to be close to the physical size, shape, and coloring of the actor though. Either one would work for our purposes since we'd only want a back or side view and don't know which suspect they should resemble."

"I can pay the man we use. We'll have to plan the scene carefully so everything looks natural. Maybe we should get an extra or two. Without making the actor suspicious about what we're doing, we have to dress him exactly like the man Cal videoed that night. His skin must be the right tone, he must have hair on his arms, he can't have any marks or tattoos, and his hair has to look the same. Everything must be identical or it won't work. "

"You should hire a makeup person too, to make it look more legit," Rainy said. "We could get along without a hair person since the man had short hair, and the rest of us can fix our own. . . . This was why you asked the captain if he knew anyone with a boat similar to his."

"Correct. I . . ."

"I get it!" Grady had belatedly come alive. "You'll do an entire scene just to get a recording like the one Cal got that night—the one stolen from Him. You only want the part where the man's there on the bow in his wet suit, and the actor won't have the slightest hint what we're actually doing."

"That's right. We'll recreate it on the boat, recapture it on video camera, and we'll possess a recording that could make someone extremely nervous. The guilty suspect will think two cameras were set that night, and he'll want that other recording."

"So you'll send a flash drive to each suspect, and it won't mean anything to any of them except the guilty party." Grady had difficulty containing his excitement. "That's a great plan."

"Not very," I admitted. "We could all die before we video it."

Rainy had been thinking too.

"We might have trouble getting the copy to the suspects. Important movie people always have plenty of hopefuls trying to slip them pictures and recordings. Other complications could arise too. One factor in our favor is that Calvin had a boat scene in his movie. That's why he wanted to film the ocean that night. His scene might fit the bill with a few changes and adjustments. I foresee one big problem."

I feared one of them would ask the question I knew she was going to ask.

"If the villain bites, who will serve as bait? Who will meet him and probably get killed?"

"I haven't got the plan all figured out yet, Rainy."

The second AD's shout broke the silence that surrounded me.

"We need all background over here who booked as hoodlums—right away."

"Good. I thought they were calling us. We'll have a few more minutes to set this up. Get the video camera from the van right away, and check that tire too. I'll keep watch everywhere at once. Don't get separated from the main body of people no matter what."

"I need to get my tote from holding first. I want to put some stuff in it besides the camera," Grady called over his shoulder as he trotted away.

"Warren," Tim said nervously, "they called again for background. I think you're one of the hoodlums."

"No—Tia said that Rainy and I were booked as extras."

"Hoodlums are extras. They wanted big, rough-looking men for the hoodlum scene. . . . The casting agent looked at your picture and size and put you down as a hoodlum. It should say so on your voucher."

There it was, plain as day. I was a hoodlum. I still stared at the words when the second AD returned.

"Hey, you over there, aren't you in this scene? We need all hoodlums now."

"He means you, Warren." Rainy sounded more jubilant than I felt right then. "We'll be okay, Warren. We'll use extreme care. This scene will draw people's attention and help us get the pictures we need. . . . Mess up all you want. It will give us more time."

I could tell Rainy squelched a giggle as she and Tia deserted me. I marched off to my execution knowing she had gotten her revenge for my earlier harsh words.

For at least an hour, we crossed up and down sidewalks and back and forth across streets. Everyone knew what they were doing except me. I didn't know when to start or how fast to walk. While formulating plans to kill the next person who shoved me, I heard someone yell, "Checking the gate." Two minutes later, another voice announced, "Print, moving on." I knew those golden words anyway. They had aced their scene, and I could get back to the others.

Before I could escape, the AD announced that hoodlums would move to a new location—a three-sided set adjacent to the street scene they had just filmed. Cameras and crew filled the area where the missing fourth wall would have stood. It looked like all the important people of the production milled around this area and quite a few extras had wandered over to watch. The three-sided room, full of nice furniture, would have passed for a room in a model home to the eyes of the camera. The AD looked us over and chose ten hoodlums to go in and trash the room when they called "action." Luckily, this time he didn't choose me.

The rest of us stayed on standby, so freedom still eluded me. It seemed preposterous for me to indulge in this foolishness considering our life and death situation, but I couldn't think of a better plan than the one I had described to them. That plan would only work if we knew our suspects perfectly.

Just then they started the scene. I watched a bunch of wimps struggle with chairs and tables. They looked about as convincing as my grandmother would have looked in the same situation. It took two of them to tip over a sofa. I heard a loud, disgusted, "Cut," and could tell someone agreed with me.

Crew rushed in to right everything. They swept up the rubble of a broken lamp, replaced it with another, and added a few more lamps and chairs. I was so engrossed in the whole process that I jumped when the AD tapped me on the shoulder.

"We want you in there too. The director said there wasn't enough action in the last scene, so be destructive. Trash the place."

Rainy had come up just in time to hear his words. She looked at me and winked. "Here's your chance. Bring back an Oscar, Warren," she whispered in my ear.

"Which one's Oscar? I'll bring them all back if you like. I'll tear them to shreds."

"Just abuse the set, please. It's called acting."

For a minute, I put aside all thought of the deep game we were playing—even ignored those cameras and all those people who waited to humiliate me again. When they said "action," I hesitated only until others began to rush into the room. That told me my time had come. I became SWAT officer Warren Roberts—doing what he did best.

I threw the sofa across the room first. It wasn't an accident that I sent it in the direction of a couple of the namby-pambies who studied a chair as if they feared it might attack them. I laughed loudly when the sofa hit the chair and sent it tumbling over directly between the two of them.

That felt good, so I songfully punctuated the rest of my deeds with a bluegrass banjo opus I used to listen to in my patrol car for an adrenaline rush:

"'Dive through the middle, don't shove or push.' Table coming through, watch your backs. 'Keep goin' round the mulberry bush,' yeah. Look out. I'm rolling. 'Oh by gosh and oh by Joe. This may be the last time, I don't know.'"

This work had just become fun. Like a demon, I ravaged everything in sight. One extra raised a lamp in the air to make a marvelous presentation of smashing it on the floor. Before it left his hands, I struck it with my fist and laughed again when the china fragments fell all over his head. I felt tempted to crack a few skulls, but remembered in time that this was acting. I had really gotten into it when they hollered "cut," and I was actually disappointed when they said, "Checking the Gate . . . print . . . moving on."

The first face I saw when I left the trashed set was Rainy's. It wasn't the familiar face I knew. This face looked pale, frightened, and unsure. Had danger arrived or already struck? I looked around quickly for the others and found them. They had watched the scene and now smiled at me. Grady gave me a thumbs-up. I found Rainy again, and she had adjusted her face to a more approachable one.

"Quite an improvement in your acting, Warren."

"Acting? That was me!"

"Yes, all six-foot-six of you, on camera. You certainly won't maintain any anonymity after a scene like that. You . . . startled me. I didn't know you were capable of such violence . . . or such loud, off-key singing."

"Honey, you saw me that day with the Nivs."

"Not really. I was busy fighting for my life. Just now . . . you were demolishing for the fun of it."

"Not just that, Rainy. They'll pay me at least sixty dollars for my day's work, and at the rate I'm spending, I need it."

She laughed. She could relate to that. Maybe she wasn't angry with me anymore.

"Warren, whether you did it for fun or money, the fact remains it was perfect for our purposes. All eyes riveted on you, and we got our pictures, moving and otherwise, of the suspects. They're mostly back and side views."

"That's what we need, but how'd you see my show if you were taking pictures? I could have done it better, you know."

"I'll admit I forgot my job for a minute or so—when you sent that sofa sailing through the air. But I managed to get a few quick shots and still see everything you did. You'll probably cause the production to have trouble with the stunt people. You went beyond the duties of an extra, but the head people loved it, and this movie doesn't have much budget for stuntmen anyway. Thank goodness you didn't injure anyone."

"Hey, Big Boy, they want you back for the boat shoot. It comes up in a few days," the AD called to me.

Big boy, I thought in disgust. There was a day I would have broken someone's head over a crack like that. I could go back and rough him up.

"You did great today!" he hollered and waved goodbye.

Maybe the guy wasn't so bad after all. Hmm. This was Hollywood, wasn't it? The guy wasn't so bad. He was just doing his job. I almost liked him. Rainy laughed again and brought my ego back down to normal cop arrogance.

"I loved your priceless expression. I know you're not a poker player."

The other three came up, and Grady tapped his jacket where

he hid the camera.

“We got all three on the camera. I’ll put it back in the van before someone sees it and takes it away from me.”

“Don’t worry about it. That was a wrap. Put the camera in your bag so we can check out and go home . . . wherever that is,” Tim added. “See, there’s already a line.”

That’s when I saw them. They had rushed to be first in the checkout line.

Chapter 7

Those guys turning in their vouchers may have worked today as extras, but they definitely weren't extras. Something about them appeared vastly different. If viewed separately, I might not have noticed, but now they looked like a family of brothers—a big family. Four Nivs already sauntered toward the parking lot, and I counted two more at the checkout table. I turned quickly toward our vehicles. Three leaned against the front of Tia's van as if it belonged to them. If numbers meant anything, it obviously did belong to them. Another two of the same mold stood by the door of my rental. It was a grave lack of precaution on my part to park near the van. I must be getting senile.

Swift calculations told me that at least eleven gang members waited for us. Six had worked as extras and probably watched our every move. The other five, the ones already in the parking lot, would never have passed wardrobe's checkpoint. They either waited all day in their vehicles or drove in later. I knew Rainy and I were old, familiar faces to them. Now I would have to assume they recognized Tim, Grady, and Tia. Quick-thinking time had arrived.

Tim and Tia had brought our tote bags from holding.

"Let's hurry and get in the line before it gets any longer," Rainy pleaded. "I have to catch someone before they leave."

It was in our best interest to make the gang believe we were unaware of their presence, so I followed the others. While we waited in the line, I tried to break the news softly.

"Act as if we're discussing where we should go for dinner and don't look around at all."

They stood directly in front of me, but I saw their backs stiffen.

"I've counted eleven Nivs. The last two just left the checkout table. The others wait by our vehicles. They haven't slashed any tires or given us any excuse to call in the police. If the police did come, or if I started anything myself, there could be havoc with all these extras around. And we still wouldn't know the identity of the man who wants to kill us. These gang thugs don't look like they will run off easily. They look insolent. What's worse, they appear confident. I could wait till it clears out somewhat here, but no way can I take eleven of them without casualties. We wouldn't all make it."

Rainy turned half around to me so all of us could hear.

"The production's not through shooting for the day. They wrapped the extras but will move everything else to another location and shoot two more scenes. Some of the production trucks and trailers have already left, and the crew is rushing to pack up and follow. It will become hugely lonesome here in a few minutes."

Rainy had gauged the situation accurately. The entire production made ready to pull out. I looked toward the parking lot again and saw nothing subtle in the glances the Nivs shot our way. I turned back and studied the terrain in the opposite direction and found only rocky wilderness as far as the eye could see. I chose a spot in the distance and told Rainy where to look.

"That rocky knob will be your goal. You will have to be quick—while production trailers still block you from the Niv's view."

We were nearing the check-out table, so I stayed in line with the rest of the extras to keep the gang's suspicions down. Another step and the wall of the tent would hide all of us from their view. I felt certain they thought we were still unaware of them.

"Rainy, this will be tough. All of you hurry around behind this tent, make sure no one sees you, and then move fast to the second production trailer. Since there are four of you, one of you can watch in each direction. If no one shows up in ten seconds, run straight away from the trailers and into the underbrush and rocks. Move as quickly as possible toward that knob. Don't worry about a detour to fool anyone. No one knows where you're headed anyway. They won't get on your trail at all if they don't catch a glimpse of you—so stay low and under cover as much as possible. Keep your cell phones on silent mode. If you see anyone, anywhere, call me on your phone. Otherwise, I'll meet you at that knob as soon as I can get there. If I don't get there . . . use your best judgment."

When she stared up at me, unruffled by the instructions I had just delivered, I felt like leaning over and kissing her—strange feeling for me. All at once the line moved forward a few important feet, and I hurried them away. I watched carefully yet discreetly to see if anyone followed them. I allowed three minutes for them to disappear, but I couldn't allow more or the gang might grow suspicious and send someone for a look-see. Even now, I gambled—but a gamble was sometimes the only choice you got.

Poor actor that I was, I still had to give it my all. When the three minutes ended, I trotted toward the rental car like I had forgotten something. Halfway there I pulled up sharp and let them think I saw them for the first time.

One Niv deliberately reached down and let air out of a tire—grinning brazenly at me as he did it. I knew Rainy and the others hadn't been seen yet because all those eyes watched me. Two faces looked familiar. That told me that this operation wasn't a big one with a bunch of branches. These guys traveled to the spot where they were needed, even if it wasn't their turf. That was good news. If it had been a huge gang, like the Crips or Bloods, we couldn't stand against their numbers and organization.

I prepared for the next scene of my fraidy-cat performance, when all I really wanted to do was rush them and smack a few grinning faces. I glanced over my right shoulder in the direction of the check-out tent, doing my best to have an urgent look—like I wanted to signal my friends but didn't want anyone to see. Finally, I glanced at the cars but didn't make eye contact with anyone. If they saw I wasn't afraid, they would become suspicious and might venture afield before I had given the others enough time to escape. I had to draw the entire bunch in another direction and then lose them, outsmart them, or outrun them. If I succeeded, I could circle to Rainy and the others.

I pivoted slowly and began an even slower walk back to the

tent. I saw no sign of Rainy and the others, not in the tent or in the distant countryside. They must have made it to cover. At the tent door, I stopped and pretended to be unable to locate them. With a sudden quick movement as if I had found them, I headed around the tent in the opposite direction from what they had taken. I ducked in behind a second row of production trucks and trailers that were preparing to move out.

There were two production rigs to pass before I came up behind the one pulling the portable-bathroom trailer. I counted on the Nivs seeing me during the split second where I passed from one rig to the next. All at once the whole line of production vehicles moved.

Now I must convince the Nivs that my friends had already eluded them in a similar fashion to what I was trying, only on an earlier vehicle. It might not work, but it would at least give Rainy and the others a few more minutes. I rushed on to the fourth production truck and climbed ineptly aboard, clumsily letting my feet slip down a couple of times to make sure they saw me. It wasn't difficult to look bungling because it was a high climb onto a moving truck. I took a quick look and saw that some of the gang had already gotten into a car, bent on following. They'd taken the bait.

There was only one production truck between me and the Niv's car. They hadn't wasted any time getting mobile, and the road was wide enough they might try to pass. I'd have to take the first drop off I could find. A sharp left turn would keep the driver's eyes focused on the road and hide me for a second from those following. I would have to move quickly to get out of sight in time.

Such a spot came at once, a steep, rough, barren drop-off, but I took it anyway. I landed hard, inches beyond the edge of the pavement, and let the momentum roll me off the edge into I didn't know what. When I painfully stopped my plummet, I was still in the open. The truck next in line behind mine now made its turn, and the Niv's car would be behind it. I took giant sliding steps toward the only cover nearby and flattened myself behind it barely in time. My battered body wanted to lie there and not move, but with half of those Nivs still back there, rest was unthinkable. Some of the gang might have headed into the wilderness. Even these ones following me might turn back at any time. I couldn't leave Rainy and the others unprotected.

Though I studied carefully in every direction, I couldn't find the landmark I had pointed out to Rainy. That left no choice but to backtrack along the road until I could locate it again. The steep incline and lack of cover were the worst possible travel conditions—slow, painful, and risky—but there were no other options. If the Nivs saw me come back, they would know for sure the others hadn't left with the production vehicles. There would be no other reason for me to return since they knew that I knew they had our cars.

The roadside began to rise beside the pavement, so I scrambled to its highest point. I still couldn't locate the landmark, but I knew what direction to take now. The remnants of the production were leaving, but a few vehicles remained there parked besides ours—probably the Niv's cars.

I chose my route and slid back down the rise. It was time to begin the roundabout trek toward my goal. The Niv's were probably city boys and that would help. If they did attempt a ground search, I could outsmart them in this terrain. This was my turf, even more so than the concrete wilderness all cops know. Still, I had four novices to protect and a leg that handed in its resignation papers three days ago. I needed to move much faster than any part of me wanted to go if I intended to reach my babysitting job in time.

These Nivs probably had enough sense to find a high place and scan the area. I would have to watch for such maneuvers. The deep gray lining of my jacket blended better with my surroundings than its blue exterior so I turned it inside out. There was no time for elaborate camouflage efforts, but I did rip a few brushy branches from nearby trees and stuff them in my belt.

Though the heavy exercise kept me warm, I could feel the air change from cool to nippy. A light mist of rain had set in. It probably snowed further up in the mountains. Although this rain and chill would be hard on Rainy and the others, I was jubilant over the bad weather. I could stand twice the misery any of those young punks could endure. Unpleasant or not, it might mean our lives.

Every few minutes I stopped dead still, listened, and searched in every direction. I even put my ear to the rocky ground to check for vibrations. It was difficult to realize that danger had invaded this silent, peaceful wilderness. The drizzle became heavier and more like sleet. It became necessary to choose my path carefully so as not to leave any tracks on the wet ground, though most of the area was rocky and unrevealing. I doubted that Rainy and the others had found time for caution or safety measures. That new thought goaded me to more speed. My imagination played act one of Gang Catches Prey. The picture wasn't pretty.

With two thirds of the distance covered, my surveillance of the surrounding area increased enormously, but I didn't dare slow my pace. A rock rolled nearby, and I embraced the ground. My Glock was ready when I rolled to my side to study everything in my line of vision. I waited, but no further sound came. I waited longer and identified the sound of heavy breathing. That sound was followed by definite footfalls.

It would be easy for me to take out a small party of them, but that would tell the rest of the gang that we had for sure taken to the wilds. They might send for more reinforcements, and I had no idea how many that would mean. I reminded myself, repeatedly, to use patience.

The cold rain pounded against me. Lying prone invited the chill to work through my body. Stiff limbs wouldn't help if the situation suddenly called for drastic action. I flexed the muscles in my arms and legs and fingers without moving my body.

The footfalls started again—possibly three or four sets of shoes. The vibration became lighter and soon I heard a mumbled phrase but couldn't make out the content. They had moved on, and it sounded like their direction was away from where I headed. Cautiously I tried my limbs, rose to a squatting position, and studied in every direction. Finally, I detoured in the Niv's direction to get some idea about this group.

After five minutes of travel, I saw movement ahead and froze. I had counted wrong. There were five of them. It was difficult to make out much about them at that distance, but I noted a red jacket and a white toboggan, which might tell me later whether more than one group roamed the area. They were still moving away from where I needed to go, so I let them get out of sight before I started on again.

This time I moved at high-speed to get out of the immediate area before they doubled back. There were at least six more gang members to account for since those ones who followed in the car couldn't still be fooled at this point. Another group was probably already in the woods and more would come.

The landmark knob of rock was finally visible. Taking the brushiest terrain that meandered in that direction, I ran. It was painful travel, but I covered ground fast now that I could use less caution.

I exploded upon them with no warning. Tia literally jumped but didn't make a sound. What a miserable looking lot they were. They sat on their totes, shivering with cold and white with fear. We were much too close to danger, so I motioned them to follow and headed straight out into nowhere with only a distant peak to guide by.

It grew decidedly rockier and the sleeting rain came down hard. I looked back and saw that all four of them looked ghastlier than before. They needed a place to rest—and soon. Rainy carried two totes and I felt like a beast not to have noticed. When I reached for one, she handed me the other. There wasn't much daylight left, and I had no idea what lay ahead. It looked like row upon row of mountains and rocks and trees. I took for granted they would rather be cold and lost than dead, so we kept traveling.

We must have covered four more miles when we came to a shelving rock that would at least give some cover from the rain and sleet. A pencil's thickness of water ran off one place on the ledge.

"Better drink all you can. We don't have any containers, and tomorrow may be a dry day."

That was my gentle way to break the news that we would spend the night out here.

"We're alive anyway," Rainy replied to the general round of groans. "The ground has been a bed long before this."

Tia brought a thermos out of her tote bag and handed it to me with shaking hands.

"We can fill that. I took it with me on set so I could fill it with coffee for all of us—in case we didn't get another motel room tonight. I'm sorry. We drank it all on the way here. We should have saved you some."

"I'm fine. I'm sorry there's nothing to offer you for dinner. I don't know where we are, what's ahead for us, or how long we'll be out here. There was one group of five Nivs searching for us a few miles back that way. There will be others. We won't try to travel any further because it'll be dark soon. . . . No one brought any snacks from craft services, did they?" I said jokingly to lighten their moods.

Four sets of extremely serious eyes told me that no such luxury existed. I hadn't cheered them.

"Is there anything in your bags that might offer a small ounce of comfort for someone?"

"Nothing for comfort, but I've got some tools—sort of," Grady admitted. "You know I told you I collect weapons, unusual weapons, and . . . and I'd put some in my bag to show you if we got off early enough."

"What kinds of weapons," I asked with new interest.

"Throwing weapons."

"He has an arsenal. For two days he's been trying to show them to you," Tia explained. "He's always boring us with demonstrations."

"Sometimes I even hit the target."

Grady laughed sheepishly, obviously not bothered by Tia's comments, or else used to them. Their mood had lightened slightly, and that was good.

"Anything we have is a luxury and might have a purpose. Let's see them. We can't have too many weapons."

He pulled open the top of his bag and inside sat a good sized jack-o'-lantern, complete with half burnt candle. I lifted it out and watched Grady's face turn red.

"What on earth, Grady. Why'd you steal one of the production's pumpkins?" Tim asked.

"I didn't steal it. They threw them all out when they wrapped us for the day. I took one that wasn't broken and stuffed it into my bag . . . so that Warren and I would have a target to set up and could try my throwing weapons. That was back when the day was going great—before he saw the . . . the gang. Everything happened so fast then. We just ran, bags and all. And I carried all that extra weight for nothing. Guess I sort of short circuited."

I wanted to laugh. Finally, I did and at least Rainy joined me.

Grady showed me his collection.

"These are only a few of the pieces I've collected. I have more in the van but I couldn't get to them. These ones I've actually tried. I . . . I saw you carried two guns and . . . well, these aren't much but I thought . . ."

"A throwing axe! Nice. Small and light but well balanced. Have you tried it?"

"Some. I'm okay. I'm better with the Shurikens. I brought throwing stars and throwing spikes with me."

I looked them over interestedly—more to humor Grady. The axe could be useful. The other items probably wouldn't be. The tiny sharp pieces of metal couldn't do much damage next to something heavy like the axe or a club.

"Stick all those in your pocket or belt in case we have to leave in a hurry. Let's lighten your loads and get everyone warmer. I want you to put on any spare wardrobe you have in your bags. It will save carrying them with us tomorrow and you'll be warmer tonight. It would be wise to put your wet clothes on the outside."

They were quick to follow my instructions while hugging the narrow bit of dry wall under the ledge. Tim had brought three extra shirts and gave one of them to Grady who only packed one. Tia and Rainy both put on an extra pair of pants and extra shirts. I was glad wardrobe had required background to bring more than one choice for this shoot. Rainy brought out one of Cal's shirts that she packed for me. Her jacket looked so inadequate that I told her to put the shirt on underneath it as an added windbreaker.

"If you have excess clothes that you can't wear, wrap them around your neck or your head. They'll help hold in your body warmth. Anything left in the bags?"

"Just our purses and the cameras," Tia replied.

"Keep the empty bags with you and use them for pillows. And leave your cell phones off to conserve energy. If for some reason we ever get separated, turn them back on—but in silent mode. We'd better try to rest now. Tomorrow could be difficult."

I sat as far back under the ledge as possible with my back against the wall and watched the rain drip off the edge. The nook was narrow but I could stay almost dry. Occasionally the wind changed direction and made it impossible to keep out the rain. For a while I was lost in my own thoughts and plans. There was much to consider, and I had to be ready to act when the time came.

"Do you think we could have a f-fire later—when it darker," Tia asked. "A s-small one?"

"No fire. I'm cold. We're all cold. . . . Death is cold."

That sobered everyone for a few minutes. Only Rainy sat there stoical in her own discomfort, but with sympathetic eyes turned on her suffering friends. That was when I noticed the other bag that no one had touched. It sat between Rainy and Tia. I had just opened my mouth to ask what was in it when Tia read my mind.

"You wouldn't be interested in this bag. It's just female stuff."

"Oh . . . all right."

"It's the cat," Rainy admitted, exasperatedly. "When we went to get the cameras, I put him in an empty tote so I could show him to some of my friends on the set. I was trying to find someone who would take care of him for a few days. But I didn't have time to ask anyone. Everything happened so fast—like Grady and his pumpkin."

She unzipped the top and the cat stuck its big homely head out and looked around. When a blast of cold, wet air swooped under the ledge, it ducked back into the bag. Even a cat had better sense than to be out on a night like this one. I wished I had a bag big enough to house me. The altitude made it twenty degrees colder than in Long Beach, and the rain was unrelenting.

Rainy shivered and the others were wilting on me. They needed something more bracing than a few dry pieces of clothes, but a fire was risky when we had no idea where our pursuers lurked. They might be as lost as we were, but if they weren't lost, they would probably go to where they had parked their vehicles and wait there until morning. If I could be sure of that, a small fire would be an acceptable risk. With the wind whipping around, wood smoke could come from any direction and could be anybody's fire to these city boys. Even if they waited somewhere close by, they wouldn't likely associate the smoke with us, and they would never be able to travel this terrain at night. If only they were brainless enough to use a big flashlight and let me pick them off one by one.

"All right, I'll chance it and light a small fire. I have matches in my vest, but I'll need some dry, hard wood so it won't smoke much."

They all looked out at the water soaked world, the cold sleety rain, and hunched back further under the rocky ledge. Their suffering was genuine, and I worried about hypothermia.

"Grady, loan me your axe."

That brought Grady and Rainy to their feet. Tia and Tim stirred and tried to make the effort.

"I don't want any of you to come out in the rain. If your clothes get wet, you'll never be able to fight the cold. Stay under the ledge, but exercise, move, do calisthenics, anything to get your blood flowing. I'll build a reflector to hide the fire. It will help send warmth back against that rock wall. We won't catch much of the warmth because this wind will snatch most of it away."

There were plenty of trees nearby of the evergreen variety. I cut three stout poles about three and a half feet long. About ten feet out from our home, I spaced them like fence posts, eight feet apart, and leaning slightly toward us. There wasn't enough dirt to sink them deep, so I built rocks up around the base of each one to steady it. When I had those support poles solid enough, I went back and cut evergreen branches to lean against the sloping poles. There was no lack of available foliage, so I built a thick, solid wall. Already it had blocked some of the wind.

I barely had enough daylight left to find some dry tinder and a few small logs to start the fire. Rainy came out in spite of my orders and took over starting the fire. She had the candle from Grady's pumpkin, which made the task simple, especially since the drizzle had slowed to a mist. I hurried to get more firewood, and Tim and Grady quickly followed suit. We soon had wood enough to keep the fire going all night, but the heat felt so good we went back for one more load. Grady's axe proved invaluable.

We had only enjoyed the fire for a few minutes when Rainy surprised all of us by bringing over Grady's pumpkin. She placed it where the flames weren't so high and raked a few more coals around it.

"It will be burnt in places and half cooked in others but it is food," she said apologetically. "If I had a pot, we could boil it."

I poured a little water into the pumpkin and made a rock wall around its off-fire side to enclose the heat and help it cook more evenly. There wasn't much else we could do except sit and wait. We all stared at that jack-o'-lantern face until its head sank ludicrously and Rainy proclaimed it was now or never.

"It will fall apart if it cooks any longer. We'll eat the soft parts."

I broke off part of the pumpkin and cut it into chunks with my knife. While I portioned out those first pieces, I heard Rainy's voice, softly reverent.

"Thank you, Lord, for this fire, this shelter, and this meal. Amen."

We ate ravenously, though it certainly couldn't compare to pizza. When we consumed all the soft part, I tried to eat one of the half-hard chunks. Burnt and tasteless, it landed in my stomach with a thudding crash. Finally, I followed the others example and put little chunks on green sticks. The fire scorched those pieces that didn't fall off our sticks, but just the same I ate until I felt sick—till the pumpkin's emaciated, grinning face laughed at me in my wretched misery. We left nothing for morning, and I was definitely glad I wouldn't have to eat any more of it.

With the food gone, we all sat hunched forward, soaking up the heat—all but Rainy, that is. She had crumpled over on her hard bed and had fallen fast asleep, too exhausted to do more. I shoved her closer to the wall and wrapped my jacket around her. She never woke.

Tiredness wracked through my own body like actual pain, and I gave in to it when I saw three other sets of eyes keeping watch. It wouldn't be safe to sleep longer than ten minutes I told myself as I fell asleep on the stony ground beside Rainy. Ten minutes later, my natural clock kicked in with its alarm and I awoke. When I saw that nothing had changed, I gave myself another thirty minutes. Without rest I'd never survive what probably lay ahead of me.

Again my inner alarm woke me in exactly thirty minutes. The others slept and the fire had dwindled to a few red coals. After replenishing it generously, I moved to a spot slightly apart from the others so I could keep watch without any campfire light or sounds of breathing to distract me. Not much warmth reached me, but an overhanging rock kept me moderately dry. I leaned back in a stupor, half-awake, half-asleep, but totally alert for any unusual sound, movement, or scent.

Near dawn, Rainy joined me and soon fell asleep again on the ground beside me. I dozed deeply for a long hour and awoke startled, angry with myself for being so weak and careless. When I saw that all was well, I built up the fire again. The air had grown penetratingly chilly but the precipitation had fled during the night. As soon as the sun brought us a little light, we needed to be on the move.

When I stared down at Rainy, barely visible in the light from the fire, strange feelings came to me—strange for someone who had been alone for such a long time. When my wife died, I promptly liquidated most of my stock of emotions and lived bankrupt ever since. For nine years, I had felt nothing except the thrill of the chase—and I hadn't experienced much of that lately. Now both the action and the feelings had come to me all at once, and the effect staggered me, almost intoxicated me.

A gray shadow slid out of Rainy's tote. He walked over to me and rubbed against my hand that rested on my leg. I petted his bony neck, and he purred loudly. The sound woke Rainy, and she smiled up at both of us. She reached for the cat and gave it a strong hug. That was when I decided she maybe only smiled up at the cat.

I watched the gentle way she held it against her. With just enough light to see the tenderness in her eyes, I realized I felt that way toward her. To me she was that helpless, plucky cat, and I wanted to hold her close, protect her, and yes—take her home with me. I had been without anyone for a long time. Now I had grown hungry, unquenchably hungry, insatiably hungry. At that moment, I actually felt willing to stay in LA and make a fool of myself—for a while, anyway. I would do extra work and eat craft services if necessary. Maybe I had finally cracked, or maybe I ate too much raw pumpkin.

Chapter 8

If our pursuers thought we spent the night in the woods, they would probably start their search from the parking field at dawn. We had traveled a good distance from there and should continue heading away from that direction no matter where it took us. If we didn't dawdle, they wouldn't catch up with us. If they came upon our shelter and burned-out fire, they probably wouldn't surmise it was ours, but just the same we wouldn't leave them any clues.

"The cat just ate the last of its food. I hope we get out today." Rainy folded the empty bag.

The others rose stiffly at those words.

"What about us, Rainy? We like to eat too. You're lucky he's so scrawny," Tim teased. "Otherwise he might already be on a spit."

That comment didn't exactly please Rainy, but it showed that their spirits were up.

"We leave in five minutes," I told them. "Bring your empty bags with you. Don't leave anything here and drink all you can before we start out. We may not find more water. Does anyone know the layout of this area? We want to get to a road or a town as soon as possible. We don't want to travel in the direction of the old film set. Luckily, the sun will guide us for a while."

"Tim and I made a roadmap before we came to this event, but its back in my van."

"I remember the area," Tim said. "The lakes should be south of us. The same highway we came in on runs along the north shore of the lakes and then at the east end it turns north. That means if we go south or east, we'll hit something. The film set was west of here, and north contains a whole lot of nothing. There could be some smaller roads or trails in between the highways.

"I take it this area boasts no towns?"

"Small towns, big lakes. I think Big Bear Lake and Lake Baldwin cover about fifteen miles from west to east."

"Let's head south-southeast and choose the easiest terrain we can find. We'll try to keep landmarks in sight so we won't lose our bearings if a cloud cover comes in, but I'll make a compass if we get lost. Let's move fast and get out of here quick."

I didn't tell them we had been heading more northerly all along. We would likely spend another night in the woods unless we found a trail and easier traveling. However, trails were places where the gang could patrol in the luxury of their vehicles. I also didn't tell them that civilization would bring worse danger. These woods might seem like a vacation next to what we could face when we emerge from the wilds.

Before we left, I took all the cut branches and dropped them down a steep incline. After covering the fire with dirt, I scattered the rocks. If anyone passed that way, they would never guess it had served as a camping spot.

From that point on, we traveled up and down more than south or east. I carried the cat bag. Rainy thought that was unfair, but I explained to her that the skinny critter probably didn't weigh as much as my boots. I advised them to use caution, but it wasn't long until I noted they had left that department to me. They followed behind, looked down at their feet, and epitomized weariness.

At two in the afternoon, I called a halt near a trickle of water. We didn't talk, but I signaled them to rest. They understood because they all dropped to the ground and went promptly to sleep. I leaned against a rock but didn't dare follow suit.

After about thirty minutes, I caught a slight whiff of smoke in the air. Smoke could travel a long distance, so it might mean anything, but it increased my caution. The only breeze came from the east. I breathed deeply a few times and soon detected the smoke again. With new concern, I nudged each of them with my boot and motioned them to silently follow.

We backtracked to where I remembered a rocky area with plenty of small caves. When we came to one that would hide them from sight on three sides, I risked a quiet conversation.

"I smell smoke, probably not close, but I need to investigate. Stay hidden here and don't make any noise. Rainy, turn your phone on silent mode. If you run into trouble, call me. I may be gone a good while, so take turns keeping guard so everyone will get a chance to rest."

Following the scent on the breeze, I looked behind me often enough to remember my return route in case darkness set in before I could return. I climbed the first rise I found but couldn't see much because of the trees. When I descended its other side, I saw the smoldering remains of a campfire. About forty yards beyond stretched a road that was, no doubt, accessible to the public. I studied it from above for a long five minutes.

No fires were allowed in this area, so it wasn't the headquarters of any regular campers. A small, rocky mound hid the spot from the road, and the three nylon bags laying close beside the fire heralded someone's eventual return. From my point of observation, I couldn't assess the narrow tire tracks in the soil, but I assumed a motorcycle or cycles made them.

I crept slowly down and made a slow circle of the area before I ventured to the edge of the road. It looked empty, so I hurried back to their fire to see what story the sandy soil and tracks might tell me. Evidently, three motorcycles had parked behind the rise, so that told me the Nivs were patrolling roads in the area. They had no way of knowing for sure we were in the wilderness, so someone had become very desperate. They had to cover every possibility because they couldn't risk losing us.

On top of one of their packs rested a box of two dozen donuts that no bug or Niv had violated yet. I just stood and stared at it for a good minute, as if it were a mirage that would disappear if I reached for it. Eventually, the knowledge that I had found treasure and had the survival skills needed to take it with me and leave no clues sank into my stunned brain.

With a small stick, I drew coon tracks in the soil around their camp. Then I really got into the game and drew some whopping big bear tracks. Even if they knew nothing about bear tracks, the size alone would make them jittery come nightfall.

When I had drawn enough tracks to sufficiently frame all the critters in the area, I investigated the packs—at least those that a coon would be able to open. More food appeared. It was still in plastic bags from the grocery store. There were candy bars, marshmallows, beef jerky, and an unopened package of hotdogs. There was no ice chest around, so they must have brought it recently and must have intended to stay the night.

I took one of the plastic bags and dumped all the donuts into it except for a small piece of one, which I dropped in the sand. I gave the box a toss into the brush nearby—close enough they would be sure to find it. I raggedly ripped open the hotdog package and dropped them loosely into another plastic bag. The wrapper I pushed partway into the loose sand by the fire. The candy bars and marshmallows received the same treatment and joined the donuts in the plastic bag. Finally, I demolished the rest of the plastic bags and scattered them around.

To complete the maneuver, I pulled clothes from their totes—a sweat shirt, jacket, and toboggan—and left them in the dirt as if an animal had pulled them out while looking for food. That was all I could steal and still blame on a family of coons, so I took my two bags and hurried to where I had left the others. Our situation grew more complicated, but at least we could face it with full stomachs.

When I came upon their hiding spot, complete silence met me. It scared me for a minute as I imagined the worst. I burst into the niche only to come upon four anxious individuals with different sizes of wood clubs in their hands. At once, I knew I shouldn't have left them without weapons. They had a right to defend themselves if I failed.

"Dinner." I announced in a low voice, breaking the tense spell. "I borrowed it from some Nivs who are patrolling a lonesome stretch of road just ahead of us."

"Then they know we're in here? And they know we're close if you . . ." Grady couldn't decide how to finish it so Rainy took over.

"Did you . . . kill them?"

I realized I had been much too sudden for their taut nerves.

"I didn't see anyone, so I left animal tracks around their dying campfire, spread the contents of their packs out over the dirt, animal style, and took most of their grub, just like some hungry coons would have done if they'd come upon it first. The gang doesn't know we're in here, but someone thinks we may be in here, so the gang is out in full force."

We feasted on cold hotdogs and donuts, saving the candy and jerky for later.

"I see no good plan or clear route we can take. If they knew for sure we were here, I'd break heads, one by one. Since they still act uncertain, we should play it cautious. We've done well so far. With about three hours of daylight left, we have time to back away from that road and head south until we find a good place to hole up tonight. Sorry we can't use the road. It would make things much simpler. If I knew our location, I'd call for rescue. But if some car or copter searched and asked questions of the wrong people, we might be serving death warrants to other innocent victims as well as ourselves.

"Anyone have any other ideas? I could wait until these guys come back to their fire, incapacitate them, and take their cycles away. We could ride out of here in style. . . . I would like to see their faces when they find the mess I left."

"More of them may wait further down the road. None of us have much experience on motorcycles, and they'd certainly know we were here if we did anything like that."

Rainy gave the answer I hoped she would give, and the others obviously agreed. We changed our course and walked through an area of rougher terrain. At least it wasn't the dry season for the area. We found enough water to fill Tia's thermos and to take a good drink before nightfall. Another hour of toil brought us to a satisfactory spot where we could hole up for the night—a tiny bare spot of ground against a rock wall with plenty of evergreen foliage to block the wind and hide us at the same time.

"No fire tonight. We're too close to civilization. If you want to cut a few branches for beds, do it now. We have about twenty minutes of light left. No talking or loud chopping. Those sounds carry a long distance."

We sat back and ate candy, marshmallows, and beef jerky. I watched Rainy pull off a strip of her jerky and pass it to the cat. He threw it into the air a couple of times as if it was a mouse and he wasn't sure if it was alive or dead. He then devoured it from head to tail, licking his paws when he was done. He made it look better than it was. When his gaze came to rest on my jerky, I crammed the last chunk into my mouth and looked at him innocently.

Once all the food was gone, they went directly to sleep even though a few minutes of twilight remained. I parked myself on the ground at the only entrance to our wilderness bedroom, behind a short, bushy evergreen. I found a sloping, smooth rock there and leaned back against it with my legs stretched out. I intended to sleep, had to sleep, but couldn't get too comfortable or I might miss warning sounds.

I had hardly shut my eyes when something dark and furry startled me by leaping aboard and making itself comfortable on my lap. I had never heard anyone call him by name so I decided then to call him Cat. He was warm, so I let him stay, but I would rather have used him for a pillow. For a while, his purring drowned out all the other sounds around me, as if it came from somewhere deep in a great cavern. No doubt it did, considering the size of his lanky frame.

I missed the fire as much as the others, but even under the present conditions my life had improved from a week ago. My eyes drifted over to Rainy, who had buried herself in evergreen branches. Yes, my feelings went beyond the excitement of action. All four of these temporary orphans had invaded my life, and Rainy had invaded my heart.

Darkness settled in and an owl's hoot brought to me the realism of our situation. I stared up at the starlit sky and before I could get sentimental again I fell asleep. I was deep in sleep when a loud hiss came from somewhere near my midsection. Sharp claws reached through my clothes and punctured my flesh. Cat stood bristled on my diaphragm and let out another loud hiss followed by an eerie, high-pitched song or moan, I wasn't sure which described it.

"Whoa! Get going," an alarmed male voice articulated.

The sound of footfalls and bodies rubbing against brush was followed by more mumbled exclamations. I heard the words "wild cat." By their wildly waving flashlight beam, I could tell they were retreating from our area. I didn't move, but the Glock stayed in my hand. There was enough moonlight to see Rainy's and Grady's heads raised. I hoped they could see me. I motioned silence—and waited.

The sounds of our night visitors continued but grew fainter. Obviously, Cat heard them too because he stayed perched alertly on top of me. When the sound died away, I reached out my left hand to pet his fur-covered bones. He purred, rolled into a tight ball, and went to sleep, but that ended sleep for me. I knew we couldn't stay there and risk the same again. The evening had hardly begun. Those guys might find their courage and come back with catnip. They probably already felt ashamed at running from the hiss of a tiger. City boys—how I loved them!

I lifted Cat's limp, sleepy body into his tote-bag home. The space was so inadequate the poor cat couldn't stand upright, but he didn't complain, and I closed Him in. The others sensed the change and climbed out of their beds.

"Let's risk moving toward a place where it's less lonesome," I said softly. "We'll follow the edge of the road, cautiously and quietly. It's not eight o'clock yet. There's a long night ahead of us and too much risk if we stay here."

I hung the strap of Cat's tote over my shoulder, but Grady took it from me and pointed to my piece, which I still held in my right hand. I nodded. He was right. I should stay unencumbered. They all brought their clubs. We set off and kept to clear ground until we reached the road. It looked deserted, so we stayed near the edge and moved quickly and cautiously. After about two miles of fast travel, we reached the top of a rise and could see the lights of a town ahead.

We saw no campfires or motorcycles, but if they were off the road like the camp I raided, we wouldn't see them till too late. I had hardly completed the thought when the headlights of two cycles turned our way from the direction of the town. We left the road quickly and moved behind cover. The cyclists acted like kids out on a lark, not surveillance experts, but I didn't let that fool me. In the wrong circumstances, those kids could become lethal. They stormed past, and we scurried back to the road edge before their dust settled.

"We should be able to reach that town before everything shuts down for the night," I explained quietly.

"We're not going to get a motel room . . . are we?" Tia asked hopefully yet with horror in her voice at the same time.

At least they understood the danger.

"Not on your life. But maybe we can get out of this area and find a better and safer place to sleep."

That was the best way to tell them I had no plan. The sight of civilization rejuvenated all of us, and we even jogged at times on the downhill sections. We reached the outskirts of the small town by nine o'clock.

"Not enough movement for us to attempt much. They're sure to scrutinize every taxi on the road."

We hadn't gone far when Rainy took hold of my arm and pointed to a church steeple on the next block.

"A church, Warren. We might find help there."

"Not there, baby. It's Saturday night and the place looks empty."

I looked again and decided to swing by it. It wasn't the type of accommodations I sought, but it could work admirably. It had no close neighbors and sat in a commercial area that looked deserted right now. There were two parts to the building—the church itself and a small section attached to it that probably housed a classroom or office.

"Wait here in the shrubbery while I slip close and see if anyone's home."

I checked along the back walls first but found no opening that invited welcome. The front and side church doors boasted substantial looking locks. Of course, I could open any door, but tonight I wanted to leave absolutely no evidence of entry. The windows on the church or on the attachment could be jimmied if nothing better presented itself. Cautiously I moved around to the church's attachment. It possessed a simple lock on its one door that graciously bid us welcome. My knife opened it in thirty seconds and left no marks. I motioned the others to join me, and now Tia had her motel room.

Rainy had saved the candle from the pumpkin, so we lit it to search the room. The area evidently served as church office, classroom, and church kitchen. Tightly closed blinds covered its two windows, but I didn't trust them to totally hide light from the outside world. We found tape and enough black plastic garbage bags to cover them. Now we could have light and not worry about intruders.

The church people had left the door leading from that room into the church unlocked, so as soon as I had studied the outside world adequately, we moved into the church itself. The two windows in there had blinds also, which we covered before we switched on the church lights.

"There you go now, row upon row of hard wooden beds plus two bathrooms—luxury indeed for a band of vagrants. Someone find the thermostat and turn up the heat. We can make a reasonable amount of noise in here since I doubt it would carry outside these walls. Avoid leaving fingerprints."

I hadn't finished my speech before Tia and Rainy found the refrigerator. It housed a half-full bowl of a potato salad of some denomination, and eight sandwiches in a plastic bag. They looked like chicken salad—no doubt leftovers from a church supper. There were five of us, so I mentally divided the sandwiches in half, came up with sixteen halves, and took my four halves greedily. That left them with an even twelve, which they could easily divide among four.

Rainy found plastic plates, cups, and silverware, and Tia found grape juice and a bag of tiny crackers in the cupboard—no doubt used for church communion. We took our feast into the church and consumed it quickly—all except Rainy. Rainy took hers to the piano and pattered out soft snatches of melody while she ate. I watched her give an entire half sandwich to Cat, and I felt guilty right down to my half-empty stomach. I had eaten the one that should have gone to the gray beast. She finished long after the rest of us. She looked so happily full, but she must have seen the hunger in my eyes—at least the food hunger.

"I know how you love to eat, and I've asked God for food ever since that first night down at the beach. We've had fish, pumpkin, hotdogs, donuts, candy, jerky, and now this nice church meal. I'd like to play a song or two on this piano, just to celebrate. And if you're still hungry, we can call for pizza delivery or anything you want."

It sounded so good I was tempted to do it, the pizza, that is. My stomach would get us killed yet—maybe the pizza delivery person too. I started to tell her that the pizza and the music should wait for a more appropriate, safer time, but their feelings were up, and I didn't want to ruin that, especially since risk was minimal.

"If anyone here isn't willing to risk their life for a song and a pizza, tell me now because Rainy's at the piano and I'm calling for delivery."

I heard instant applause—quiet, but applause nonetheless. I looked up the church's address in the office and used that phone to order the goods. Gambling that the delivery person didn't belong to this church, I told them to bring the order to the side church door.

When I got back, they were in the middle of a song I had never heard. I stood there awkwardly until they finished singing. I gave up mentioning about fingerprints again.

"Don't you want to sing a song with us while we wait for the pizza and our fast approaching death by untold numbers of gang members?"

I liked her realistic joke about our situation. I played along since everyone seemed lighter.

"I don't know many church songs. Maybe a funeral song would suffice."

She started Rock of Ages, and I followed the best I could. I knew the tune, but the only words I recognized were Rock of Ages, so I hummed the tune, interspersed with my three words through thee long verses. When we finished, Grady walked up to the podium and found a collection basket, which he proceeded to pass around to the congregation. Tim and Tia shook their heads good-naturedly, but Rainy took a bill out of her purse and dropped it in. I knew she couldn't afford to give that money, and Grady seemed upset by it.

"I'm just in fun, Rainy. Shouldn't you hold onto all your cash until better times? Later on we can send money to the church and pay for their hospitality."

"It amounted to almost nothing. Besides, you can't out-give God. He multiplies everything you offer Him."

Her sincerity was so convincing, for a minute I felt like putting my Glock in the collection basket. I could sure use a second one. Her statement must have moved Grady too because he reached into his pocket and brought out all his change.

"He might as well have mine since I can't buy anything with that little bit of change. That breaks me. Maybe we can get to the post office pretty soon and pick up our checks."

That pleased Rainy so much I wished I had something on me besides a credit card. She immediately played another melody on the piano.

"Tim," I called softly so as not to interrupt the song, "Draw me a rough map of this area." I handed him a piece of paper and pen I found in the church office. "I especially want to know the location of the parking field where we left our vehicles and how far it is from here."

"I'd guess it's six or seven miles, maybe eight," he said as he penned a rough diagram.

My body said, "Don't try it! Stay in the church and rest," but duty drowned out its wise counsel. Tim completed the map just as Pizza Man arrived. With Rainy still working away on the piano, we gave off the distinct impression of a church social or departmental meeting.

My credit card paid for the pizza, and I offered to add an ultra-generous tip if he would drop me off at a point I hastily chose from Tim's map—one within short walking distance of the parking area that our cars might still inhabit. He liked the idea of extra money.

The fragrance of hot pizza rolled my way from those still unopened boxes and almost brought tears to my eyes. I wanted mightily to take a few slices with me, but that same fragrance might carry and give me away to waiting noses. If everything went as planned, I would soon walk into enemy territory.

When the pizza deliverer headed for his car, I quickly turned to the others. "Grady, loan me your axe. All of you stay put, stay quiet, no more piano, and get some sleep. If I'm not back before Sunday school tomorrow, go to the police and tell your entire story. No—don't go to them. Call them and have them come to you." I hurried out to jump in Pizza Man's car before he left without me.

I kept the man talking about himself until I recognized the intersection where we turned to go up to the shoot on Friday morning. When he let me out, I headed toward the only lit up store in the area. After he turned his car and moved out of sight, I hurried up the dark, obviously seldom traveled, road. Soon I would know the fate of Tia's van and my rental, and I would know if any gang members still waited there.

Upon nearing the dirt parking lot, I increased my watchfulness and slid into cover at the side of the road. Moonlight revealed the outline of cars ahead—two cars and a van. With a full night ahead of me, I tried to exercise some patience by visualizing empty pizza boxes and sleeping fugitives. My rental and the van appeared to be unoccupied and unhurt. The third car, a customized, fancy rig, sat about fifteen yards to the right of the van. The glow of a cigarette shone through a half-open window.

I made out four people in the car and the remains of a burnt out campfire nearby, which told me their story and condition. These members stayed to watch the vehicles, hoping we would foolishly return for them. They were probably enduring their second night here and were probably tired of the whole camping experience—especially the wood gathering, the cold, and the uncomfortable beds. With disenchantment in the ascendancy, they all got into their car.

All at once their engine started and confirmed my reasoning. They would run the heater, off and on, for warmth and would bitterly contemplate another uncomfortable night. Under such conditions, they wouldn't reach a point of sound sleep, not with four people sitting upright in a mid-sized car. Slowly I moved around to the other side and saw that they had flattened all the tires of my rental. I expected the same for the van, but found only two of its tires down. That left me enough room to squirm under it. From there I could hear a few mumbled words at times. My stomach growled and told me I should have eaten some of the pizza. The loud rumble of my innards would give me away, not my pizza breath.

The breeze coming from their direction brought traces of marijuana smoke. I stretched my legs and tried to find comfort. I needed information. These guys probably didn't know the real reason they pursued us—beyond revenge, that is. Likely, just the gang leader had contact with the wet suit man, and I doubted that he had been told the actual truth. If our wet suit man would eliminate six people who knew less than nothing about his crime, he wouldn't carelessly proclaim his dirty deeds to others who could, later on, make his situation worse.

Experience and reasoning told me the Nivs, including their leader, didn't know the truth. The best I could expect out of this night's misery was to hear a name that would lead me to more information.

It soon looked like I had sacrificed for nothing. Two hours on the hard ground and nothing had happened. More time passed, and I thought I caught the name Britt Turner. It could mean something or it might mean nothing. Some of them had worked as extras on the set where Britt played the lead, and they might naturally discuss it. That seemed likely since they referred to him by his complete name. If they knew him, or worked for him, they would call him either Britt or Turner—not both.

It would help if they said the name of their gang leader. He would at least know who hired him—the only information I needed. If I could get one of them alone, I could bust the information out of him, but so far no opportunity presented itself.

The hours rolled tediously on. No other cars showed up. I must have fallen asleep because my cell phone's vibration in my vest pocket startled me. I glanced out and everything appeared quiet with my four neighbors. Evidently they slept. Anyone could be calling, or it could be Rainy. She wouldn't call unless it was important. I worked it out of my pocket and found a short text message from Rainy: Three Niv's outside.

Swiftly as possible, I slid from under the van and staggered stiffly erect. It was time to turn loose the monster. I walked straight up to the car, yanked open the door on the dozing driver, and dragged him out into the dust. The blunt side of Grady's axe rapped his head one blow, and he sank unconscious. The guy directly behind him opened his door to get out, and I slammed it so solidly on him it lifted the car's chassis. When he let out a howl, I opened the door enough for him to extricate his legs. Immediately I rammed it shut again. He scrambled to follow the other back seat occupant out the right side door. The guy who was in the front passenger's seat had already vacated and came around the car toward me. The instant that

Wounded-Knee in the back seat leapt free of the car, I jumped into the driver's seat and took off.

One door still hung open, so I swerved in a half circle and nicely grazed one of them. He slid about fifteen feet, and the open door slammed shut. The other two Nivs ran for cover, and I let them flee unimpeded. I might regret that later, but now I had to get to church—on time. I pushed the souped-up vehicle to its limit. Lucky for me, no cops patrolled that area right then, and no early-morning motorists drove about yet.

My heart sank when I saw three cycles outside the church and realized the front door stood part open—so much for my neat entry job. They had beaten the lock into submission with clubs, but they hadn't carelessly shot it open and drawn outside attention. The church light was on, and I could hear sounds of a struggle inside. My Glock filled my right hand, and Grady's axe filled my left as I pulled the church door closed behind me.

Grady and Tim had profited from my exhibition on the movie set. They possessed the church's wood podium, one on each end, and took down their assailant with it. I saw no gun—only a knife and an extremely ugly club. My eyes searched for Rainy and Tia. Noise came from the other room, and I left the guys to take care of their assailant.

The Nivs must have gained entry only minutes before I arrived. Two of them bore down on the girls. The bleeding gash on Rainy's shoulder awakened a second monster for me to unleash. This monster wasn't noble or brave. It simply wanted to kill. I discarded gun and axe, grabbed them both by the backs of their jackets, and spun them around. I hit one solidly on the chin with my knee and he instantly left the game. The other one ate his spiked metal club. He screamed so loudly I had to slug him. When he crumpled and fell asleep, I stood there for a second in disappointment. I still wanted to play, and there lay a couple of quitters.

Tim and Grady attempted to pin their guy down, but he still had plenty of life in him.

Just as I yelled, "Save that one for questioning," Grady came down hard with his wood club and number three quit the game.

That left nothing to do but drag him into the room with the other two. We couldn't wait around for one of them to awake. These guys may not have called for aid, but the ones who loaned me their car would definitely have drummed up help by now.

"Tim, where'd you put that roll of tape?"

He handed it to me, his eyes big and wondering.

"Both you guys make sure no one's outside and then bring those cycles into the church and let the air out of their tires. Turn out the church lights and tear all those plastic bags off the windows.

"Now get out of here, all of you. You don't need to watch. No sense having to punch out the same faces twice. It's time we cut their numbers. All of you . . . out. Get your stuff together so we can leave." When they didn't move fast enough, I shoved them into the church. "I'll be a minute—a short minute."

I gave my sternest warning look to Rainy and Tia and closed the door on them. All three gang members remained unconscious, so it made my job easy. I tore the clothes off number one, bound him with tape to where he couldn't wiggle a finger, and shoved him aside so I could start on number two. Rainy busted through the door while I taped him.

"Warren, don't m-murder . . . them . . . oh."

"Rainy, I said stay out."

"S-Sorry. I thought you meant to kill them."

I ignored her and continued with the tape. When the door closed, I had my grim chuckle. Number three depleted the roll of tape, so I didn't bother about their mouths. They wouldn't shout for help. I stuffed their handguns in my vest and threw their other weapons, their clothes, cell phones, and wallets into the last of the plastic garbage bags. Their chances of getting free stood at nil, but if they accomplished the impossible, it was a known fact that most people hesitate to run naked onto a city street. Of course, if they felt like dressing first, they could wrap up in the restroom's toilet tissue, about the only covering I left them besides the window blinds.

I quickly wrote a note and put it where church patrons would find it upon entering the premises: These three men broke into the church. They are gang members and dangerous. Call the police.

"Good luck, boys," I said to their sleeping bodies when I left the place.

Chapter 9

These three Niv's might be out of the running, but no telling how many hunted us right then. With only the Niv's car to carry us to safety, we needed to vacate the area promptly.

"Here, kitty," Rainy called, and searched the church for her cat while the others carried the bags to the car.

She looked tired, worse than tired, and she definitely hurt. In addition to the cut on her shoulder, I saw a wicked bruise above her left eye and blood on her wrist. Her clothes probably hid other wounds. She needed a doctor, but first I had to get us safely away from this area and dump the borrowed vehicle.

The cat ran out of hiding and headed for the tote like he had found home.

"Everyone get in the car, quick." I helped Rainy and her pet into the front seat. "The Nivs will recognize their own auto the minute they see it, so it won't do any good to duck down unless we drive into a shooting situation. Meanwhile, keep watch."

"It was my fault they saw us. I opened the door at the wrong time," Grady confessed, breaking into my thoughts.

"Anytime would have been the wrong time.

"We were worried about you. I planned to run down toward where we left the vehicles and see if I could learn anything . . . or help. I had barely opened the door when I saw three guys there on their cycles. They probably just stopped to talk with each other, but when they saw me duck back in so quick, they became suspicious. I don't think they could have recognized me, though there was a light behind me."

"That was your second mistake."

"I know. We turned out the lights right away and made a hole in the plastic so we could peek out the window. One of them walked up to the church door and knocked. When the other two joined him, Rainy called you. They were definitely suspicious, but still uncertain. They had some kind of confab before they went to work on the lock. Rainy told us to take our clubs and hide, that maybe you'd get here in time."

I couldn't comment. The sick feeling inside me said this narrow escape was much too narrow. What would have happened if the hills had cut off phone reception, and I hadn't arrived in time?

"Tim and I hid up by the podium so we could see them when the door opened. They stood there for a minute as if they were undecided what to do. One of them found the switch and turned on the light."

"Their hesitancy probably saved you from gunplay. If they had known for sure whom they had cornered, they would have charged in ready for slaughter. They couldn't be sure you weren't someone like a janitor who got scared when three people loitered outside the church at this time of the morning. They might not have tried the door at all if there'd been a vehicle parked outside to show that someone could be inside working—getting the church ready for Sunday service."

"I guess it would have been smarter to shake a mop out the door or throw a bag of garbage out. . . . Anyway, Tim and I ducked down when the light came on. They must have only glanced around the church before they headed for the kitchen. When we heard Tia scream, we jumped out of hiding and charged the closest one with the . . . well, you know the rest because you came in then."

"I take the blame, Grady. I never should have left. I took an unnecessary risk and accomplished nothing except to lose a pound or two by not eating any of the pizza."

"Did you see my van?" Tia asked.

"Both vehicles sat on flat tires but looked undamaged otherwise. A car full of Nivs kept watch in case we came back, but they knew they would get hauled in as suspects if a patrol car saw them parked beside vandalized vehicles. Hopefully, that means no one messed with your van's contents."

I glanced over at Rainy again and noted her closed eyes. She either had fallen asleep or was unconscious. We had driven a good distance from the town, and I was about to plan our next action when a car pulled onto the highway about a mile ahead of us, coming our way. That was gang and no mistaking. With no place to get off the road, we owned about a minute of anonymity. I pulled close behind the pickup truck in front of me and hugged the right side of the road to prevent recognition as long as possible.

They passed us and hit their brakes, but it didn't do them any good because there were cars behind and to the side of them. They pulled off the road onto the shoulder and it would only take a minute before they found a chance to circle back. I accelerated and passed cars rashly. The owner of our car had modified it to handle such a challenge, and I used everything it had. Rainy came to life and drew in an extremely audible breath when we barely missed a head on collision with a tractor-trailer.

"I'm sorry, Rainy. I'll be more careful."

"Be less careful," she gasped. "I'd rather stare into the headlights of a semi as I leave this world than a club with demon eyes behind it."

Even as she talked, I counted two cars now in pursuit and gaining. If they got close, they might use guns or might get in front and behind us to purposely slow us—which would be worse. I could contend with one car but not two. Our situation grew grave.

"Hold on!"

I demanded everything the car possessed and passed seven vehicles in a blur—in a distance hardly adequate for passing half that many. When I squeezed back into traffic, I knew I had taken the Nivs by surprise and gained on them. I saw a narrow road that turned off to the right. With no time to analyze the wisdom of such a move, I made a sharp right turn and almost sanded the paint off the left side of the car on a rock wall. No telling where the road led, but I couldn't stay on that other highway and let them come up on us. They obviously had fast cars too, maybe faster than ours.

"Watch behind. Tell me the second you see them. We may have gained a minute or two. They'll miss the road we took, but they'll come back and find it. I need a place where we can make a stand. Anything will serve our purposes better than this car."

"I see a car. It's probably them," Tim hollered. "It's barely in sight."

My experience with gangs told me they wouldn't act foolishly bold or brave. Otherwise, they would all be in jail and there would be no gangs outside. These guys were steeped in crime and had gained experience because of it. I had to think like them so I could anticipate their next move.

They wouldn't sacrifice their lives or their fine autos, no matter how much the pay or benefits. They wouldn't necessarily follow instructions to the letter either. That made them unpredictable to some extent, but after their encounter with guns at the garage had failed, they had grown more cautious or else had a deeper plan that still eluded me. One point for sure, our deaths wouldn't look accidental if we had club and knife marks on us any more than with shells imbedded in us. If they planned to take us alive, or half-alive, they might as well quit now. I wouldn't let that happen.

"They're about the same distance," Tim said breathlessly. "Maybe gained some, but not much."

"Everyone get your club and stick it in your belt or pants. Get me a small, plain club from that bag of Niv's junk."

When I heard some poorly stifled groans, I knew I should have explained more adequately. I tried to use language they would grasp.

"We won't fight them with clubs. We'll use our clubs as props and our acting skills to convince them we have no guns. I'm guessing they'd prefer to bang us to death or take us alive, but I know they'll shoot if it becomes necessary. We need to get behind cover or out of range before they use their pieces."

Directly ahead of us I saw what looked like a possibility. I braked, almost putting us through the windshield, as we careened into the side of a raggedly rough incline."

"Those still alive scramble up that hill. Whatever you do, don't slip," I shouted as I shoved Rainy ahead of me. "Cat will be alright in the car, Rainy. Don't stop unless I tell you to."

I stayed below them. At the first sign of a leveled gun, I knew what to do and knew I could do it better than our pursuers, but I wouldn't start that type of business because they would definitely shoot back and might hit one of us.

"If shooting starts, move like lightning to get behind the largest rock you can find and stay put."

We had made good progress up the hill when both cars zoomed into our parking lot. They piled out like kids at a picnic and scrambled up like monkeys high on speed. We could never outrun these young punks. They carried plenty of weapons in their hands, but the only guns I could see were stuffed under their belts.

Tia screamed, and I jumped sideways to break her slide, but Grady got to her first. I slid five feet down but managed to catch an anchored rock. Nine gang members climbed the side of the hill. Some climbed swifter than others, but they all moved admirably. I tried to keep my eyes on Rainy half of the time. Although she climbed hurt, she outstripped us all. I knew from experience that no one's energy could last forever, and I was ready if she faltered. The slope didn't slope anymore. It had become downright steep and almost as dangerous as our pursuers.

"I thought you said none of us would die falling off a cliff," Rainy hollered down to me, loud proof that she was still alive and game.

"If I did, I meant it. Let's live, Rainy. . . . Everyone climb toward the right," I bellowed up at them with my loudest voice, "up, and to the right."

The gang heard me and headed toward the right—and that was right where I wanted them. The hill wasn't leveling off but I saw scattered level spots where I could make a stand.

Some of the gang had come close enough to use guns now, but they hadn't brought them out. They must have felt tremendously certain of themselves. One Niv arrogantly threw a small rock at me and grinned as if it was a big joke. When the rock fell short by ten feet, I could have laughed loudly. Then I did. We had reached the middle of the rubble area that I had sought from the beginning. If those rocks hadn't been up ahead of me, I would already have emptied a couple of guns. And these jokers thought they could knock me down throwing puny rocks with their puny muscles—uphill no less! Grady could have done better.

"Come on, come on!" my voice roared out on its own without asking my good sense if such arrogance was wise. "Hey, Rainy, watch me SWAT them out. These ones are for you."

I laughed and rolled rocks and threw rocks. It felt so good, I sang, loud and lustily, in time with my work. At least I sang the three words I knew of the song that would most please Rainy.

"Rock of Ages . . . Rock of Ages . . . Rock of Ages . . . Rock of Ages . . . And another one . . . and another one . . . Rock of Ages . . . hey! Aren't you going to stay for the chorus? Come back up here. Rock of Ages . . ."

Tim, Grady, and Tia had come down closer and had gotten into the act.

"Use the rocks like large throwing stars, Grady, and go for it."

He did just that, and his aim proved well above average. We had to pry some of the rocks loose, but we still managed to keep the slope alive with rocks of all sizes, and they did their work. It quickly became a fiasco. No one below had time to pull out their pieces. By the second verse of the song, I was rolling.

"Rock of Ages . . . Rock of Ages . . . Rainy, they won't stay and let me finish my song."

I turned to find Rainy and saw that she had crumpled against a rock. She attempted a weary smile, but I saw beyond it. She needed her wound patched before she lost any more blood, and she needed rest—days and nights of it.

"Hold the rocks," I ordered, "and get behind cover till they move out. Whatever you do, don't get in range of their guns."

A swift, painful slide down the hill brought me within good Glock range. We needed one of those vehicles and not the one we drove here because I busted its tire when I stopped. Luckily, the closest car faced the hill head on. That gave me command of all four doors. I sent lead into the legs of a Niv who hit the level and headed for the driver's door. I had no qualms about killing one of them after how they had treated Rainy. I wanted them gone the quickest way possible, but I also needed to sting enough of them to insure they wouldn't pursue further.

I kept the rounds coming and stung two more when they

approached the car. Another brought out his piece, and I left a memento in his shoulder. A fifth one got off two rounds before I perforated him. By that time, they'd all caught the message and hurried to squeeze into the remaining car, burning rubber out of there in the opposite direction from where they had come in.

Rainy and the others had disobeyed. They clung to the hill right behind me and were ready to go. Tia told Rainy she would get the cat. She helped Rainy into the back seat where she slumped against a corner. The Nivs had thoughtfully left the key in the ignition. I punched the trunk button and hollered for them to stow everything from the other car in the back.

"Tia, get me the license number of both these cars."

While they took care of that, I checked the load in my Glock and put it on my lap. The two in my vest and the one on my leg hadn't been used, so I was ready for action in case the Nivs got their nerve back. I doubted they would. Five of the nine sustained bullet wounds, and they had only one car. They would want to go somewhere and get patched up. I intended the same for Rainy. At the main highway, I turned left to head back toward the town, but Rainy revived enough to call me on my move.

"Don't return to that trap. Get as far from there as you can get."

"We're going to a doctor, or a hospital."

"We're going to the first populated area we find and rent another car. Then you'll find us a motel room. . . . The bleeding stopped. We'll buy some medicine and bandages . . . and cat food."

I didn't realize someone so little and beat up could sound so stern and resolute, but I was stubborn too.

"Warren . . . I want to live," she said desperately when I didn't stop. "Get me a soft bed . . . and a pizza."

She had said the magic words. I u-turned the car. With Tim giving directions, we reached civilization and a rental car agency in record time.

"If you touched their car anywhere, wipe off your prints while I rent us another ride. Grady, you'll follow us in the rental, and we'll dump this one somewhere along the way."

It didn't take long. Less than thirty minutes later we dropped the Niv's car in a spot where it wouldn't be found for a while and where it would confuse them about our whereabouts. After I called and reported my other rental stolen, we hurried off in the new one to find a motel room.

We found accommodations in a good neighborhood with plenty of eateries all around it. We could hole up there at least a couple of days. Rainy was asleep so I carried her in and put her on the bed. Tia and Tim knew the area and volunteered to drive somewhere for supplies and eats. They looked gray and tired but were up for it, and Grady went with them. Cat and I sat and stared at each other hungrily and waited for their return.

After a short time, I began to study the junk we collected from the three new church attendees. It didn't take long to write down all the numbers on the cell phones and the information from their driver's licenses. They had little money, but I expected that. Most gang members weren't flush. They could probably make as much money flipping hamburgers. Only the leaders and the suppliers made real money.

There wasn't much else of any use. I put their clothes and wallets in one plastic bag, all their weapons in another, but kept the handguns. Those would be adequate for an emergency. I also kept their cell phones and what ammo I found in their pockets. Those could prove helpful somewhere down the road.

I felt Rainy's eyes on me but was afraid to look at her. She needed a doctor. She needed a better deal than this one. She needed a better protector. I shouldn't have let her get hurt.

"You ought to sleep until they get back. You've had it worse than any of us—and no sleep at all."

That was Rainy, thinking of others before herself and making me out a hero. Didn't she ever complain?

"I slept. I was asleep when you left the text message."

"Where? Under the car?"

"Under the van. There wasn't room under the car."

"I hope they remember to get food for the cat."

"And for us?"

"Thou preparest a table before me in the presence of mine enemies."

"I hope no enemies show up when the food shows up. I'd like to eat till I can't hold any more—without interruptions." I sat down beside her on the bed. "Do your friends believe . . . like you do?"

"No . . . they must be simply scared to death."

Her words surprised me, even caused me to feel somewhat inadequate. "You're not scared to death?"

"God sees our situation. He even sent someone to help take care of us."

Now I felt completely inadequate. This woman, who had twice been almost killed by those brutal devils, wasn't terrified by our circumstances. And if God sent me to help her, I had certainly fouled up the job.

"Maybe you expect too much from God. He might fail you as badly as I have."

"You haven't failed. I recognize your symptoms. You need food and sleep. God can take us safely through this."

"Why doesn't He then?"

"Maybe He wants us to go ahead and make our tiny movie and try your plan. Maybe He intends for you to bust a few more heads."

My SWAT philosophy was to never give up, never quit, never stop, even with six bullets in me and a broken right arm. I could see that Rainy would have made a good SWAT officer. She wouldn't quit—not on me, not on anything.

"You'd better get some sleep too. We don't know what kind of hell lies ahead of us."

"You're bedside manner isn't exactly what the doctor would prescribe for someone in my condition."

"I tried to take you to a doctor."

"That's not what I meant. I meant you shouldn't say things that worry me. You should act optimistic and encouraging and speak soft words to me."

"Pillows, cotton, mink . . . foam . . . clouds . . . marshmallows . . ."

"Thank you," she said and fell asleep.

I promptly followed her wise example. Centuries later the cat leaped on me and hissed, his fur and tail bristling. His attention aimed at the door where someone struggled with the knob. When it opened to disclose our three shoppers, he immediately grew calm and went to scratch at the packages that smelled like food.

Rainy laughed, and the sound buoyed my spirits.

"We got chicken so we wouldn't have to wait for it, but there are pizza places close by if anyone's still hungry after we finish this. We got a dozen donuts too—for our cop friend." Grady laughed.

He shouldn't have laughed. He didn't realize how much I loved my donuts or how many nights they had comforted me while the rest of the world slept. Tia opened more bags to disclose all kinds of snacks, cold drinks, and hot coffee. Obviously they had grown comfortable with using my credit card. Cat got his bag of dry food, but he seemed more interested in the chicken. Tia brought out the medicine for Rainy's wounds and treated them while we divided the grub.

We ate until the food was gone, and though it was still early afternoon, we all fell asleep. Rainy woke us four hours later and said we should work out our skit so we would look professional. Otherwise, we might cause suspicions.

"With a few minor changes, Cal's boat scene should work perfectly. Grady isn't in that scene, so he can run the camera. We'll write in a part for you, Warren, so you'll have an excuse to be present."

"No—no acting for me. Can't you teach me how to use the camera?"

"Not well enough to fool people who've been around this stuff most of their lives. Besides, the video must be perfect. We'll give you a background part. You've had experience with that."

"How can we make copies of the new script?" Tim asked. "My computer's in the van—along with Calvin's original script. It will look strange if we don't have printed sides for the shooting."

"We'll write it by hand tonight. There's a self-service printing place near here where they rent computers. Tomorrow I'll type and print it there," Tia volunteered.

After two hours of work on the writing, we rehearsed. Rainy still looked white and tired, but she wouldn't stop until we had it right. Luckily, the scene called for me to stand still and look dim-witted most of the time. At one point, I had to carry an unconscious

Tim across the deck. At least they gave me an adequate excuse for being there, considering that my main talent was brute force.

I watched them come alive as they performed the work nearest to their hearts. I began to realize how it was with them. Many people had come out here to make it big in the movies, but few had stayed. These four were among those who stayed, not because they had found their place in the industry but because they couldn't go back. They had tasted a tiny portion of their dreams and couldn't give up the excitement of pursuit. A nine-to-five was too mundane, too depressing, because they had been in front of the cameras and liked it there.

I felt that way when I retired from the force. Police work was in my blood and it hurt to turn away from it. Now I had taken a big bite of my old life and discovered it hadn't lost its flavor but had become more potent with age. After all, most of me still worked pretty well, I told myself as I hobbled out of the room to call Capt. Nobel.

We arranged to use his friend's boat for shooting on Tuesday night. That would give us almost two days to prepare. The captain asked about any developments, and it was difficult to get off the phone. Finally, I followed a hunch and told him the whole story, including what we meant to accomplish with this shooting. The hunch was good, and the captain would help. While we still talked, another call came in—Lauri's number. When the captain and I had finished our plans, I walked to a nearby fast-food place to call her back.

"Warren, you scared me when you didn't answer. Sorry I'm so late getting back with you. With the funeral and relatives, I couldn't get away to do anything. Is everyone still all right?"

"We're all alive but had another close call—a bad one, Lauri. No debilitating injuries though. I believe we're safe for the present, but you definitely don't want to get involved."

"Bob was my husband. How could I not get involved? Am I supposed to believe his life meant nothing?"

"What about your life, Lauri? Who will protect you?"

"I checked on the phone calls and found a few suspicious calls—all from a burner phone bought in Chicago. It's probably not still in use. I also found a couple of incoming calls from that phone about the time Bob sent you on the job, and two more the morning of the day Bob was killed. Also, I saw where Bob had called the number a few times, evidently to get more information or to relate your progress. I found the calls you made to Bob the evening he was killed. About that same time, Bob called your mystery man twice, the last call probably only an hour or so before he was shot."

"I guessed it would be something like that. We're dealing with a smart, wary, and extremely dangerous man. That's enough investigating for you."

"Did you see the gang insignia on Bob's desk?"

She totally ignored my concern and advice. I never did have a way with women.

"You know I saw it."

"Well?"

"The Nivs, a small white supremacist gang. I didn't know it was still active in Chicago, but it has a branch or two here."

"There's only one on the West Coast, according to the information I turned up, and the one here is considered extinct. They've shown no activity for some time. But you know that wasn't what I asked."

I had forgotten that Lauri did the greater part of Bob's investigating. She no doubt already knew more about the Nivs than I did.

"I've had two run-ins with the gang here, but I believe they've simply been contracted to kill us. Got to find the one behind it. . . . He's the one who probably shot Bob. I'm fairly certain that mark on the desk was strictly for show—maybe to lay the blame elsewhere."

"You're sure it's a man?"

"Hairy chest."

No sooner had I said it than I realized she had baited me into revealing half the plot. Lauri was bound and determined to involve herself and die with the rest of us.

"Any more identification, Warren? That's not much to go on."

"That's all, Lauri," I said resignedly. "If I had anything more, I would already have gone to the police. If I went with the scant information we have now, I'd be signing death warrants for myself and four others. There were five of them, Lauri, but one was dead before I got out here."

"Warren, if something happened to you, I wouldn't want to let this drop. Give me the complete story, the identities of those you're protecting, everything you know or suspect."

"I'll be glad to do that right away if you promise to not get involved and to use the information only if I disappear or die. Is there a safe way I can send it? Someone could get to your mail before or after you received it. Likewise, someone could break into your place and read your email. I know I'm leaning toward the cautious side, but until I know more it will have to be that way. I'll need a safe place to send it, and I want it to stay in that place after you read it—understand?"

"I understand. I'll arrange something and call you back."

"If I don't answer my phone right away, don't assume I'm dead. I may be busy or on a movie set. We're not allowed to leave our cell phones on when they're filming. I found out the hard way."

"It sounds like you're having fun. I can't exactly picture you acting though . . . unless you played a cop."

"The assistant director said I was great."

"What line did you say that earned that kind of praise?"

"I . . . never mind, Lauri, it's not like that. . . . I'll make up a report on this case, and you let me know how to get it to you. Got to go now, Lauri. There's an important matter I have to take care of right away."

Chapter 10

My important matter was the cashier at the fast-food counter, but I had temporarily thwarted Lauri's attempt to get more information from me. The others had finished their rehearsal when I returned to the room with a large bag of tacos.

We ate while we studied the video and pictures they took that last day on set. They were clear shots, but they didn't help us to eliminate any of our three suspects. When we considered only back and side views, any of them could be the man in the wet suit.

Tia studied them closely. "If we could see them shirtless, we might know."

"We can always have Warren go rip off their shirts," Rainy replied, her white face suddenly turned rosy.

"We'll simply have to go for all three. We have no choice. Rainy do you have that paper with the descriptions and lists of names we collected the other day or was it in the van?"

"I took it in my tote that last day to study while on set, so we've at least got that. We've also all added our observations from that day and any conversations we overheard."

"Tell me everything about this producer, Don Denlin. What do we know about him?"

"He's the executive producer on the Torment film. He doesn't like the location or how the movies being done or how much it's costing or how slow it's going. He doesn't get on with the director but doesn't want to release him. He's also one of the secondary producers of the film where Cal went off the cliff, and He was on that set of the movie the day it happened."

"How about the director? Ertsly, isn't that his name?"

"Allen Ertsly. Likewise, he's constantly at odds with the producer. They argue all the time. Everyone has heard him say the film sucks and will bomb for sure."

"Is he the kind of director who's careful not to have accidents happen on his set?"

"He's rather slipshod, though the key grip is directly responsible for safety. They'd both be blamed if an accident occurred. I saw a heated conversation between those two the day of the boat accident, but couldn't hear what was said. They fired the key grip that same day."

"Was it the same key grip I met on the Big Bear shoot?"

"No, the job is too demanding. A key grip couldn't adequately handle two big shoots at the same time."

"Better write down that Ertsly likes explosions in his movies," Tim added. "He's known for being fanatical in that line."

"How about Denlin? Is he into fireworks?"

"Definitely not. That was one point of contention between them. He complains that it costs too much and they don't need such grandiose exhibitions."

"We've ruled out the boat captain so that leaves Britt Turner. What do we have down about him and his possible motive, Rainy?"

"He's a relatively new star – has had three lead rolls. He got his first starring role in a movie because of his champion-swimmer status. The movie did well and landed him another roll—one that his manager never should have taken because it went straight to video and didn't do well even there. Torment looked like it was doomed to fail too. I doubt his popularity could survive another box office failure."

"Does he realize Torment could hurt him?"

"He's not big on brain power, but everyone has heard Ertsly rampaging about how the movie will flop. Even a fool would realize his career was headed for trouble."

"Did this accident help the movie or his career?"

"Both!" Grady responded. "They kept a camera rolling through it all. It caught the explosion, and it showed Britt bringing in person after person to the crew boat. They showed it on the news repeatedly. It was . . . rather spectacular. Anyone would be curious to see the movie after what the news showed."

Grady's eyes actually shone. Anything heroic drew his attention, even if it was only acting. Lately, though, I had watched him channel some of his dreaming into action. He was developing rapidly into a stronger person, and a lingering bruise on my head attested to that.

"I'd give anything to see a replay of that day. Anyone know who filmed the footage?"

"I know both of the cameramen," Rainy volunteered. "If we were on set, I could find out which one filmed it and could ask some questions. I doubt we could see the footage."

"Shouldn't we put Britt's manager down on our list of suspects?" Grady asked.

"I doubt that the percent he earns would warrant the risk of setting off a boat explosion. Besides, he couldn't be sure that his client would save lives or even stay alive in such a situation. It would have been necessary for him to involve Britt too, and I can't see two people jumping so easily into such a risky plan and then displaying enough conscienceless ambition to commit unlimited murder. Murder looks rather horrendous to most eyes."

"I guess your right about that, but a gang member wouldn't hesitate to kill. Members kill from the very beginning, even if they're only children—sometimes young children," Grady responded with passion I had never seen in him. "Maybe someone hired a gang member to sink the boat. Maybe a Niv wore that wet suit."

"Good thought, Grady, but years of investigations tell me that only one person embarked on this scheme at the beginning. A gang member wouldn't know enough about the shoot to do everything at precisely the right time. I've seen how uncertain a shoot can be. The person who set the explosion knew all about filming and about this film. That would eliminate the Nivs. I believe this started with one cautious individual who grows less cautious and more desperate every day. We do need to find out his connection with this gang though."

While we discussed motives and descriptions, Tia checked the casting lines. I thought she knew I wouldn't let them take any jobs until we solved this case.

"Hey, they just called for all extras who worked on the boat scene the day of the accident. Thursday they shoot a scene at Long Beach, and they need all of us for continuity. They read off the names of those they haven't reached yet and asked anyone who knew them to please get the word out. Our names were on the list—our real names."

"Of course," Rainy said thoughtfully. "We didn't cancel our old registrations but did change our phone numbers, and now they can't reach us. We should call in. With our own shooting finished by then, nothing should hinder us. It would give us a legitimate excuse to be on the set, and I could ask the camera person anything we wanted to know."

"You forget, we would have sent out the flash drives with the video footage. Too dangerous at that point for any of you to go public, especially on a movie set."

"On the contrary, it's the one time we should stay together. No one should meet this murderer alone. Besides, we're actors and are expected to show up, and the cameraman could give us some pertinent information."

"I don't care what the cameraman says at this point. It would be dangerous to speak to him once we send out the clips."

"This call back will afford our best opportunity to fill in the blanks." Rainy continued to ignore me. "We'll take our list of names and talk to anyone who might know something. The shoot is downtown Long Beach, so how could such a public spot become dangerous?"

No one stepped forward to contradict her. They left it to me again.

"Booking the shoot is, of course, an option," I started diplomatically, "but the risk is . . ."

"Every minute we sit idle, our risk increases. Once we release that video clip, we stick together. We all want to end this risk." She didn't wait for my permission but went on with her own plans. "Tomorrow morning we'll change to our old identities. If Warren will let us continue to abuse his credit card, we'll buy hair dye and try to remember how we looked before the explosion. Tia, you call them tomorrow morning and book all of us. No one will be answering phones there today."

"But Rainy, how can you make your hair grow longer? And what about Tim?"

"It's not a great concern. Remember, no one took photos of us on that set to record our look or our costumes. They'll probably ask us to fix ourselves as close as possible to our look that day. And people will be missing too—those who will refuse to work on that film again. Tim's hair has been growing for about five days. In a few more days, it won't look like he shaved his head. Mine just needs the color changed. I'll style it more like I used to wear it. No one will notice."

"You can take back your old identities, dye your hair, call the camera person, call anyone you want, but once we send out those clips, you will all stay in this motel room. No one works on that set this Thursday." Was I a man or not?

"It's a shame we can't book you on the shoot too, Warren. We'd hate to leave you alone at the motel. You might take a call from the suspect and need our help." Tia sounded almost brazen.

"You're the ones who will need help. Rainy trusts too easily. She might invite the murderer to share the motel room or offer him a lift somewhere."

No one would meet my eyes. Rainy's stubbornness had infected them.

"I'll hang around the shoot and keep an eye on things since I won't be working." They could think they had won anyway.

"Maybe we could disguise you," Rainy suggested. "You're so big and prominent and recognizable . . . and . . . and cop like. They'd notice you prowling around the set."

"He can use my wig," Grady offered.

"How about if I buy a cop uniform?" I asked in jest.

"That's it! You could go on set and ask questions," Grady said excitedly. "It wouldn't matter that you can't act. Just be yourself."

Rainy immediately burst both our bubbles with one stab.

"No one would forget the face of the man who threw that sofa."

Ignoring her words of discouragement, I tried on Grady's wig.

When even Grady laughed, I abandoned that idea. I consoled myself with coffee and a donut while they went through one last rehearsal before we turned in.

Next morning the girls bought dye and other hair products. Tia changed into a blond and Rainy became a true redhead, which made her eyes look three shades greener. They booked themselves on the Thursday Torment shoot in spite of my loud grumbling. Rainy's PA friend gave her the phone numbers for Britt Turner's photo double and his stand-in so she could see if either one wanted an acting job that Tuesday night. While she talked with him, I got a phone call from the casting agent for Torment. They wanted me on the set for Thursday's shoot—just as the AD had told me. And I had thought he was joking.

Later that morning, we all bought a change of clothes and a few items for our shoot on the morrow, including a white towel the size of the one in the recording and chalk to mark the exact path the actor would take. After wearing the same clothes for over three days, clean clothes would feel great. Tia handled the printing, I bought some extra ammo for my pieces, and we loaded up with food before returning to our room.

Cat welcomed us home with excessive affection. Evidently bored with motel life, he had played with his water and food and had spread both all over the small kitchen area. He jumped onto Rainy's lap while she called our prospective actors. The photo double couldn't do the acting job the evening we needed him, but the stand-in, Tug Thomas, welcomed the opportunity.

"I'd rather have him anyway," Rainy said after talking with him on the phone. "I barely know the photo double, and he's too friendly with Britt and the director. He might talk about our film and make the wrong person suspicious—or give the whole plan away. I believe Tug will keep quiet about it. I'll tell him we want to keep it secret because we plan to present it to Cal's mother as a memorial before we market it. That's not a lie, because I'd like to do just that when we climb out from under this other problem. We'll tell Tug that we'd almost completed it when Cal had his accident.

"Yeah," Grady added, "Tug's all right. The other day I talked with him on set, and you could tell he felt bad about Cal. They were friends of a sort. He'd probably work this job for free if he knew the real reason behind it."

"If he knew the real reason, he'd probably run from us like from the IRS," Rainy said drolly. "No one wants to die. I believe he'll do effectively for what we want. He's a swimmer and about the age of the producer, in his late forties. He's also in good shape and could pass for someone in his mid-twenties, someone like Britt. Ertsly falls somewhere in the middle of that age range, so Tug should do nicely, especially since it's only a back and side view.

"I forgot to tell you, I also got my friend, Wayne Grimmel, to do makeup, which will give the shoot a more legitimate look. He said he'd take care of our hair too, but I told him we'd probably do our own. He's been working on the Torment shoot, but he says our night job doesn't interfere and he needs the money. I didn't call any extras. We already have Warren for that, and I thought we'd spent enough money. Will the boat have lights we can use—for the part that's not supposed to be in the dark? And can someone get us a wet suit?"

"I'll tell them to have a few lights ready, and Captain Nobel will find us an exact duplicate of the suits he carried. I'm sure the man in the recording wore one of the yacht's wet suits. I've let the captain into our confidence, so he understands fully what we intend to do. I thought one more head working on our side wouldn't hurt, especially since he saw the explosion first hand. Do you need anything else for the camera?"

"All set. Formatted the SD card and charged the batteries. Cal's camera case only contained a flimsy tripod he used for emergencies, but it should serve adequately for this short scene. Oh, I forgot. There should be food—at least something for the two people we hired and whatever boat crew participates. The rest of us can pretend to eat and save money . . ."

"We'll all eat, and I'll order pizza. Will that do?"

"That will be perfect. I hope this works. It's costing you so much."

"Don't worry. I've got a job for Thursday." I grinned.

"We all do, Warren. And we probably have some checks waiting for us in our post office boxes. We'll all help pay for this," Grady announced.

The others immediately nodded their acquiescence as if they had already discussed it. I had only meant to get a laugh when I said I had a job for Thursday. I didn't expect such a serious reaction.

"Don't argue with us, Warren. We intend to pay back everything you've spent on us—if we live, that is," Tim seconded.

Rainy and Tia just smiled. I hoped I could live up to their expectations. It felt strange to have friends after being alone for years.

Tuesday morning Captain Nobel sent us an invitation to come early and rehearse.

"I want you to plan it exactly like the video showed it. My uncle owns this yacht. I told him what we want to do, and he will help any way he can. You can trust him fully. We'll tell the crew we are shooting a movie scene. They won't even see what we do."

When we arrived at the yacht, we met with Captain Nobel alone.

"Captain, we've told no one about the real reason for tonight's shoot. The person who will wear the wet suit thinks he's being paid to act in an independent film. We wrote lines for him to say so it wouldn't look suspicious. We'll show you exactly where the actual man stood both times he became visible in the recording."

"Yes, I need to know that. We're fortunate that tonight the water will look similar to how it looked in the early morning before the accident."

"It's important for the actor to do exactly what was done that night, but it doesn't have to be shot from the same angle. We want them to believe that Calvin had another camera set, and that he had another recording of the man in the wet suit. You know how the bow of your yacht looked, so we need you to make sure there's nothing in this recording that will give away that this boat isn't the same one."

"I understand. That is why I thought we needed time to get this right. Will anyone else come besides the actor you mentioned?"

"A makeup man, Wayne Grimmel. We've kept him in the dark too. You must realize what a total gamble were perpetrating. We knew of nothing else to try. I've told you the three men we regard as suspects. If you know of anyone else we should consider, tell me now. We can deliver a copy of the scene to them as well."

"They told me I am a good suspect." His droll expression

lightened all our spirits.

"You're too short." We all laughed and it felt good. "We need someone with a build similar to that of Britt Turner. The director and producer both qualify."

"Either of them could have done it. They are both dishonest. They hate each other yet they become buddies to put the blame on me. They know I am not responsible. I thought at first that the explosives people had caused the accident. I had no way to find out for sure or ever prove it. Now you tell me of this recording we will make, which gives me a tiny bit of hope and a chance to fight back. I thank you for that—whatever comes of it. We will leave port now to work this out. It is better if not too many eyes watch us."

"The others won't be here till six, so we have all day."

"My uncle has to make a run to Catalina. If you don't have other obligations, you should stay aboard. You'll find berths below if anyone grows tired, and the cook will prepare your meals. Later we will show you where the accident happened."

We wallowed in luxury for the rest of the day. The cook didn't just feed us, he fed us bountifully and kept hot coffee available constantly. The rehearsals went well until Rainy reminded us of a prop we forgot. Our villain carried a small duffle bag under his arm when he first went over the side of the boat. That presented a real problem. If we used one the least bit different from the one on the original recording, it would instantly prove our recording was a fraud. When we went to Captain Nobel with the problem, he laughed at our concern.

"Come with me."

He led us to a small garage type room where all types of water toys, wet suits, and other diving gear were stowed. They had numerous small diving tanks hung on the wall in black nylon bags, and the bags were large enough to hold additional diving equipment. He said they used the bags when they took a diving party out in the yacht's tender. Each person carried a personal bag of gear.

"You see, both my uncle's yacht and mine were built almost identical. He owned my yacht and sold it to me when he got his new one. We worked together. If he couldn't take out a party, he would send them to me. We bought most of our equipment from the same place too. This bag will exactly match the one carried by the man on your recording."

During our final rehearsal, Rainy called for a pause.

"Grady, no matter how awkward it feels, use extreme care that the actor can't be identified as Tug when you shoot the segment we intend to use. You'll have to ask him to turn this way and that way so his every movement will look exactly how we need it. He may wonder why we're so exacting about insignificant matters, and we may have to do it over twenty times to get it right."

"I'll be nitpicking about other places too, Rainy, so it won't seem odd if I have him redo something countless times. He knows we're recording with only one camera and in low-light conditions. We'll pretend we're adjusting settings, and he won't know. I promise I won't pass it unless it's right. We'll tell him it's a critical part that has to be just so."

"I guess it will work," she conceded. "Even if we're fussy, it should take only a few hours, and I told him we'd pay him for an entire day. I also made it clear to him that the movie might go no further than the hands of Cal's mother. He doesn't expect to become famous over it. Like Wayne, he's glad to earn the extra money."

"Rainy, You and Tia will take Wayne and Tug into the kitchen when it gets dark. Tim and I will experiment with the lighting and other settings until we can duplicate that night perfectly. The camera will have to be set stationary for the night scene so it will look the same as if Cal had attached a second camera somewhere. Warren can just hang around in case we need him."

On the way back from Catalina, the yacht deviated from its former route to show us where the accident occurred.

"They shot the scene here. My yacht rests below us, but too deep and too damaged to salvage."

"Too deep to investigate?"

"Yes, even for someone with deep-dive experience. And the ocean would have washed away any evidence the fire hadn't already destroyed."

Tug and Wayne were waiting when we arrived at the docks. As soon as they boarded, we put out to sea. We had a short sundown scene to film, strictly for show. The other scenes, the ones that counted, would wait until the outside lighting matched Cal's recording exactly.

Tug's part called for him to wear wet suit pants for both scenes. We let him pick what he deemed a good fit, and when he presented himself for inspection, everyone approved—until he turned and displayed the small tattoo on his back.

"This is LA. I always have to cover tattoos," Wayne announced. "I have waterproof makeup with me if it's to be a water scene."

"Will I be in the water?" Tug asked. "It's not the warmest time of year to swim with only half a wet suit—especially if it's a night scene."

"No," Rainy quickly assured him, "you'll give the appearance of going over the side into the water, but we'll have a ladder and a small boat below. We've already set up the ladder so it won't show on camera. We'll pour a bucket of water over you . . ."

"Warm water?"

"A bucket of warm water over you before you climb back aboard the yacht."

"Sounds good. By the way, wasn't Cal in the film? Won't that present a problem about finishing it? He and I used to talk about it all the time. He couldn't wait to get it done. Life's not fair, is it?"

"He'd completed most of the movie, especially the scenes featuring him. We went over the footage and saw that it will take very little recording to finish it. We made a couple of miniscule changes, but it works."

"I hope his mother lets you release it—not because I'm in it," he was quick to add. "It would be . . . fitting. I know it would please Cal. And I can see you're putting money into this venture."

"Like we said, there aren't many scenes left."

"Let me know if you need me again after tonight. Also, if you have any boat scenes, let me know. I dock my boat here at the marina, and I'll work something out with you to save you the expense of hiring one. It's not a yacht, but it might do."

"Thank you, Tug. We'll remember that," Rainy assured him.

Their first segment of the shoot went well. Grady became Mr. Perfectionist and acted exasperatingly critical on some portions. He called for scenes to be redone, repeatedly, for apparently no reason.

He told his actors to turn this way and then to try it again turning more the other way. He had Tug change the position of his arms and his body a half dozen times for one tiny segment. He seldom gave a reason, but Tug good-naturedly went along with it.

When they completed their sundown scene, Tim and Grady took it to a private room Capt. Nobel made available. There they reviewed it on a big-screen television. When they returned to the upper deck, they pronounced the work a success and told everyone to take a break until they could record the night scenes.

The girls went below to feed and entertain our two paid guests, and I stayed with Tim and Grady while they set up for the night work.

"Did I act irritating enough to get away with what we have to do now?" Grady asked slyly.

Tim laughed. "If he doesn't quit before we start the scene, I think you can bend him like a pretzel, and he won't question anything."

"I hated to act like that, but this won't work if we don't have it exactly the same."

"I didn't complain, Grady. Your performance deserves an Oscar."

"He's right," I seconded. "We have to get this next part correct if it takes all night. You paved the way nicely. Before you call either of these next wet suit scenes complete, make sure all four of you view them and see no problems."

"We intend to," Tim assured me. "Grady, I'm going to stand where Tug will stand. It looks dark enough out. Record about fifteen seconds of me, and I'll go below and review it to see if we're ready."

After they finished their experimental recording, and Tim had left with the camera, Grady came over and sat near me.

"I'm beginning to have hope this will work."

"We haven't many avenues left if it doesn't. I could try to get hold of the gang leader and beat the truth out of him. I could disguise myself and beat the pulp out of each of our suspects until one confessed. Trouble is, the murderer wouldn't confess unless I half killed him, and the innocent couldn't confess because they didn't do it. I'd end up maybe three quarters killing them trying to find out. .

. . I hope this works too!"

"If you . . . if there's no other way, I could change my looks and try to get into this gang," Grady offered hesitantly. "I know about gangs. . . . My younger brother belonged to a gang . . . and he was killed. My mother was killed a day later. I think it had something to do with the same gang. Maybe I owe it to them to try . . ."

I read his uncertainty, his hesitancy. He couldn't do it. He had grown in the short time I knew him, but not that much.

"After you went through their initiation, which would resemble hell, you'd likely be expected to kill someone. Are you up for that, Grady?"

"Not the killing part."

"Then you'd die before you could learn anything helpful."

"You're right. I think I could do the dying part better than the killing part. I guess I couldn't kill that way, not someone innocent. But I'm willing to risk myself any way that's necessary—if it will help."

"You're risking yourself now, and our situation could become worse. When we deliver those copies, anything can happen. But I understand your offer. Thank you."

Tim returned and pronounced it time to get on with the show.

"The lighting compares favorably with the original stuff. Let's go ahead. It won't get any better."

He called everyone on deck. They appeared relaxed and in a jovial mood, which would help in what lay before us. Grady turned on a dim light for his preliminary instructions. He enjoyed playing cinematographer and director of our artistic deception.

"I realize that most of you know where and when to move, but I want to run through it one more time before we start. Tug, I'm going to step off your movements for the first part. Try to follow my exact actions. The camera will be stationary and the movement has to be precise. I've marked your path so you can walk confidently, long strides, yet step lightly—to give the illusion you're in a hurry but are still being secretive and quiet. The character knows where he's going so there's no hesitation."

Grady went through the movements of the beginning part

of the scene, putting in a gesture here and there. When he got to the part that counted, we all held our breath and tried not to look in Tug's direction. Grady went through it smoothly and clearly. I saw his slight look toward Rainy and her almost nonexistent nod of acceptance. Evidently Grady had gotten it correct with the right speed and look.

"Do you want to see that again, Tug?"

"I believe I've got it. Let's rehearse it once, and I think I'll be good to go."

The rehearsal went satisfactorily. Grady gave further instruction to Tug and Tim. Wayne constantly moved in to administer a makeup repair or adjust someone's hair. It felt like a real shoot. After he recorded the scene for the sixth time, Grady, Rainy, and Tim went into the TV room to view it. Tia and I had the responsibility of keeping Wayne and Tug entertained.

That was a difficult job since I wasn't an actor like the rest of them. What could I say that wouldn't sound ridiculous or give us away? Like Rainy told me, I always came off like a cop. I couldn't even pretend to be an extra.

"I saw that scene you did out at the Big Bear shoot," Tug said. "A stunt man couldn't have done it that well. Either you spend a lot of time in the gym or else you've worked as a stuntman before."

Here it came. The best I could do for a big dumb cop.

"I'm kind of new at this line, Tug. My background is construction. I guess moving all that plywood and lumber . . . and plywood . . ."

The ship's cook saved me. He brought a tray of hot snacks, and his helper brought a coffee pot and cups. I didn't finish my sentence but rushed to put something in my mouth before I could say anything else ridiculous. At least with such good treatment, our guests wouldn't complain if we had to redo that blamed scene a dozen more times.

The others returned before the food disappeared and joined us for the remnants of it.

"Moving on," Grady announced. "We should be able to wrap within half an hour. There's no dialogue, and only Tug acts in this last piece. Watch me Tug, and I'll show how it's to look."

Grady climbed aboard the boat as if he came out of the water. Before he could look at Rainy for approval, she spoke up.

"I think it would look better if he stayed stooped for a couple of feet instead of straightening so quickly. It would give a stealthier mood. What do you think, Tim?

"Definitely—and maybe move a tad faster. I'll watch in the camera, and you go through it again, Grady. Tug might as well stay warm until we know exactly what we want."

Grady went through it again, and Tim gave him more instructions.

"Turn slightly more to your right. The audience isn't supposed to know for sure it's the same person. We're getting too much of your face."

Grady went through it a third time. Rainy and Tim both gave their approval while Tug unwrapped from the blanket he held around him. Wayne doused him with warm water, checked him over, and they were ready to shoot.

The first take appeared to be perfect. Tug put the blanket back around his shoulders while I handed him a cup of coffee. The others headed below to view it.

"Pretty windy out here for this kind of work," I sympathized.

"I'm used to foul conditions. They don't bother me, and they've treated me good. I'm game if it takes another three hours,"

It wouldn't take another three hours because Grady bounded back up and announced they had a wrap.

"Everyone come down to the kitchen where it's warm. We're heading in. We'll actually get a night's sleep."

"That's good news," Tug responded. "I have to be on the Torment shoot at seven in the morning. Any of you working that shoot tomorrow?"

"Not till Thursday."

We were tempted to ask this likeable actor more questions about the accident but had sense enough to keep quiet. Neither he nor Wayne should associate this work with that shoot or they could unintentionally ruin our plan. We made small talk until we pulled into the docks. Rainy paid them in cash that I withdrew earlier for that purpose, and both men seemed pleased and more than willing to work again if needed.

Chapter 11

Wednesday morning, we bought half a dozen flash drives for the video segments we needed. The tricky part would be to deliver them to the right people and make sure they watched them promptly. I didn't even want to think about the second tricky part, the part where I waited to see what bounded through the door we opened.

We didn't find any satisfactory way to deliver the flash drives, so we opted on overnight mail delivery. The package needed an irresistible title that would take it beyond a possible pile of other mail and past a probable secretary. After a dozen choices, we finally wrote: "NEW Torment Reef accident footage—Urgent/Personal." The overnight delivery would probably accomplish more than "urgent" printed in red letters, but we used both anyway.

I left my phone number on the flash drive and nothing more. It would make no sense to the innocent, and hopefully they would chuck it in their wastebasket and say nothing about it to anyone. At least by mailing it, we knew the suspect wouldn't receive it in the presence of another suspect. We had to convince Mr. Guilty that he, and he only, received the video clip, and that we knew the truth. He would think blackmail, and he would call!

We had left the post office and stopped at a shopping center when my phone rang. It sent a jolt through me that continued until my brain told my reflexes to relax. No one could receive the package until tomorrow. . . . The call was from Lauri.

"Warren, I have a rental car. Tell me where to meet you."

"Did something happen, Lauri? I can't get to Chicago now.

We just put a plan in the works that ties me here for a couple of crucial days."

"I'm here, Warren, at the LAX. Actually, I'm leaving it. You can give me the case report in person."

Why, God? Why did you let this happen to me? were the words that chased through my mind. I shook my head. I was beginning to think like Rainy—No offense, Lord.

"Here?" I dumbly asked.

"I need the address of where you're staying, and I'll want a room too."

"I . . ."

"Before you try to bully me, I want you to know I intend to stay till the end. Remember, I'm still in fragile condition, so don't cross me."

I was the one in fragile condition. She sounded about as fragile as a bulldozer. I gave her directions to a small restaurant, two doors down from where we were shopping, and hurried away to locate Rainy. I found her in the cat food section of the store, of course.

"Here, take the keys to the car. Go anywhere you need to go, but use caution. I'll see you at the room. I have to meet a friend at the Chinese restaurant here, and it may tie me up for a while."

"Have you got your penknife on you?"

"Penknife?" I was experiencing one of my stupid days.

"Never mind, Warren, the joke's already ruined. See you later."

"Wait. Do you have that paper with you—about the suspects?"

"In my purse. I transferred the information to a notebook."

"I need to borrow it, but first I need contact information on all your families. If something went wrong, I want to put a full report in the hands of someone who could notify the police and your . . . your families . . . if necessary."

"It's all right, Warren. At this point we don't, any of us, consider this a game. I wrote a complete account of what's happened so far. The report contains family contact information. I meant to mail a copy of it to someone trustworthy, but hadn't chosen the person. Here, take the notebook and add anything that I left out. I feel better about this now. I'll see you later."

Over dinner and coffee in the restaurant, I studied her report. It was thorough, though un-cop-like to the extreme. I added a few facts at the bottom and laid it aside in time to greet Lauri.

I didn't find the grieving Lauri or the businesslike Lauri in this middle-aged goddess who sailed through the restaurant door. Her hair had lost its tight perfection of yesteryear and now framed her face with a short, fluffy bounce of dark curls. The dress looked new and showier than her normal style.

"I've gone Hollywood, Warren. I came to see it all."

She smiled vivaciously as she took the seat across from me. She performed a much better acting job than I could render, but I saw through it to the depths of her unsmiling eyes. When she grasped that her performance had failed, she changed back into Lauri Caine, desolate widow, but with something new added, something I could only call a resolve of steel.

"Have you eaten?" she asked when the waiter came.

"I waited for you," I lied, and we both ordered a full meal.

She took the notebook and studied its pages carefully—three times through. Finally she looked up at me.

"Bob's epitaph."

"And Calvin's. I'm trying to keep the number down to two, but your presence out here and your knowledge of the whole story will make that more difficult."

"I left town discreetly. Actually, I used my maiden name, and didn't tell anyone anything except that I needed to get away for a while and rest. This new, glamorous me is more of a disguise than a change. You didn't help me pull it off."

"I'm sorry, Lauri. You acted wisely about everything, and I'm glad to see you. At least you're close by where I can watch out for you too."

"I see why you haven't dropped this mess on the police yet. You have nothing whatsoever to go on. . . . When did you mail the flash drives?"

"About an hour ago—right before you called."

"You may not get any responses till tomorrow afternoon or evening. How have you prepared? Can I help?"

"You could take me to a couple of places. When you called, I left my rental with the four I'm protecting."

"Good. I want to visit a few spots too. First, I need to make a copy of this report, and then I'll need a post office. After that, I'd like to see the movie location you'll work at tomorrow, that big Hollywood sign, that place where they have the footprints of the stars, and some of the stars homes. I'd especially like to see Nicholas Cage or Viggo Mortensen, if you can arrange it."

"Friends or relatives of yours?"

"I can give you the names of a few eating places where the stars frequent," Rainy said. She had come up behind me and scared me into tomorrow. "Warren hasn't lived here long enough to know his way around. He's been busy acting."

"Rainy, this is a friend from Chicago, Lauri . . ."

"Lauri Burch. Glad to know you Rainy. It seems I asked the wrong person about the Hollywood scene."

"If you have time, you should take a tour and see some of the star's homes and other interesting spots. Let me write down some names and addresses for you. A map would be helpful too."

"Rainy, Lauri and I have to go a few places now. I'll see . . . call you later."

I stood and didn't have to pretend my impatience. If these two became acquainted, my job would become doubly difficult. It would draw Lauri into the danger, and I didn't have time to protect one more person. Lauri must stay a nonentity. I walked over to pay my tab at the register and watched Rainy bid Lauri goodbye. From clear across the room, I could tell I had hurt Rainy's feelings.

"You ended our conversation rather abruptly, Warren. I wanted to ask her more questions. So she's the one who helped you fight that gang the first time? I can see she's still somewhat banged up."

"All three times. For safety's sake, Lauri, no one should know your identity. It might involve you and give our killer another goal."

"I own the right to become involved. At this point, no one's loss equals mine. I won't put your lives in further jeopardy or make your job more difficult, but I do want a room at the same place where you stay."

Lauri had her way. We stopped and secured a room before we

took care of the other business. She mailed a copy of the report to a contact of Bob's in Chicago, someone who would hide it until told otherwise. She also made a copy for herself, insisting she needed it and would hide it adequately. She had her way there too.

Actually, she had her way about everything for the remainder of the day except for one detour I requested—a police supply store. I bought a few items that could be useful and a few more that likely wouldn't be, but it felt good to have them on me. Late in the day, she suggested we invade one of the star hangouts Rainy had recommended.

"Let's try Pink's. Your friend said it stayed open until two in the morning. We can sit there and eat hotdogs all evening, and maybe I'll see someone famous."

"And maybe the wrong person will see you with me and register a new face to eliminate. And maybe someone will follow me to the room and . . ."

"I withdraw the request. It was selfish and foolish. Take me to a movie, and I'll keep reminding myself I'm in Hollywood."

All I wanted was sleep, so the movie would work. I had slept sitting up quite a bit lately. I fell fast asleep before the previews ended, and had no idea what movie we had watched when she nudged me awake at its end. I felt embarrassed but didn't know what to say.

"I'm sorry, Lauri, I . . ."

"That's all right. It was just like having Bob back for a couple of hours."

She smiled, and I knew she understood. When we returned to the motel, I joined Rainy and the others in our room. Noting all the bags, it looked like they had done plenty of shopping. A knife lay beside Rainy's purse, and I looked at her in surprise.

"We picked up our checks from the post office and bought a few items that might be helpful in the next few days. We also got our own rental car. We thought you'd feel better if we went to the shoot tomorrow in a separate vehicle that hadn't been seen by anyone yet. We'll use care when we leave the set so no one will notice or follow."

I heard a distinct chilliness in her voice, which I hoped resulted from jealousy and not from my rudeness at the restaurant. Now I could pretend that Lauri was an old girlfriend who came all the way out to California to see me. Considering Lauri's attractiveness, it would make me look like a real catch if I could keep up the charade for a few days.

"Lauri is Bob's widow," I burst out. I never could play those games. "We have to keep our distance from her or we'll put her in danger too. She copied your statement of everything that's transpired so far, including all our contact information. If anything happens, she'll get it to the authorities."

"We know," Rainy said with enough coolness and distance in her voice to let me know she hadn't forgiven my rudeness. "While you watched a movie, she called and explained everything. She told us not to tell you. . . . It would be nice to go to a movie again. . . . We have some leftover pizza . . . and donuts . . ."

"I don't want anything. I'm going to bed."

And I did. . . . Women. . . .

They had set up the shoot adjacent to the marina in downtown Long Beach. We arrived inconspicuously in our two cars amidst droves of extras. Rainy wisely dropped off the others a few blocks away so that they could walk in separately. No gang members knew either car yet, and I wanted to keep it that way for another day or two. We arrived early but not before Tug, who waved when he saw me. Hopefully he would heed our request and not accidentally leak any information about the shoot.

The director worked nearby. I studied his face and demeanor carefully so I would recognize the slightest change, any panic, nervousness, or suspicious actions. When I felt I knew the man thoroughly, I turned my attention to the extras. A quick amble around the shoot turned up no familiar or unfamiliar Niv faces. Tia must have noticed my intense scrutiny because she joined me.

"Do you think gang members will show up today?" she asked.

"They can't risk the boldness here that they dared out at Big Bear. If any Nivs show up, we'll lose them before we return to our room. Don't worry. I'll find a way."

"Rainy told us to stay separate today so we would look less suspicious."

"Just remember this—the murderer knows all of us, even if

he hasn't received his copy of the video yet. One of those three men knows we all came here today. Watch them. Try to read their faces, and the guilty one might give himself away. Today might be his day for action, so keep each other in sight and don't leave the set even to visit the parking lot."

"Rainy has to check the car occasionally. She called a friend yesterday who agreed to watch the cat for a few days, so we brought him with us. The girl works background here today and promised to take the cat with her when we wrap. We parked close by so Rainy should be safe."

"Tell her I'll go with her, and tell the others to keep plenty of people around them—people they know. . . . One question before you go . . ."

Tia's gaze must have followed mine because she quickly gave me the scenic food tour.

"At either of those concession trailers, you can order what you want for breakfast and take any drinks you want. That table over there was set up for us too. You can plunder it for your breakfast if you like. It has bagels, cold cereal, muffins, pastries, fruit, and canisters of hot foods like eggs, bacon, potatoes, sausage, gravy, biscuits, and hot cereal. You can use the machine on the end and squeeze your own orange juice. If none of those food offerings work for you, you can line up in front of that man over there, and he'll make you an omelet any way you want it. . . . I'll go tell the others your safety rules."

I made the rounds of all the food supplies and finally topped it off by filling my pockets full. I had good reason for such gluttony. Although I had categorically belonged in the overweight bracket when I first arrived in LA, my belt now rode on its last notch and could no longer meet the challenge. If someone called me to work right now, the weight in my pockets would put me in real danger of flashing, probably directly in front of those intimidating cameras, and all for the sake of two cokes, an apple, three candy bars, and a bag of corn chips.

Luckily I had cop training and could eat and work at the same time. My neck grew stiff from monitoring my four rookies who right now worked on a scene. It wasn't my fault no one wanted me.

During a break in the shooting, Rainy came over and sat by

me for a while.

"Not much news to report yet. The director and producer actually act friendly toward each other for a change, and the only boat shoot today will be on a docked boat—that one over there. You have it rather easy today, don't you?"

"They haven't called me for anything yet."

"They may have you down for only one scene. I've sat all day on a set, and they never got to my scene at all. It goes that way sometimes."

"I noticed that Tug waylaid you earlier."

"We certainly made a friend the other night. He's hungry to do more with us. . . . He asked me out to dinner tonight."

"I hope you didn't accept. You need to stay put at our room as soon as this shoot's over today."

"I thought we might all hang around here—with you. If you don't want our company, maybe we'll take in a movie. We've done nothing but work or hide for so long."

"I'd feel better if you went straight to the motel, but even a movie theater is safer than here . . . or around me. Anything beats that."

"Are we supposed to let you take all the risk?"

"There's no risk," I lied. "Someone will take the bait, I'll get a chance to identify him, and we'll turn the investigation over to the police."

"And if no one bites?"

"We'll look for another suspect. Or it will mean that the suspect already has a plan in effect for getting rid of us and isn't worried about any harm we can do with an incriminating recording."

"It's beginning to sound less risk free."

"It could definitely turn hazardous if I had to protect all of you. If I can take my time, unconcerned about your safety, my risk stays minimal. Our murderer must dispose of all of us. If he can find no one but me, it will confuse his plans, and now that we have that recording, we're somewhat protected because he will also need to locate the original recording."

"Good speech, Warren, but I'm not gullible. If he can't find all of us, he'll concentrate on taking you out."

"I'm not that easy to eliminate."

"And we're not that easy to lose. We're in this together. We may not be up to the challenge, but . . ."

I laughed and upset her.

"Rainy, I've got three times as much chance of staying alive if I work alone." Now I was telling the truth. "I don't mean to hurt your feelings, and I'm glad for your loyalty, but if you want to live through this and want me to live through it, you'll stay out of sight after today and not surface until it's over."

"We'll see. Right now, I intend to cozy up to some of the people here and see if I can learn anything more. My friend, Jeff, is here. . . . He asked me out to dinner tonight too."

"The PA? But I'll get you room service," I called to her stiff, offended, departing back.

It looked like pizza would no longer tempt her. I wished she wasn't so darn good looking. The red hair really made her come alive, and I wasn't the only one who noticed.

With a cup of hot coffee in one hand and a bagel in the other, I made the rounds of the set. Gang members were decidedly lacking on this shoot, maybe because it was a call back or maybe because they risked recognition at this point. That meant I would have to watch the perimeters of the shoot. If any Nivs came, they would watch from a shop window, the marina, or the parking lot. Since this shoot was set up in a public area, a good many curious onlookers hung around, but none resembled a Niv.

I ventured off the set to saunter past the many piers of boats at the large, impressive marina. Evidently only boat owners had access keys to the locked entry gates at each pier. The yacht we borrowed for our shoot was docked at the end of one of the longer piers. I checked the public bathrooms, visited each of the marina shops, and finally walked the length of the large, public parking area. When I couldn't see through a vehicle's window, I watched for the least movement of the chassis that would signify someone was inside. I found no sign of gang activity, so I slipped back onto the set and filled my coffee cup.

"Are you Warren Roberts?" a voice from behind asked and shocked me into realizing I wasn't cautious enough.

I turned to find the extras coordinator and breathed a sigh of relief. It wasn't likely anyone had viewed the flash drive yet anyway. I nodded and expected him to say they needed me on the next scene.

"The director wants to talk with you—now."

Every nerve on me came alive. Was it about the video clip? If he was the guilty one, he already knew me. He could also compare the phone number on the flash drive with the one the casting agency had for me and confirm that I sent the flash drive. A director could get such information in a second.

When I approached Ertsly, he motioned me aside into a production tent. I was ready for anything.

"Warren, you're not SAG are you?"

"N-no."

"You did a SAG day player roll about five years ago. If you do a second day player role more than thirty days after the first one, you have to join SAG/AFTRA immediately. We want to use some of the audio from the scene you did at Big Bear Lake. You need to join today. We face a big fine if you don't get down to SAG/AFTRA headquarters before they close."

My mouth must have hung open for a whole minute. And I thought I was ready for anything!

"You'll have to scare up the money for it somewhere." He evidently read me wrong and pegged me as a starving extra with no money. "I believe they take credit cards. You'll get day player pay for that day's work, and that will cover much of your registration fee. We may give you another day player spot later on. Everyone liked the scene. I need you to get down there right now and take care of that. Let me know as soon as you're back."

"I never did any other d-day player rolls," I stuttered.

"Here it is—a SAG commercial with exhibitions of SWAT training. They paid you day player rate."

He shoved the paper in front of me.

"Oh," was the most profound statement I could deliver.

So that insignificant SWAT demonstration and those few lines I had said actually amounted to a union job. Four of my SWAT team had given a presentation in front of a camera, explaining what we did. While I still cogitated, he handed me the necessary papers and left the tent. Was this for real or was it some devious plot to get me away from the others? Where was Rainy? I found her close by, ready to protect me if I was answering a response to the video clip.

"That's how it works, Warren. What a break for you. Now you can be a full time actor and won't have to do construction work anymore," she said facetiously.

"Rainy, I . . ."

"Go right away. It should only take a couple of hours, and you'll get back before we're wrapped. If you don't go, it will look suspicious and ruin everything. Most actors would kill to become union—especially with a day player roll. Besides, no one will probably view the flash drive till this evening or later."

"I'm not out here to be an actor."

"If you make waves now, you'll draw attention to all of us. Trust us to act wisely. If we're wrapped before you get back, we'll leave with all the other extras and use extreme caution. Don't blow everything now when we're so close. Besides, now you have your big chance to do your own thing and not have to 'step around' us. You'll have the ring all to yourself. That's what you wanted, wasn't it?"

I had forgotten those words I said to her eons ago, but she hadn't. I had only wanted to keep her safe. Against my better judgment, I left. Rainy always caused me to use bad judgment. Why did I listen to her?

When I still sat in the SAG/AFTRA office three hours later, I asked myself the same question. At least my suspicions of the director had dwindled. No killers waited for me on any back streets and no one had followed me. When I walked out of the building, it was still early enough to reach the set before wrap time.

The producer met me when I arrived with my proofs.

"I see you got it all taken care of."

"All signed up."

"Good."

That was that. This Don Denlin obviously also knew I had to join SAG/AFTRA. It probably wasn't any plot to eliminate me, or anything to do with the recording. And I was now considerably poorer—but I owned this useless plastic card I would be ashamed to carry in my wallet alongside my master police officer badge. I could already see an officer laughing when he pulled me over for a traffic ticket and saw my credentials.

I set out to find the others, but they had all evaporated. Finally, I checked the boat where they shot earlier that day. The upper deck looked empty, but someone could be shooting in the lower quarters. I started to board when an official looking person stopped me.

"No one's allowed past here."

"Are they shooting now?"

"They're through for the day."

"I'm looking for four friends. Maybe they're still below."

"Everyone's gone. They wrapped about half of the extras an hour ago."

I hurried to the extras coordinator and learned that they had all four signed out. Their car was gone too and panic squeezed in on my brain—until I remembered we owned cell phones. A half dozen tries later told me their phones were turned off. Maybe they hadn't remembered to turn them back on when they left the set, or maybe they actually went to a movie, or . . .

I called the motel room and got no answer, as expected. I was ready to call Lauri when I got a text message from Rainy:

"Out of reception for a while. Don't worry. See you tonight."

At those words, my heart jolted with the violence of an actual blow to my chest. I realized I had been a step away from rash action. Probably they watched a movie, and evidently she was still angry with me and didn't want to talk—hence the text message. New concerns smothered me. Maybe they went to get Tia's van. Areas by Big Bear had no cell phone reception. Maybe they purposely got their own rental car so they could go out and get Tia's van. That van contained everything they owned. I should have taken care of that, but I hadn't wanted to invite more danger.

I grew restless again. I went to extras holding to turn in my voucher and pretended the production had wrapped me.

"They want you tomorrow morning at ten," the PA said and set me free.

Tug saw me and motioned me over.

"You don't know if Rainy's still around anywhere, do you? I wanted to show everyone my boat. I gassed it up so we could go for a ride if anyone had time."

"They wrapped and left, Tug."

"Too bad. Have you got time? It's only a few piers down."

"I'd like to see it, but I can't right now. . . . When I see Rainy, I'll let her know you were looking for her."

"Tell her the offer's still good about using my boat for their film. I'll help anyway I can."

I figured she was the one he wanted to admire his boat. That's how it would be if I were in his shoes, and I couldn't take time to humor him now. My crew had picked a bad time to flaunt their independence. Tonight, of all nights, I needed to know their whereabouts. I swung past the motel, but our room showed no sign of anyone having been there since morning. I called Lauri, but her tour bus hadn't arrived back yet.

At the end of three hours, I called all their phones again with still no luck. Maybe they decided to watch two movies. My nerves wouldn't survive a double feature. In less time than an intermission, they could all be dead. Something told me Rainy wasn't angry enough to endanger all of us. She simply wouldn't do that. Why hadn't I realized it before?

Had the murderer caught them? Would he call and bargain their lives for the new recording? Heck, I didn't even know if anyone had seen the copy yet. I felt reckless again, and that boded no good for someone. I couldn't wait for a phone call. There was a gang leader, somewhere, who should know something. I would find him or let him find me.

I experienced the bleakest feeling in the world when I called those four phones again and got no answers, but I continued to call regularly. Finally, I called Lauri again.

"Lauri, they all four disappeared. I was forced to leave the movie set for a few hours. When I got back, they were gone. I had one text message from Rainy's phone saying they'd be out of reception for a while and would see me tonight, but tonight has arrived and they haven't. I've called them a couple of hundred times—nothing."

"If someone captured them, he could easily send a text message with Rainy's phone, and he'd be smart enough to fix their phones so they couldn't be located. I don't think the police could help us there."

"Maybe you can learn something about that gang, like maybe where they hang out around here. That report I gave you lists some of the Niv's cell phone numbers and has a list of numbers I found on their cell phones. Maybe those will help to locate them."

"I'm working on it, Warren. Call me often so I know you're alive. If you go three hours without contacting me, I'll take it to the police."

"Sorry to ruin your trip, Lauri."

"I came for this—didn't you know that?"

Chapter 12

The only plan I could formulate sounded ridiculously simple—and exactly what I needed. I would go to every place where I had seen gang members. If I saw any person that looked like they belonged to that gang, or if I recognized any members that I'd seen before, I would take them any way I could. One way or another, I would find information.

With Tia's van my first destination, I was surprised to find it exactly where we left it and my rental still sat beside it. Evidently, no one ever drove into that lonely spot. I easily broke into the van and brought out Tia's air pump. I worked on the tires as noisily as I could, left my car lights burning brightly, and generally made a racket that would wake the dead. Finally, I sang, but even that didn't produce any results.

I called a wrecker service and waited there, even lit a fire. The wreckers pulled both cars to a garage, and no one showed up to prevent it. With that task out of the way, I found no reason to wait longer.

My next stop was the garage where Rainy and I survived our first gang encounter. With all the lights on in the place, I made plenty of commotion. If any gang members lived close by, word would circulate that one of us had come home. The house in front remained vacant. I walked around it twice and then walked up and down the sidewalk inviting trouble. Only darkness met me.

Lauri's call broke into my fruitless efforts. She gave me a neighborhood to check, including all the streets and cross streets I would need to know.

"There's been action by the Niv's in that area, Warren. Don't know if it's their headquarters or if they even have a headquarters. I'll check some more."

Good sense told me I stood out too much to mix and mingle with the locals in such an area. I would look like a hungry cat invading a town of rats and mice. They would likely all disappear, and I would learn nothing. I needed to wear some urban camouflage if I hoped to melt into my surroundings. I drove on to our room, half with the hope of finding them all there. My stomach turned over at sight of the room's emptiness.

The bag of garments and weapons I had taken from the gang members lay there on the floor. I studied every item. One knife with a wooden handle had the word "Lock" cut into it. I found the word "Chief" on one of the cell phones. They might be nicknames. It wasn't much to go on.

The clothes items weren't made for someone six-foot-six, but I managed to squeeze into a jacket by splitting the arms and back in a few places. I looked weird enough to scare myself. With Grady's wig perched on top of my head, I was grotesque to the extreme. I took my own jacket along, not sure I could pull off this kind of charade—though I did own this card that said I was an actor.

My vest contained two of the four guns I carried on me, my leg holster and a pocket held the other two. I hid knives and razor blades anywhere I could find a place. I even taped a blade under the strands of hair on the wig. I had prepared for war and even prepared for capture—my last resort to find the right person.

I left the car a good distance away from Lauri's selected neighborhood, and going on foot to its commercial streets, I scrutinized the patrons of dive after dive. When I found someone who could be a Niv, I stayed awhile and asked for "Chief" or "Lock." After each exit, I made a quick reentry to see if any noticeable action ensued. I stalked up and down what must have been a hundred streets and alleys, and felt like an old time gunman daring his opponent to come out and face him. My bad leg pronounced me a lunatic who should inhabit a wheelchair in some nursing home.

Finally, in one sleazy bar I glimpsed an occupant's quick

departure into a back room. The cast on his arm told me much. I barged through the door into an empty room and through another door into an empty alley. I found no sign of the man in either direction, only a drunk sitting against a cement block wall hugging a bottle, but he wasn't the same man.

"Where'd the man go who ran out of here?" I asked in my most menacing voice.

Two sullen eyes stared up at me. Almost too late, I saw that the color of the bottle's fluid didn't match the name on the label.

Any other time, I would have dived in the other direction. This time I dove directly at him, knocked the bottle from his hand as he hurled it. It hit the cement wall behind him and did what it was supposed to do. I reached both arms around him and rolled, using his body to protect my face while we moved clear of the fireball.

He got the worst of it. I ripped off my flaming wig and still glowing jacket. The back door of the restaurant opened, and I put a bullet into it. It closed instantly. The Molotov cocktail man groaned, and I lifted him in front of me as a human shield. I had already seen the tattoo on his arm, which told me I had found the right place.

I dragged him down the alley, but he cried so loudly I knew I would get no sensible information from him. Before he drew more attention than I could handle, I left him to groan alone and began a wide detour. Thanks to Lauri's thorough directions, I eventually arrived back at the same location, though I now advanced from the opposite direction. Directly in front of me with their backs turned my way stood the one with his arm in a cast and another with an Uzi. I jabbed my Glock into the back of the armed one and held my thirty-eight on Mr. Cast.

"Don't want to kill you tonight. Take me to your boss. I have information for him. Someone has cheated and framed him, and someone plans to kill him."

"He'd kill us if we took you to him," the one in the sling spilled, confirming he wasn't the dangerous one. I knocked the other one senseless, took both their guns, and dragged Mr. Cast by his long hair to a more private sector.

"Make a sound and the biggest bandage in the world won't help you. I'd enjoy killing you, but if you take me to your chief, I'll let you live. I won't even tell him who told me. But he'd thank you when he hears what I have to say."

"I don't know where he is."

I put his bad arm in a hammerlock and lifted him off the ground with it. My gun barrel poked against his eye.

"This is the last object you want to see, right? . . . Move fast and keep us out of sight. If anyone sees or hears us, I'll kill you. You've got exactly three minutes to lead me to him."

The pain caused him to begin to wretch. I eased up slightly.

"Thirty seconds gone."

Suddenly I discovered I had stepped on an ant's nest. They poured in from everywhere. With that many assailants, a hostage would do me no good, and I couldn't help anyone if I died. I dropped him and ran in the only direction clear for travel. Being retired from the force didn't mean retired from working out. I could still move quickly and could jump. Granted I sometimes ran with a limp—but I owned a fast limp. My bad leg didn't handicap me at all, it just hurt—immensely—as I limped faster than ever before in my life.

I wondered at the strangeness of the confrontation. No one fired a shot. That meant word had gotten out, and my disguise hadn't fooled anyone. They followed someone's orders that stated I wasn't to die by gunfire, at least not by gang gunfire. Two came in front of me and tried to block me. I used my forearms like battering rams and threw them out of my way. One hit the wall and the other skidded across the cement. I didn't look back to see if they got up.

My car waited for me in another direction, but I could detour to it later. Even as I ran, my mind worked in time with my stride, but no matter how I arranged and rearranged the pieces, I couldn't create the complete picture. If I didn't make it out of this neighborhood, I would never find the missing parts or my missing friends. Risking capture no longer seemed a viable option, not with this many captors on my tail. Quite possibly, they weren't thinking capture anyway. They might just want the fun of clubbing me to death.

I zigzagged through front doors and out back doors, and sometimes reversed the procedure. No politician ever met so many people in such a short period. The last of them dropped from sight about twelve blocks from my car.

Twelve more blocks of limping took me to my car, but already I felt like going back. I couldn't wait the four hours till morning and watch the sun rise with Rainy missing. She couldn't be dead. Her God wouldn't allow that, would He? I had never blown a job so totally in all my life.

The street looked empty when I pulled away from the curb, but I knew that a hell full of violence lay only a good run's distance away. I had made the rounds there for four hours and given them plenty of time to get organized. It had been successful beyond my wildest expectations, because now I knew where to go. If I couldn't get to their leader, I could grab anyone that strayed from the herd and force some degree of information out of them. Maybe even now they had Rainy and the others locked away somewhere.

When I entered a safer area, I gave it more thought. They hadn't shot me, so maybe the others still lived. If they had taken me to the leader, I would have faced grave trouble because I knew of no plot or betrayal—except a gang symbol on a desk in Chicago. I possessed a cop's hunch that usually proved as accurate as fact. I felt that someone was using the Nivs, deceiving them, and not telling them the whole story, but I didn't know the whole story either. I needed more information, quick, or I had to invent another believable lie. Only then could I go back and demand, "Take me to your leader." In the meantime, they could stew over the last false information I gave them. I planted a seed anyway.

My watch said it was almost time to contact Lauri, I took another look around the marina in Long Beach first and searched every nearby parking area for their car. With no luck, I followed the route they might have taken to the motel. A thin line of light escaped under Lauri's door, so I tapped quietly.

"Come in, Warren. . . . You look awful. Better sleep."

"I'm okay, but I'll sleep a few hours. If I don't call you in four, you try me. I might need a wake-up call."

"Warren, this may not be correct, but try the name Armind Jones for the gang leader."

I remembered hearing the name Armind at some point during the night. I had run the gauntlet of clubs, knives, and Molotov cocktails and accomplished little. She spent the evening on a phone or computer and found the gang leader's name.

"Anything else about him—his address, phone number, favorite color?"

"He served a prison term, been out four years, and deals in violence and drugs—like most gangs. I'll see if I can learn anything more."

"Just a minute. I want to get you something."

I searched our room and found the papers for their new rental car. It was just luck they weren't in Rainy's purse. Lauri waited at her door when I got back with them.

"Would you report their car stolen? Make sure someone notifies you if it's found. If you get any text messages from me, run to the police. They won't be mine. Good night, Lauri."

The room felt too empty. How could I sleep there? If they were alive, I couldn't imagine what their night was like—I didn't want to imagine it. If I slept in my regular place on the floor, I would miss Rainy's presence across the room. If I used the bed, I would probably bawl, and that word wasn't in my SWAT vocabulary.

I sat down on the bed she used. A shiver rolled over me though the room felt warm. Her tiny Bible sat there on the bedside table. I picked it up but couldn't open it. Finally I stuffed it in my pocket, got in my car, and drove back to Long Beach—the far end of Long Beach where Rainy and I feasted on fish one night a century ago.

Parked at a distance, I walked to our mound of sand. The night sky displayed a trillion stars, but no other light reached me. Irrationally I turned page after page of her Bible and stared at dark blurs. The pretense comforted me. I knew something comforting lay in those words that I couldn't see. I knew, because Rainy used those words, and she was always a comfort. Right now the darkness hid those words from me—the same darkness that hid Rainy from me—but I was suddenly certain God knew where she was. There in the sand I finally slept.

It was still dark when I got up and washed the sand from my hair at our outside shower. For a change, I wasn't hungry. I called Lauri and told her I would be at the set and would get information if I had to drag each of the suspects away and batter the information out of them. I didn't tell her I also planned to go back to the gang's hangout and find this Armind Jones.

"You can't do anything if you're in jail for assault. Do it the right way, Warren."

"That's what Rainy would say—and she might be dead now."

I hung up quick. I couldn't control my voice through another sentence, not through another word.

Tons of extras wandered around the Torment set. I signed in but didn't intend to work. I carried a cup of coffee but didn't intend to drink it. This movie set was the last one I ever wanted to invade. I must have looked rough with my bloodshot eyes and day's growth of beard because people stopped and looked at me twice. I felt rough.

I put discretion behind me and went straight to where the director, producer, and Britt would hang out, but found none of them.

"All hoodlums go to the hair and makeup trailer."

The word hoodlum hit me like a shock. I glanced down at my voucher and found the words printed neatly by my name. When I looked up again, the PA stood in front of me. He pointed to the trailer, and I meekly got in line. I would have to play the game a few minutes longer, or I would be thrown off the set with no way to learn what I needed to know. By hiding out, I had avoided both the hair and makeup people two other times. Today I would have to endure whatever took place in those perfume-reeking rooms.

From a fancy barber's chair, I gazed at the wall of mirrors in front me. The face I saw scared me. My hair stuck out bizarrely and assorted wounds and burns decorated my neck and face. I hadn't realized I looked so beat up—probably because I hadn't bothered to look in a mirror, probably because my innards racked with too much pain to ever feel those superficial scratches.

"How was your hair fixed when you did that last hoodlum scene—the one where you trashed the set?"

Had everyone heard about that?

"Like this. I looked exactly like this."

"I don't remember you. Probably Dana did you. I'll just touch it up some."

She pulled chunks of my hair straight out and sprayed this

awful spray all over my head. She wasn't the least bit gentle about it. It hurt and it stank. She proclaimed me perfect and sent me to the other end of the trailer to take another barber seat in front of mirrors. I was relieved to discover that Wayne would work on me.

"It doesn't look like you need much of anything, Warren. I think that look works. We'll dust you up so you don't shine. Been working any more on that independent film?"

"We've been too busy, but we'll get to it."

"If you get a chance, call me when you do your scene today. I'd like to see it. I missed the last one but sure heard about it. Maybe I can get out of here and catch it."

With pure relief, I left the trailer, but I still felt somewhat dubious about what I must endure to remain on the set and learn what I needed to know. I had certainly gotten myself into a corner. The voucher in my pocket proclaimed I was SAG now. That meant I was an actor—but I couldn't act. That meant I could eat the best food—but I wasn't hungry. That meant I would be paid to work today—but I planned to leave long before any hoodlum scene took place.

"All hoodlums get over here on the double," came an announcement from somewhere and proved that my resolves and rash thoughts were for aught. I had to play this game for a while longer since the flash drives should now be in the hands of our suspects.

I followed, but only because it would eventually lead me to the person I sought. The director and AD were still setting up the scene. After a careful study of Ertsly's face, I decided he looked pale and worried, a much different man from the one I scrutinized yesterday. Something had changed for him. Maybe he and the producer fought again and I was looking at suppressed tension or anger. The producer looked totally at ease though. The AD called for everyone's attention.

"We want all hoodlums to run full speed down this path we've marked. You're being chased, and you're terrified. If someone feels they can make it over that wood wall, go ahead but do it quick. Everyone else scatter to one side or the other, but not until you're almost up to it. We've placed a soft landing on the other side for anyone who can make it over. When you see my hand drop, run."

That was clear enough. For once I knew for sure when to start. His hand came down and I was off. No one ran ahead of me or beside me. There was just that wood wall beckoning to my pride, and directly on the other side lay freedom from that dreadful camera. I took a giant, flying leap and connected with the wall victoriously, both hands on top, ready to swing my body over with just the power of biceps and my somewhat massive shoulders. The wall crashed over and landed unhurt on the padding meant for me. I came down hard on the wood—not a soft landing.

Flat on my face, I saw the other hoodlums run past trampling the now deposed wall and escaping the beast or whatever was chasing us. I struggled to my feet and limped to safety.

"Cut"

Some kind of big discussion went on between camera crew, director, and producer. People laughed. I saw them review the take.

The AD was kind enough to come see if I still lived.

"That wasn't how the scene was written, but they liked it so much they may use this new version. They have to see if the footage is good—make sure none of the padding shows and none of the extras broke character."

"If it's not perfect?"

"We'll reset and do it again."

"W-which version?"

"Moving on," someone called loudly.

"This version," the AD laughed. "You're lucky. It's a keeper. . . . I'll send a medic to check you over."

With new pain pounding through my abused body, I wasn't in any frame of mind to take the call that buzzed on my cell phone. I didn't know the number. It could be a suspect calling about their new flash drive or it could be a call about Rainy and the others. It took everything in me to answer that call.

"Hello."

"I got your clip last night. I'd like to meet with you. I'll be free in about forty-five minutes—but won't have much time. Can you meet me at Renee's? It's a restaurant at Shoreline Village in Long Beach—directly beside the downtown marina."

"I'll be there."

Luckily he hung up before I could be injudicious enough to ask who called. I would have to get there first and see who arrived. It might be awkward in a restaurant. What would I do if all three suspects ate in the same place? Right when it was time to slip away from the set, I saw Lauri. She sat beside Rainy's PA and gave me a welcoming smile. I motioned her to meet me, but before she came, she turned to Jeff, patted his shoulder, and gave him an even broader smile than the one she gave me.

"I'll be back in a minute, Jeff. I need to take care of some business first. Can I bring you back a coffee or anything?"

He evidently didn't require anything but she earned a return smile—a rather sickening smile if my judgment counted.

"Follow me," she said guardedly as she walked past and stepped behind a tent. "I'm an extra today, but I'm here to learn what I can."

"How'd you manage that?"

"Who do you think got you all the information you needed to join the casting agency? . . . I wasn't on a tour yesterday."

"We got a bite on the clip. I'm to meet the person at Renee's, a restaurant directly across from us in the Village."

"Which suspect?" she asked breathlessly.

"No idea. I'll leave my phone turned on. If you see any of the three head that way in about thirty minutes, call me."

"Be careful."

The eyes that warned me to watch my back weren't those of a frivolous female trying to drown her grief with a new adventure. Something dead serious lay in their depths. I understood it better now because I was near the bottom of the pit she had already descended. She would play with PA Jeff or even with Mr. X, the murderer, if it would help in her investigation, but Bob was written in capital letters across her perfect brow, and it was plain the hurt hadn't eased yet.

When I got to Renee's, I was surprised and relieved to find it was a sandwich stand on the boardwalk, not an actual restaurant. For those who wanted to sit and eat, a few small tables sat along the boardwalk overlooking the water. It wasn't a good place for a hit, but I still studied everything within sniper range. Finally, I bought two of their BBQ beef-on-a-bun and found the most distant table that would still allow me a view of the restaurant's customers. The food in front of me grew cold while I watched and waited. My appetite might never return if Rainy didn't. Lauri called while I dumped the sandwiches in a garbage container.

"The producer and Britt got in a car and left. The director is walking your way."

Ertsly was the man I least suspected, had even considered taking him off the list. I went to my table and waited. In five minutes, he came in sight accompanied by another man. That caused me to hesitate. They both looked around and finally went to the stand and ordered. They took a table almost as distant as mine only in the other direction.

My approach startled the director, but instantly his surprise turned to irritation. Hopefuls had hounded him before.

"Don't have time to talk with you now. Wait for me back on the set."

"You said meet you here."

It felt good to act like a cop again instead of a bungling extra. I read his face as it changed from confusion to comprehension and finally to fear. I waited and let the silence envelope us. In the end, the other man spoke first.

"That's not one of my divers. If that was one of my men, it wasn't from this shoot. And we never set up charges at night. It's much too risky."

I looked at Ertsly and held the silence until he felt bullied into filling it.

"This is Dave Long, the owner of Priority Pyrotechnics. They're one of the biggest pyrotechnic operations around here. They have an unimpeachable reputation."

"Our company has done this kind of film work for over twenty years—in some of the biggest films made. We don't make mistakes, but if we did, we'd admit to them."

"Did you see the explosion? Do you think pyrotechnics caused it? You're the expert," I finally said. Obviously, the man wouldn't be here if he didn't have concerns along that line.

"Dave, I don't believe I'd answer that until we know what this is all about and your attorney's present," Ertsly advised.

This investigation wasn't going anywhere even close to the direction I had expected. The director was clean. I felt certain of that. This other man loved his company, but wouldn't commit murder for it. I was almost sure of that. But they might have valuable information I needed, so I kept it going.

"A camera was set on the bow of the yacht during the early morning shoot a few hours before the accident. By chance it picked up these scenes. You don't have to answer my questions. I work for a private investigator who is looking into one of the deaths. I believe neither of you had anything to do with this explosion, and I guarantee he'll accept my opinion as fact."

I pulled out my retirement badge, firearms permit, and a few other impressive cards just to help my cause—everything but my SAG card.

"SWAT! That explains those scenes you did. I thought you might be some kind of blackmailer . . . or worse."

The director actually laughed, and I felt I had an ally that could be a help at some point. With my friendliest look plastered on, I turned to Dave who still studied my credentials.

"I'd appreciate your opinion about the explosion, Dave. You're the professional."

"I didn't see the explosion. I did see footage of it, and it looked like something we could have set—but we didn't. Anyone familiar with pyrotechnics would recognize the kind of explosion that came off, so this information I'm giving you isn't anything secret. That fact has worried me. I've expected someone to throw the whole matter in my lap. In some ways, your recording actually relieved me because it showed the way it no doubt happened. I've racked my brain about this accident. I've thought all along it wasn't from a problem with the yacht's engine, but if the captain cleared his name, they'd for sure jump on us next."

"Were there explosives on the yacht that night?"

"None whatsoever—at least none we'd brought on. We did have scenes coming up that would have required that kind of material, but it wasn't time for those yet, and they wouldn't have been on board the yacht."

"Would it be possible for someone, the man in the wet suit,

to do something under water that could cause what happened?"

"Easily. He probably would have set most of it up prior to the shooting. I know half a dozen ways he could have accomplished it, and he wouldn't need to be an expert. Anyone with a slight knowledge of explosives could have set an explosion. He'd need to be a pretty good swimmer and diver, though. We do use divers from time to time."

"That Joe Clark who works for you looks like the man in the picture," Ertsly mentioned. "Do you know his whereabouts that night?"

"Joe's been with me a long time. I trust him completely."

"Dave, I brought those pictures with me that we took from the recording. Why don't you call Joe over here and see what he says?" Ertsly suggested.

Dave made his call while Ertsly brought out the pictures. The two men closely scrutinized three, high-resolution eight-by-ten's, obviously taken from our fake production. Now I grew nervous. What would these two experts see in our sham?

"He does look exactly like Joe," Dave remarked. "I'm not sure what job he was working on at that time. He could handle such a trick with no trouble, but why would he do it? Heck, I know Joe. He wouldn't do something like that. He said he'll be here in a few minutes."

"How about you," I asked. I looked directly at Ertsly. "Could that be you in the wet suit? Consider it for arguments sake. When I make a report, I need to account for everyone who could match this picture."

I could see immediately that it was a new thought to him. He took all three pictures and studied them one by one. Finally he laughed.

"I'm safe . . . with an alibi that would definitely hold up in court—even better than the fact I was around people all that night who would vouch for my presence. Look at the man's upper arm in this one. My back and upper arms suffered torture by the waxers about a week before the accident. This man has arm hair up to his shoulder—it might not be much hair, but it's still visible."

"Good, you're off the list. What about Don Denlin? He's

about the size and build of this guy."

"I wouldn't mind if you pinned this on Don, but everyone knows he can't swim. We can't even coax him to go out in the boat when we're shooting a scene."

"You know this for a fact? It's not some tale he's spread around to put himself above suspicion?"

"Never thought about that. I haven't known him long, and I'd almost be willing to frame him if the opportunity presented itself. That's not to be repeated, by the way."

"I'll ask the same favor of both of you. No one is to know about our meeting today—absolutely no one. We don't want the guilty person to do anything rash or disappear. Don't let anyone else look at the recording or pictures until I get back with you."

"Here's Joe now. Hey Joe, we're over here. Need your help on something. Can you identify the man in these pictures?"

I studied his face and saw nothing but innocence there as he paged through them.

"Looks like Ford, doesn't it. Yea, I'd say that was Ford. Where'd you take it? Has he stolen some more of your business?"

"No, nothing like that. But thanks Joe. We needed someone else to confirm it. You're sure, are you?"

"Yep, pretty positive. We worked together for quite a few years. If you don't need me for anything else, they're waiting for me on that Mathews job."

"That's all, Joe. Thanks for coming by."

As soon as he was out of hearing, both of them laughed. It was a laughable situation, but all I could feel was deep dark dread that I wouldn't find the right man in time. Still I had to be thorough.

"Who's Ford?" I finally asked.

"He used to work for me, then quit and started his own firm. Ever since then, he's been trying to steal my customers."

"I'll vouch for that," Ertsly added. "He asked for the pyrotechnic job on this film the day after the accident."

"But the picture doesn't make me think of Ford. Naturally it's difficult to judge since there's nothing much to use as a scale—mostly just ocean. But Ford's only about five-foot-four. I get the impression this man's taller. I could be wrong. Ford would certainly stand to gain from any accident by my firm. A big blunder like this one could ruin even a company of our repute."

"Dave's speaking of really big money—enough money to risk something like this."

"That's right. I don't think Ford would purposely put anyone's life in danger, but he could have miscalculated. I could probably find out if he was involved."

I felt like I was listening to Grady again. It all sounded so—so Hollywood. Would our next step be to call Ford to come look at the picture? Would he say the wet-suit man looked exactly like John Doe who had an even better motive? I didn't have much confidence in anything at this point. It all sounded reasonable, but something didn't feel right. There was still the producer, but not if he genuinely feared the water. And there was Britt Turner. It was difficult to believe that such an innocent-faced, bland individual could set an explosion, much less plan a murder.

"Dave, if you can find out anything discreetly, go ahead. Otherwise don't dabble. This could get dangerous. Thank you for your help."

"I know ways to check at a distance with no one the wiser. I'll call you if I learn anything."

When he left, I turned to the director.

"Ertsly . . ."

"Call me Al."

"All right, Al, if you'd get me copies of the footage you filmed of the accident, it could help. Meanwhile, I have to check out a few more things."

"Will you be back on the shoot this afternoon?"

"I may come and go. If you see me, treat me like an extra."

I did go back because it had come down to Britt Turner. I hadn't mentioned him to Al because he might unknowingly give something away. Before I barely reached the set, I got a call from another unknown number.

"Hello. This is Denlin Productions. I want to speak with the person who mailed the clip of the boat accident. They didn't leave their name," a businesslike woman's voice announced.

"I sent it."

"Mr. Denlin says to tell you he can't use it. The quality's poor and the material's dull. He thought possibly you'd sent us the wrong clip. If you have anything spectacular, or even interesting, he says you should send it on. He might be able to use it for publicity."

"Thank you. I'll check to see if my secretary sent the wrong one."

That eliminated the producer from my list. Now I needed to find Britt.

"You're getting good at that—acting, I mean," Lauri said as she grasped my arm.

"I'd always thought of it as lying."

"Am I the secretary who may have sent the wrong flash drive?"

"Guess you are, Lauri. Add to your report that the director and producer are both clean. So are Priority Pyrotechnics and their owner, Dave Long. There's another, newer, pyrotechnic firm run by a Ford who used to work at Priority. He's a weak suspect, but put him down anyway. His old boss plans to check into it. Have you seen Britt Turner?"

"They haven't gotten back yet. I've watched ever since you left."

"The director can be trusted, and he now knows an inkling about the situation—in case you need some quick help. Meanwhile, see what you can learn about Britt, and I'll do the same. Add this address to your report too." I discreetly passed her a slip of paper. "It's the hot-spot of the Nivs, or it was last night anyway."

With each passing minute, it felt less and less like the others were still alive, but despair hadn't won yet. My mind and emotions kept me halfway in the middle of a dangerously desperate state. I wanted to fight someone, chase someone down, but there was no one. There was only this desolate feeling of time passing. I gave myself until eight o'clock that evening before everything we knew, and everything we thought we knew, would go into the hands of the police.

When Britt and the producer got back, Denlin appeared to be in a good mood, but all I saw of Britt was his back as he entered his personal trailer. Evidently it wasn't time for his scene, since his stand-in, Tug, still stood for the cameras as they set it up. I felt like walking in on Britt and shaking the truth out of him. I could do that, or I could go to the gang's hangout and beat information out of someone.

Tug saw me and walked over. He was the last person I wanted to talk with at a time like this, but it was too late to make my escape.

"That hoodlum scene was a scream. You're a natural, aren't you?"

"Natural bungler. I didn't expect the wall to come tumbling down."

"I still give you credit. If you hadn't attempted it, and given it your all, it wouldn't have happened. Are you wrapped for the day yet?"

"They said I'd be wrapped soon. I'm waiting for word."

"I'll be through shortly, too. If this scene goes without a hitch, I'll be done for the day. I'm taking my boat out, just for the fun of it. Why not come with me and get some fresh air?"

"I'd like to, Tug, but I'm to meet my friends when I get off here, and we have business to take care of."

"You've got my cell phone number. Call if anything changes. I won't leave right away. If Rainy or any of the others can come, bring them along. We'll make a party of it."

I nodded my goodbye. It made me feel good for a few seconds to pretend I would meet Rainy shortly, but he ruined it by that amorous gleam in his eye. I felt like saying, "Give it up, man, she's mine," but I didn't know whose she was right now. By now, she could be God's, but I figured I still had a right to hope . . . and fight.

Chapter 13

For the thousandth time, I studied the set, the trailers, and the parking lot. My gaze stopped at a familiar face close by a parked car. He had been at Rainy's garage on our first Niv confrontation and had been on the set at Big Bear. Maybe they weren't such a large gang after all. I had seen repeats of faces more than once. I studied carefully every square inch of the parking area that was visible, even as I started a long detour. My guess was that he had already seen me, so it was important he lose track of me if I was to take him by surprise—and alive.

When I neared his vicinity, I saw he had moved to the fringes of the lot. Was it a trap? Did more of them hide close by? At this point, I didn't care if twenty of them bore down on me. Here might be the information I needed, and I felt as reckless as the derailed SWAT officer I was. There were no other people in sight, so I stooped low and worked my way around the autos. He stood directly on the offside of a pickup truck. He looked around with a tense expression on his face but didn't see me.

I dove under the pickup and pulled both his feet from under him. He had no chance to make a sound before he landed hard on his face. It wasn't a time for anything fancy. I simply sat on his back with both his arms in a hammerlock. My right hand exerted pressure while my left held the Glock to his head.

"Don't make a sound. This gun speaks absolutely quiet, and I'd sooner risk it than have you draw attention to us."

I gave one sharp push to his arms and heard the groan of pain he tried to stifle.

"Who's top dog in your gang? Is it Armind Jones?"

He didn't speak but nodded his affirmative.

"It's time for you to take me to him."

"I-I don't know where he is."

I pushed again and saw that he felt it.

"I'd tell you . . . if I knew. I-I d-don't know."

"What do you know? Where are my friends? Be careful what you say because they may be the last words you ever speak."

This time I gave his arms a jerk he would never forget. He couldn't answer for a few seconds.

"N-no one has told me, but A-Armind sent men to Catalina Island. . . . It had something to do with them, I think."

"How many men? When did he send them?"

"Early this morning. There were eight. I dropped them off at the Catalina Express boat. . . . I was told to stay on watch here."

"Are they alive—my friends?" I asked, and my voice came out almost a hoarse whisper.

I was as afraid to ask as he was to answer, but I gave him a good reason to answer quickly.

"I d-don't know. I-I think so. . . . Why else would he send so many?"

I pulled him to his knees, his arms still in a hammerlock.

"Let's see how long it takes you to find Armind. We'll look for him together. Where's your car?"

"That b-blue one . . . over there."

There it sat with three other gang members standing behind it. A group of tourists approached from the other way, and extras from the set were heading to their vehicles. A shootout was out of the question. I ducked down again and dragged him with me.

"Where on Catalina?"

"I don't know anything more. That's all they told me. It's . . . not a . . . big place. I d-don't know," he howled breathlessly, and I eased up on his arms.

His friends had seen us and were coming to offer aid. I left him lying face down on the pavement and exited swiftly around the parked cars and back to the set. Lauri stood there with deep concern etched on her face.

"I saw those men over there—saw where their attention was placed and knew it had to be on you. I was dialing the police when you popped up."

"They may be alive, Lauri—somewhere on Catalina. It's a gamble, but I intend to go there. You know I don't forget faces. Eight gang members should be on the island. I only need to find one."

"Their tourist season hasn't started, so it won't be overly busy."

"That will help. You know what to do if you don't hear from me for any length of time."

"I've already made arrangements for that. Wade Jennings, a Chicago cop friend of Bob's, is on his way here to help."

"I know Wade. Good man."

"I'm to meet him at the airport in about an hour. I'll brief him on the latest happenings. We'll probably go to the local police at some point. I need to leave now, but call me when you get to Catalina."

She left before I could ask her if she knew anything about transportation to the island. Wayne and Tug talked nearby, so I barged in on their conversation.

"Do either of you know the fastest way to get to Catalina? I heard someone mention an express boat. Does it run all the time? I don't mind paying a private boat, or renting a boat, but I want to leave as soon as possible."

"You could go on the Catalina Express, but you'd have to wait for their next scheduled run. And they don't run during the night. If you planned to stay there late, you'd have to wait until morning to return to the mainland. Why not let me carry you over there. I go there all the time."

"I'll pay you for the trip, and gas, if you can take me there and wait around till I need to head back. I don't know how long it will be."

I couldn't risk getting stuck there overnight in case I was following a false alarm. Suddenly thankful for a friend like Tug, I hoped I wouldn't involve him in the danger.

"We'll dock in Avalon's harbor, and you can call me when you're ready to leave. There's some cell phone reception in Avalon, but you might have to search for a spot where you can get a signal. If you find that you need to stay till morning, that's all right too. Catalina's one of my favorite places."

"Can you leave right now?"

"Give me about thirty minutes to wrap up a couple of small matters first. You can wait here, and I'll call you when I'm ready."

"I'll be here," I hollered to his retreating back.

"You'll like Catalina," Wayne said, before I could go aside and call Lauri. "I've been there a few times. It's a nice ride, and if you leave now you'll have plenty of daylight left for the trip."

"How far away is it?"

"About twenty two miles. The trip will take maybe an hour and a half. I'm glad you're letting Tug help out. He's sort of an outcast around the movie set. He had some fame once, about twenty-five years ago, but it lasted so briefly that hardly anyone remembers him. I recall because I've done makeup here for almost thirty years. Tug had one good movie followed by a failure. After that he dropped out of sight."

"I guess that's common in this business," I said with disinterest, but thought at the same time about Britt and how he faced the same prospect. Now maybe the publicity from the accident would bale out both him and the movie.

"It shouldn't have been the end in Tug's case. He got involved in a scandal, women, drugs . . ."

"You hear that sort of stuff about Hollywood personalities all the time. It doesn't appear to hurt their popularity."

"It probably wouldn't have. He might have survived the scandal and the bad movie choice, but he made enemies among important people in the industry. He stepped on the wrong feet when he tried to climb back into the limelight. After that, he couldn't get anything, not even a day player role."

I nodded and tried to appear interested, but greater matters weighed on my tired brain. My lack of response didn't bother Wayne. He had worked as a makeup man for too long. Like a dentist, he was used to monologues.

"Few people on this set remember him. He never gets anything much better than background work or an occasional photo double or stand-in job these days. It's a shame because he was a good actor. He's kept himself in good shape too. He's the same build as his son, though I've heard that the son looks more like his mother. She left Tug after the scandal, and he's never remarried. I guess Tug kept in contact with them because he certainly taught his son to be a champion swimmer."

"Tug must not do too badly financially if he can afford a boat and dockage at a marina like this one."

"Yeah, you're probably right. Maybe he has another business. I don't know him that well. I just see him on a set from time to time. I was surprised to see him on this movie. He told me Britt tries to keep his distance so as not to injure his own career. You'd think Britt could at least get him a day player roll on this rinky-dink movie. It's pretty sad that all he got was a stand-in spot. He was a swimmer of repute too. That's why he taught Britt. It's kind of unusual for a father and son to both land their big rolls because of something like that."

Suddenly Wayne's words sank in.

"Britt Turner is Tug's son?"

"Like I said, most people on this set don't know that, and Britt's not about to mention it. He even chose a stage name that wouldn't associate him with his dad."

My head whirled. Had my last suspect turned into a pair of suspects? Had they planned this together, or did Tug only harbor suspicions and intend to protect his son. Maybe Tug . . .

"Tug was on the boat the day of the accident, wasn't he?"

"Sure. He joked with me the other day about it. Said he'd rescued three fourths of the people, and his son got all the credit. I guess no dad would mind that, though. I'd rather see my kids in the limelight than step into it myself."

"That should help Britt's career a little, shouldn't it?"

"I should say—more than a little. He got an enormous amount of news coverage and two primetime interviews. . . . If his popularity hangs in there, I hope he gives his dad a boost. I know Tug appreciated the chance you gave him in the movie you're producing. Maybe you could squeeze him in for a few more lines somewhere. I actually feel sorry for him. I believe he's a better actor than his son, but don't tell anyone I said that."

Shock wave upon shock wave broke over me. I couldn't believe the terrible irony of our situation, the terrible mistake we made when we chose Tug to play in our fake movie. I had to think fast. There wasn't much time left before I would face him again.

"Your right, Wayne. Tug did a good job on their shoot, and they want to use him again. Rainy meant to talk with him about that after they wrapped yesterday, but I don't know if she had a chance. I was up at SAG headquarters paying dues, and they were all gone when I got back."

"Yeah, they wrapped early. But I saw them with Tug after that, so they probably got with him about the film. By the way, I saw you in that fence scene. That was incredible . . ."

"Thanks, Wayne. Excuse me a minute, will you. I have to take a call."

My nerves had exploded and now a call came from a blocked number.

"Yes?"

"Can you meet me . . . about that flash drive?"

It wasn't anyone's voice I knew. It sounded young and timid. In less than twenty minutes, Tug would return, but I couldn't turn away from this new lead. Brit was the only one who hadn't contacted me. Was this him or a trap? Did Tug leave so he could arrange this call while he stayed out of sight?

"Where are you now?" It took effort to keep my voice calm.

"In Long Beach, on a movie set."

"Meet me behind the wardrobe trailer in two minutes. Okay?"

The location was close, safe for both of us, and on the end of the set away from where Tug had disappeared.

"I-I'll be there."

I stood behind a camera and watched a white-faced Britt leave his trailer. This good-looking, muscular man looked like someone attending his own execution. I allowed him a minute to worry before I walked around behind the trailer, ready for almost anything at this point. His face registered genuine surprise when he saw me. The killer would already know me. Maybe I had misread his look. Maybe it was just the shock of confrontation that filled his eyes.

Staring back, I gave him no help. If a surprise still hid in the

Cracker Jack box, he would have to bring it out. I was ready to shake the box if he delayed much longer—about as ready as I would ever be. This man reeked of some variety of guilt, but I saw something else there too. I wondered why he wanted to talk. Maybe he needed to know more from me before he dropped his bomb.

"I just got your flash drive. I don't know what to say. Who have you shown it to? Do you intend to go to the police? I-I can't be blackmailed. I'm not that rich. Can you wait? Could you wait till this film comes out? This will kill my mom."

I stared at him in silence. Either he was the most stupidly arrogant person I had ever met, or he was practicing acting. Right away, something felt wrong.

"I'd like you to understand the situation, even if you won't do anything. Dad has been down for a long time. For over twenty years he's worked at any job he could get. I had to pull strings to get him this stand-in job. They said he was too old to look like me. He and I both know he looks better now than he did back when he got his big break—and he's only in his forties. He's been eating his heart out all these years. He had one shot at the big time and now . . ."

He hadn't made me feel sorry for the guy, and I grew more impatient to learn the truth—if he knew it.

"He must have been afraid I'd end up like him. All I can figure is that he planned this terrible accident to put me in the public eye. His insane, misguided attempt to help me has cost all this. I figured it out after I saw the recording. I haven't talked with him yet. I don't know what to do."

Now I was genuinely shocked speechless, but he wasn't through yet.

"It's difficult to get Dad work. His enemies in this business haven't forgotten him. I learned long ago you have to be friends with everyone—even with those who aren't as important or talented as you are. There might come a time when they have power. It happens, you know. I won't make the mistakes Dad made. I expect a long ride at the top."

I wished to high heaven that this low mentality, conceited kid was the one, but now I knew he wasn't. He thought he had something special and wasn't smart enough to keep it to himself.

He was destined to be a one-night stand unless someone intervened. Years of dealing with criminals told me Britt Turner wouldn't try something of this magnitude. He was a dreamer, but a harmless one. He didn't think anything was amiss that he couldn't fix with his charm. He was convinced the world had discovered how special he was, loved him for it, and would love him forever. He was also convinced his father did the crime. I had to find out why.

"You recognized your father in the picture?"

"Immediately. He has a little birthmark on his upper arm. It's small, but I could see it. And a boating incident is the kind of scheme Dad might try. Mom and I know that side of him too well."

When the director and Dave had pulled out their pictures from the recording, I saw the tiny discoloration on the upper arm. I was surprised that Rainy and the others hadn't noticed it when they reviewed the video. I should have insisted on reviewing it with them. It was my business to note things like that. Still, it was so insignificant most people wouldn't be aware of it.

It was only natural for Britt to identify his father from our constructed video—since it was his father. He might not have felt the same if he had seen the original. Still my gut feeling told me I had found the culprit. Britt's words, Mom and I know that side of him too well, spoke louder than the picture. If Tug was the murderer, I had led Rainy and the others right into his hands with my insane idea to make that video.

"Mom said it was a brazen, reckless act that first put Dad in the spotlight and landed his movie roll. I had suspicions he was responsible for my big break too. But . . ."

I left junior babbling to himself. There was no time for him now. It was time for me to walk into whatever trap Tug had manipulated. That was the only way to find the others—if they weren't already anchored at the bottom of three hundred feet of water. I forced myself to calmness and a moderate walking speed. I tried to prepare myself mentally for anything, but anything covered too much territory. When I saw Tug coming in my direction, my heart made a tigerish leap into my throat. He saw me and motioned for me to come on.

"I packed some supplies—eats and drinks," he said jovially,

like someone anticipating a fun outing to Catalina.

I began to doubt my own feelings. Either this guy was totally innocent or his acting was far superior to his son's acting ability. He carried three large paper grocery bags, and handed me two of them while he unlocked the gate to his pier. My bags contained two-liter drinks. When I saw the size and condition of his sporty cabin cruiser, I wondered again how he could afford it. We boarded and my eyes made a swift search for clues, for any sign of struggle. Nothing met my gaze except clean white surfaces and an abundance of rich varnished mahogany.

"Follow me to the galley, and we'll put these eats and drinks in the refrigerator."

I was halfway down the steps when it hit me directly in the face. I recognized the CS gas and there must have been something else there too. My lungs shriveled to the size of raisins, and my eyes smarted unbearably. Just as my sight started to close down on me, I saw Tug with a mask over his face and a jumbo wrench in his hand—Tug, the master actor.

Chapter 14

Burning pain was the first symptom of consciousness to hit me. The left side of my face rested against a hard surface and darkness surrounded me. When I tried to rub my hand over my eyes to see if he had blindfolded me, I realized he had tied both my hands behind me and had attached those bindings to my tied ankles. My cramping legs and stiff back told me I had been in that position for a while. The hum of an engine came gently to my ears and lulled me to sleep again.

The next time I awoke, my eyes had cleared, though the rest of me remained the same. Dim light came from somewhere, enough light to show me my situation. I occupied the floor of the boat's galley, and judging by the engine's throb, it was in the aft portion of the boat. I rolled over to determine what tools and weapons he had left me. He had taken my vest and jacket. I pressed my leg against the floor. He had taken that gun too but had left the holster. Maybe he hadn't found the blade there. I still wore my boots, too, but I couldn't tell if he had found their hidden places. At least he knew nothing of the tools that I hid in strategic spots on my person.

I saw blood on the floor and knew it came from my head—probably from its collision with his wrench. My stomach felt queasy, whether from the boat's rocking or from the gas I inhaled, I didn't know. My groggy mind wanted to sleep again. I hit my head on the floor a couple of times, hard, to shake off the consuming drowsiness. A dull thump sounded below my ear, only once, followed by silence. The sound helped me focus on the reality of my situation. I had to free myself of the ropes and do it now.

At least I had prepared for a captive situation. My penknife had left with my vest and guns, but I had brought other options. The blade in my short's band would do nicely if I could reach it, but having my wrists bound to my ankles restricted my movement immensely. I wasn't a slim, loose gymnast type who could slide my body through the circle of my arms and bring my feet up close to me or do a backbend that would bring my fingers near the blade in my shorts. I felt more like the Hulk at eighty years of age with arthritis. The green color fit me too.

At the expense of an excruciating cramp in my bad leg, I ascertained that my boot no longer contained its blade. I squirmed in my ropes and worked to loosen them while my mind toiled double time. Was Tug the only one on the boat or had he brought help? I searched the room for a sharp object and discovered the intercom on the wall. No doubt, he had turned it on to monitor sounds in the cabin. I would have to struggle quietly. Right then, another thump came from below, and it hadn't come from the engine. A minute of arduous squirming showed me I lay across the hatch. It wouldn't open with my teeth, so I gambled on a quiet probe.

"It's Warren—I'm tied."

The thump came twice—definitely an answer. Someone still lived. Tears streamed from my eyes as I rolled to my side and concentrated on my ropes again. My thumb and fingers finally grasped the knot that should free my ankles from my wrists and allow me to straighten my legs. If I could untie that one, I could exert more movement to loosen the other ropes or to reach the blade in my shorts, but the small, tight knot wouldn't budge.

The hum of the engine stopped, and panic invaded my mind for an instant. My good sense told me that haste wouldn't get the job done. I calmed myself and put all my concentration on that tiny knot, to pick at it constantly, if only one fiber at a time. My hands burned in pain from work in such a cramped position. Finally, I felt a slight movement and tugged the end through the knot. Within seconds I could straighten my legs but couldn't take time to enjoy the bliss.

Because of the weight I had lost, I could reach under my

loose belt and find the band of my shorts—but too late. The galley door opened and Tug stood there. I wondered if he had come to end us. Whatever his intent, I couldn't let him find that blade. He would check my bindings if he saw that I escaped one of the ropes. I pushed my short's band back into my pants even as I spoke to draw his attention away from my movements.

"I heard a thump in your bilge. I thought you were the only rat on board?"

He grinned amiably, dragged me a couple of feet to the side of the hatch, and opened it with a much too satisfied expression on his face.

I squirmed to where I could peer into it.

The darkness of the room, and the even darker bilge, made it difficult to see, but I soon made out Rainy's form. Grady was sandwiched half underneath her and they were both bound and gagged. Rainy's eyes were open. All at once, a flashlight beam lit the area, and I could see Tia and Tim squeezed into the tight area at her right. Tim's eyes were open, but when the flashlight beam hit his face, they closed reflexively. I wondered if this wretched place was where they had been for the past twenty-four hours. Rainy's eyes told me their state. I saw the inches of cold, oily water in the bottom of the bilge. They had been cold to the extent that they had gotten beyond shivering. I breathed the stagnant air and was amazed any of them had survived this long. Tia groaned softly. That left only Grady's life in question.

"Grady," I bellowed, and got enough movement from him to know where I stood.

All four of them lived, though barely. They were all hypothermic or drugged and would be helpless in any rescue attempt I might make.

"Where are we, Tug," I asked angrily.

I literally shivered at the cold intelligence in the depths of his eyes.

"We're almost to our destination. I'm anchored here until dark—then I'll take you to meet some old friends on Catalina. I picked out a lonely section of beach. Didn't I promise to take you to Catalina? Now I need to fix myself some dinner."

"Don't close the hatch," I pleaded as he leaned over the dark hole. "There's no oxygen in there."

"I run the blowers from time to time, but I'll leave it open for now. I wouldn't want anyone to die too soon. Since all of you helped ruin my first plan, you'll help me put across this one. You've made it much more complicated than I'd originally intended, but I've about tied up all the loose ends. I believe it will come out remarkably better than I'd hoped."

"All this carnage to boost your son's career?"

"My son? You kidding?" He looked at me in astonishment for a long few seconds. "I did this for me! I've done enough for Britt. I paid for his first role. He thinks he landed the role with his charm and talents, but I bought every particle of fame he owns with money I earned selling drugs, guns, people, or anything else that came my way."

"Is that how you make your living these days?"

"That's how I've always made my living. I used to run in a gang myself, as a kid in Chicago. I had just turned thirteen when I shot and killed someone in a rival gang. He was my first . . . no telling who will be my last."

"Aren't you rather old to play gang?"

"Oh, I've traveled beyond that childhood whim. I saw right away where the actual profit lay. I graduated to supplier before I reached voting age. I kept Britt and his mother in luxury for twenty-five years and bought Britt his ride to the big time. Shouldn't any father expect generosity from his son in return? Wouldn't any son give his dad a lift back up? Instead, I receive a junk job on a junk movie from an ungrateful son who's ashamed to tell people that I'm his father and was famous once."

"No one remembers you, Tug. How'd you expect that explosion to do you any good?"

If I could only keep him busy talking while he prepared his meal, he might not notice my efforts on my wrist ropes. Even if I couldn't slip out of them, with their slackness I could cut them quickly when the time came.

"I admit I used poor judgment," he finally answered and proceeded to crack half a dozen eggs into a skillet. "Got a big night ahead of me. Need to stow away plenty of fuel. . . . I miscalculated a few matters. The explosion caused more damage than I'd planned. I've worked with pyrotechnics before but not extensively. I needed a fire to insure that people went overboard, so I used extra gasoline in the bilge to supplement the explosives. Guess I added too much, but my plan still would have worked if the camera had turned on me and not Britt. I should have realized that they'd focus on the star. I rescued most of the people, and he got the credit."

He placed half a dozen slices of bacon in another skillet and went on to chop onion and green pepper for his eggs.

"Everything else in my plan transpired perfectly, though. Two days earlier, I set off a tiny smoke bomb near the boat's engine to give a hint that the yacht had a problem. When it came time for my biggie, both cameras rolled and the transpo boat was ashore. I set the explosion off by remote control and dropped the device into the water. I even told the cameraman to keep rolling and he obeyed me."

"I can see it all now. You probably ripped off your shirt and dove into the water in front of the camera."

The man was so caught up in himself that he didn't hear the mockery in my voice—or didn't care.

"What else? I thought I'd ride the headlines again—considering all the people I'd saved. . . . Not only didn't it work, but your friends recorded me at an especially revealing point of my plan."

"Why'd you call in a detective agency to help? Obviously you eliminated Cal with no help."

"I couldn't find his friends, and I needed some quick help. I couldn't risk hiring a detective agency located here, and I know my way around Chicago. It was a smart move on my part. You handled the job with ease. But I hadn't expected the Nivs to fail me."

"What story did you tell them to get such loyal help? Did you offer them a payoff for our deaths, or are we intruders who must be killed because we endanger their illicit supply and traffic?"

"Both, actually. I told them you had a revealing video of one of our transactions and meant to blackmail us. I offered them a bonus supply of goodies plus assurance that their supply will continue to flow smoothly when they finish this job."

"Since you don't intend to deliver either promise, how will

you eliminate them?"

"Actually, I need them as my scapegoat. None of them, except their leader, have ever seen me. I've scheduled a meeting with him for when I get back."

"So you'll kill him too."

"Like I said, I grew up with killing. Why should it bother me?"

I saw it again. Evil emanated from this man. I wasn't staring up at a wild eyed radical who killed for a cause, nor was this a trained professional who killed for pay and had long ago buried regret or emotion. This man thoroughly knew the evil side of life and chose it because it fit him so well.

A groan came from the bilge, and I burned inside at the man's cruelty. Bacon scented the air to torture those in the bilge who hadn't eaten for more than a day. He probably hadn't given them anything to drink either. I watched him wolf down his meal.

"You made it easy for me when you showed up on set today. I arranged your meeting with that gang member. Didn't you think he gave in too quickly . . . and talked too easily?"

"I pegged him a coward—like the rest of them."

"I needed a way to get you into my boat. It worked well, didn't it? I've had you under my thumb all along. Only once did you stump me. I couldn't figure what you intended to do with that recording we made together—take it to the police or what. Only when we shot those scenes did I realize for sure that none of you knew I starred on your original recording. I could have saved myself an immense amount of trouble if I'd known."

"If I'd seen that original recording, you never would have gotten away with any of this. I would have seen and remembered that little place on your shoulder. One glance would have sufficed."

"Too bad. If I'd known for sure the others possessed no such powers of observation, I might have skipped all this trouble—still I would always have felt uneasy. It's time to break with the gang anyway. They've been dragging me down and will have no place in my new life."

"What about the statements we've written. You don't know where we put them."

"Room 217. I even have the key. I called to tell them I'd be staying another couple of days, and I picked up a copy of your recording to give to the police. It will show clearly what you were perpetrating and will greatly help my cause. Is there anything else I forgot?"

"What were we perpetrating?"

Chapter 15

"I wanted you to ask that," he said, and put aside his empty plate. "I'll give you a preview of the story the police will record and the newspapers will print. By the way, I'm rather good at monologues, but I'm sure I will benefit from this rehearsal."

When he rose to recite his grandiose lie, he became a different person right before my eyes.

"I managed to piece together a great amount of information from conversations I overheard while I lay bound and gassed in the galley of my own boat." He looked down at me and grinned before continuing.

"Evidently this boat captain, Capt. Nobel, wanted to get out of the drug business. It had become too hot for him. He planned to sink his yacht for insurance and sue the movie production company for additional losses because of their misuse of explosives on his yacht. Being an amateur regarding such things, he didn't realize the production hadn't brought any explosives on board. He also didn't set the charge properly. The yacht sank too quickly and caused casualties, which he hadn't intended. Worse yet, this group of five extras had a recording that showed him in the very act of setting the explosives.

"As soon as he realized they intended blackmail, he paid this rogue, former cop, Warren Roberts, to find and eliminate them. The man had talent—and a history of violence. He took out Calvin first but then decided he could make more money by joining their blackmail scheme. That forced the captain to make a deal with them. He agreed to pay them off if they'd help him make a new video—

one that would implicate another person setting the explosives. They evidently chose me because I was the most experienced swimmer and diver on the boat that day. Capt. Nobel used his uncle's boat for the shoot, but I don't know if the uncle got involved in any of this.

"Anyway, as soon as they created the new video, Captain Nobel sent Warren to trick me and the others into meeting at my boat. Warren didn't know the captain had double crossed him too. The captain's gang contacts, the Nivs, seized the boat, gassed and tied all of us, and took us to Catalina. They docked my boat just offshore near a lonely stretch of beach where they planned to shoot us and leave our bodies. We were still tied when they boated us toward the shore in my boat's tender, but as we neared the beach, I dove backward off the side of the boat.

"They shot into the water but missed me. Being totally bound, my chances looked slim. My swimming experience saved my life. I went under water, swam like an eel, and had to surface twice before I loosened my ropes enough to get free. They didn't see me either time, but the second time I heard the shots on the beach. . . . Horrible! Horrible!"

He had totally kept my attention. Now I clearly saw the real actor in action—Oscar quality talent. At least now, I knew plainly what he intended for us. But he wasn't through yet. He had only paused for effect, and I could picture him doing the same at the police department. A bunch of fools like me would probably believe him.

"I could see their flashlight beams, and I knew it was too late to help the others. Some of the gang stayed on my boat, and I guessed that quite a few gang members patrolled the island. I couldn't risk swimming ashore at Catalina to get help, so I swam toward the mainland. The water represented safety to me, even though it felt like ice, and I wore no protection. Only the thought of poor Wayne, who'd also worked on that recording, kept me going. I had to make it back and warn him, if they hadn't already murdered him too."

He punctuated his ending by shoving me over to check my ropes. I barely had time to make them appear tight. I had actually not gotten far in loosening them, so I exerted pressure outward to make it appear they cut into my flesh. He turned the flashlight beam into the bilge to confirm that everyone remained secure. When he reached to close the hatch, I rolled over the opening.

He kicked me hard in the stomach and then in the side, but I stayed put. That didn't make him happy. He reached in a drawer and brought out a crime prevention tool I was extremely familiar with—a taser. He zapped me until my eyes tried to leave their sockets, but I held my post. Actually, I was too incapacitated to move. When I looked again at his face, he had put his actor's mask aside.

For an instant, I felt myself shrinking back from the heat of that hellish gaze. I thought of times in the past when I had faced hell in the line of duty—in my body and in my mind. Those times were nothing next to this. I now looked into two yawning infernos and felt the terribleness. I saw deep into the fiery pits of his soul. The curtain had been pulled back, and there sat hell in all its nakedness.

I don't think I ever resorted to prayer, but right then, in my heart and mind, I told God that if He would help me free just one arm, I would end this. Then I begged Him—from the depths of my soul. When Tug turned away to go up the stairs, my eyes were wet in thankfulness. My arm wasn't free, but Tug had left the hatch open. That would suffice for the present. They had good air to breathe for a few more minutes.

Rolling off the hole, I called into its darkness, "Does anyone have strength enough to move? Worse times head our way. Try to move. Move anything. Get your circulation going—please."

I looked down at Rainy in the dimness. Duct tape covered her mouth. I could at least end that suffering for her if I could reach her.

"Try to lift your head a few inches."

She tried, and I was able, after a few attempts, to grip the end of the tape in my teeth. I ripped as quickly as possible to minimize the hurt.

"I'm sorry about the food," she said after looking up at me sympathetically. "I'm hungry too."

For once, she hadn't read me. The last concern on my mind was food, and the first concern was her. It seemed strange to me that when we faced only minor danger, she didn't care about food. Now, when we were at death's door, she was hungry. I couldn't understand this woman's mind.

I had brought this pain to her, but I knew it would have come to her anyway. Some other poor hired fool like me would have dropped into her life, someone who wouldn't know how to protect her any better than I did, maybe not as well. For sure, they wouldn't want to save her as badly as I did. I didn't know if that counted for anything at this point.

Why I did it, I don't know, but I looked into her eyes and said, "Pray." I rolled away from the top of the hole and waited for the engine's rumble. I must try for my blade again and cut myself free the second I knew Tug was occupied elsewhere.

Only a minute or two passed before he returned to the room, now dressed in a black wet suit. He took the rope I had struggled to untie and again secured my wrists to my ankles, tighter than before, leaving my bad leg in agony. He left abruptly, and I heard the engine start. At least the hatch stood open, but I would have traded that luxury to lose the extra rope. That hard, tiny knot might mean all our lives. I worked on it at once, even as I gazed into the bilge trying to give a silent message. Finally, I lowered my head into the opening and spoke softly so the intercom couldn't pick it up.

"I'm working on my rope. He retied the one I'd gotten off. I'll try to keep him talking again if he returns. The more we know about what to expect, the more we can prepare for it, and while he talks, I can work on this knot."

Rainy nodded her head and that undid my emotions again. My insides were hot as pitch, so hot I wondered why I couldn't melt off our ropes by looking at them or melt this man by staring him down. The heat inside me had grown so intense I didn't dare look Tug in the eyes again.

"Warren, forgive me for insisting we go to the Long Beach shoot. I'm to blame. None of us would be in here if I'd listened to you," Rainy said in a throaty whisper.

"We'll get through this, right?" I did my best to smile.

"Thank you, Warren. . . . We'll be fine."

I didn't trust myself to speak, so I rolled over and worked feverishly on my knot. I had almost conquered it when the engine cut again. Too late, I thought, even as I continued to work. I lay close to the hatch, ready to protect them any way I could, when he came through the door.

"I anchored a short distance beyond our beach. The tide's high, but luckily there's still enough beach left to hold all of you. It's finally dark outside, and since it will take two trips to get you all ashore, I need to start now. Get out of the way, Warren, so I can move them out of there.

When he grabbed hold of the rope connecting my ankles to my wrists, and pulled me aside, I knew the knot had tightened again.

He reached into the bilge and dragged Rainy out by her ankle ropes. Her head struck the opening, but he paid no attention. To him, she was already dead. He pulled her across the room and left her on the floor while he went back for the others.

"It's a shame I can't trust you, Warren. You could do the bull work for me. . . . Need to get that leak fixed. Getting too much water in there," he remarked as he yanked the next one out.

I saw the hell again and knew it would be like that clear to the end—unless I could put out his fire. I tried to conquer my feelings and entice this man to divulge more information. It might help me plan what to do, though it would almost be better if he made his move now. If I could get free of just one rope, I could possibly take out this guy. I might have to drown us both, but I couldn't handle half a dozen Nivs while all laced up.

"Why not shoot us now and dump us in the ocean?" I asked, goading him to talk.

"I don't want blood all over my boat."

"You could dump us first, and then shoot us."

"To give credence to my story, the police need to find and account for all of you. I suppose I could do it myself, but police equipment has become so sophisticated that someone might pick up a clue, a spot of blood, or a bit of DNA that wouldn't match my story. The only way to ascertain my plan works is to move you elsewhere or sink my boat with all of you in it—and I really like this boat.

"You can see I've been meticulously careful about everything. I even waited until I'd added you to my collection so you'd all leave this world about the same time. If the authorities perform an autopsy, their findings will correspond with my story. At this point, I simply can't risk any mistakes that might disprove my statement—especially my dramatic dive from the tender while still bound. That will be the highlight of this production. Can't you picture it?"

"I'd rather see it in person. Why not let me tie you so you can practice it a few times. I especially think you need work on that eel part. The Nivs won't mind the wait."

He didn't even smile at my suggestion.

"They'd mind the wait all right. They expect revenge, and they especially want you. I don't mind granting them a favor when it fits my purposes so nicely. They're already on their way to our private rendezvous. They picked up kayaks in Avalon, and they know when and where I'll leave you. I know it's ridiculous for me to hogtie you for them, since I could have killed all of you a dozen times over with no mess, but I can't trust them to handle it by themselves. Those bunglers are nothing but show when you get right down to it."

"What about when those bunglers hear your story in the news. They might realize you were their supplier?"

"With their leader gone, they'll scatter. They'll have no way to get supplies, and they have no second in command to take over. I've worked this out carefully, and the gang's already been implicated a number of times in this deal, especially when you left those three tied in the church. The Nivs won't see me or my boat at any time, so they won't know what's going on."

"You've set up all the Nivs for a fall—your faithful allies?"

"All things change. I've changed this operation half a dozen times since the beginning, mostly because of you. Because of my adaptability, I'll accomplish better results than I ever hoped for. And we'll both be in tomorrow's news. Isn't that an interesting thought?

"I'll not only be a hero, but the director and producer will love me. They'll realize I saved them from prosecution and from lawsuits arising over the accident. They could have gotten into serious trouble over their pyrotechnics since they couldn't prove there were no explosives on the yacht. I could save them millions of dollars and court appearances and possible criminal charges. And when I give the captain to the authorities to prosecute, that will endear me to them forever."

Tug slammed the door shut on the now empty hatch. In spite of their rough exit, I felt relief to see them out of their prison. More dead than alive, Grady and Tia evidently fared the worst, but at least they still breathed.

He surprised me and cut the small rope I had worked on tediously. My wrists and ankles were still bound, but I could again straighten my legs. Even while I stretched and flexed them to relieve the numbness, I plotted how to take him over the side with me, how to hold him under until he drowned. It wouldn't be easy, not against a world class swimmer, especially since my biggest claim to fame in the water was my ability to out-sink any of my buddies. Probably because of my heavier bones, I became the all-time champ at being able to sink to the bottom quickest without exerting physical effort. Maybe that talent would become a blessing before the night was over. If I could get hold of him with my knees and teeth, or somehow get my tied hands on his throat, maybe . . .

Those plans fizzled when I saw he had his piece pressed against Rainy's head.

"You two go first. You won't have as much opportunity to get into trouble on that beach as you might have here while I'm gone. Get up those stairs. Come on, Warren."

"Untie my ankles so I can walk."

"Squirm up them. You can do it. Pretend you're an eel."

He guessed right. With his gun pressed to Rainy's skull, I could do many things. I struggled up one step at a time. I still couldn't act, but I tried to appear beat and helpless. It might help our cause later. When I reached the top, Rainy had only made it up the first step. She had almost no control over her body movements. He grabbed hold of her shirt and dragged her up the remaining steps and across the dark deck to where his tender bobbed beside his boat, tied and ready. He shoved her aboard but left me lying on the deck.

"I can take three this trip. Stay out of trouble while I bring up one more."

He tied a rope around my chest and under my arms before he shoved me into the choppy darkness below to fare for myself. The shock of the cold water sent sharp stabs of pain all over me. I went totally under, and it took all my effort of pumping my legs to reach the surface. My talent for sinking didn't help at all. I would have given anything for an ounce more buoyancy.

I managed to grab only one breath before I sank again. The next time I surfaced, I saw Tug come out with Tia over his shoulder like a sack of grain. I sucked in all the air I could hold and sank again. He didn't want me to die by drowning, so I gambled he would pull me up. First I saw his flashlight beam above me, turned on the water where my rope disappeared into the dark depths. Finally he pulled me out, and I didn't have to pretend the choking and gasping for breath that consumed me.

He wrapped the rope a couple of hitches around a post. With my mouth now barely out of the water, I could save energy and watch what went on. The stars gave just enough light for me to affirm that Tia and Rainy lay in the tender. He studied me for a minute, probably wondering how he would hoist me into that little boat.

"No sense making two trips." he said with decision. "The tender should hold the five of us adequately. We can drag your weight behind. It will save time and trouble. Our visitors will arrive soon anyway."

That ruined my newest plan. I had meant to get free when he dumped me on that beach and then somehow take him down when he came back with Tim and Grady. Now I would have the gang to contend with, and maybe not many minutes of leeway before they showed. I began a quick rethink of my plan.

Tug proved his good physical condition when he carried both Grady and Tim to the boat, one after the other. He rolled them unceremoniously in and finished by tying my line onto the stern. He never looked to see how I fared while he motored toward the island. He wanted me almost-but-not-quite dead when we hit the beach. It wouldn't take much pretending on my part.

The movement of the boat and the ocean tossed me in every direction, usually under the water. I gulped breaths of air whenever I could. When the opportunity came, I grabbed the rope in my teeth and bit down hard. It kept my head out of the water often enough to breath semi-regularly. Maybe he thought I could hold my breath until we reached the beach, or maybe he didn't care anymore because he never reeled me in to see if I still lived.

The rendezvous point was located further from his boat than I had expected. I guessed he couldn't let any Nivs see his boat or it might cause snags in his later plans. When my legs finally dragged against the bottom, I took a deep breath and let the rope fall from my mouth. This time I absolutely had to give a convincing performance. He pulled the boat onto the beach, dragging me into the gravelly sand and shallow water of the shore. I lay there prone. When each small wave withdrew, I grabbed a quick breath, the rest of the time I let the water wash over me.

"Let's have some help, Warren. I don't intend to drag your carcass onto the beach by myself."

I remained silent and lifeless, like someone drowned. I had seen enough drowned corpses in my years of police work to enlighten me on how a fresh one should appear, so I duplicated the look to the best of my ability. He kicked me sharply in the ribs, but wet deck shoes can't do much damage, and I was too numb to feel anything anyway. My performance must have convinced him because he grabbed hold of my boots and tugged me up the beach a short ways while I remained a dead weight. I couldn't stop my heart from beating, but I knew that the cold water had slowed my pulse. I tried to control my breathing to match it.

Prepared for anything, I wasn't surprised when he struck me on the head with a hard object. It was supposed to render me unconscious, and I pretended it did. A few more kicks followed, which I accepted limply and gratefully. I could have kissed the wet, gravelly sand under my face when I heard his motor start. I waited for the flashlight beam that I knew would follow, and while waiting, I memorized my exact body position in case he returned. My ears soon told me he had gone a good distance out from the shore. I dared reach my soggy, numb fingers inside my pants to find my short's band. The second I had the blade within reach, the flashlight beam touched the shore. I squinted my eyes almost closed and waited. While I waited, I cut lose my wrists.

When the flashlight beam disappeared and the sound of his motor grew fainter, I cut free my ankles. I studied the black surface of the ocean for any sign of his boat or the kayaks. The Nivs would come from my right. Tug had conveyed their arrival information by his numerous glances in that direction. I stepped out further into the water and listened intently. I heard distant voices, but it was too dark to make out any kayaks. All at once, a light blinked three times from the direction Tug had headed. The beams pointed toward the beach. Seconds later an answering signal came from the Nivs—close, much too close.

We owned nothing but a narrow beach with no place to hide and no avenue of escape. Dark rugged walls of rock surrounded the area on all sides. They looked unscalable, especially considering the condition of my charges. I investigated the beach on the Niv's approach side where the hard packed ground met the rock wall. Like a half-crazy dog after a rabbit, I threw sand and gravel between my legs and behind me in a steady stream. Two, hand-sized rocks I laid aside for possible weapons. When I had accomplished two, shallow six-foot trenches, I rushed back to where the others still lay, silent and prone.

Tia was a dead weight in my arms as I ran and deposited her in the first trench, her back against the rock wall. Rainy had rolled half way to me. That facilitated my job and saved me valuable seconds.

"There may not be time to untie you. The Nivs are almost here. I'll have to cover you with sand," I whispered on our way to the trench.

When she lay close against Tia in the furrow, I ran back for Grady. Tim worked his way in the correct direction, so I placed Grady in the second trench and covered Rainy and Tia with the sand. Tim's strength soon gave out, and I helped him to the trench. I only had time to cover the trenches lightly, but it would fool anything but a direct flashlight beam—at least for a minute or two. It would have to do.

"If you see a flashlight beam, close your eyes."

No response came, and I wasn't sure anyone had heard my whisper. Only the sound of the surf filled the deep silence around me. I glanced at the spot where Tug had left us and half expected to see him there. That was when I realized that no bodies lay out on the beach to tell the Nivs they had found the correct place. If they didn't see the bodies, they might flash their lights around and discover those poorly constructed piles of sand.

With no other choice, I tore off my shirt, pants, and boots.

With a bit of sand mounded under them they might be taken for a prone person, at least until the Niv's got close. I sprinted back, grabbed one of the rocks, and reached the Niv's arrival point only seconds ahead of them.

Two kayaks glided toward the beach, each carrying two Nivs. I needed those kayaks desperately. Hypothermia could kill as easily as a shell, and Grady and Tia were about gone already.

With no time for anything fancy, I flattened myself in the shallow water at the edge and scooted out from shore barely in time. They were upon me before I had reached neck deep water, but they were so intent on the upcoming beach they never saw me in the water between their two kayaks. They passed by and I followed silently. When they reached the shallows, they shined their lights on the beach. One beam found my exhibition, and they nosed toward that.

It would have helped me immensely if one boat had beached ahead of the other, but instead they hit shore almost side by side. I came up behind the rear Niv on the left kayak and waited for the strategic moment when they would step out of the boat to drag it ashore—an awkward moment in a kayak. He would have a gun on him, somewhere, but he hadn't drawn it yet. I would have time for one quick guess of where it would be. Without a gun, my operation would fail.

They both floundered out of the kayak at the same time. I came down hard enough with the rock that I wouldn't need to use it a second time. With the out-cold Niv supported in my left arm, I searched for the gun with my right. I hadn't found it when the front Niv turned around, gun in hand. I leaped, caught him around the neck with my left arm, and grabbed his gun from his hand before he knew what had happened. I shot twice and saw one of the others fall even as I became overbalanced and fell backward into the water, the second Niv still in my arm. I rolled, holding him under and fired twice again. The return fire caught me twice and caught the kayak two or three times. I landed two shells in the shooter and he dropped where he stood.

The two lying on the beach didn't move, and the one I had rocked to sleep lay face down in the water. That meant I needed the one I was drowning. I dragged him up the beach toward the others, all the time trying to count how many shots had been fired. The Nivs would have put at least two shells into each of their tied victims, maybe more. For safety's sake, I fired a few more rounds to convince a listening Tug that we had all died according to plan. I put the gun to my recovering Niv's head.

"What signal do you give when you finish the job?"

He looked at me dumbly and coughed up water. I jammed the gun barrel in his mouth and grabbed a nearby flashlight.

"I killed all your friends, but I promise I'll let you live if you tell me the signal he expects. How many light flashes? Tell me straight, because if I don't see him leave, I'll kill you."

He didn't realize that I couldn't see anyone, but I knew Tug would wait out there somewhere, at a good distance, to receive a victory signal.

"Three flashes, wait five seconds, and flash three more. Repeat it until he flashes back."

I knew the direction Tug took when he left with the tender, but the gang wouldn't know that, so I turned the beam directly out over the water and flashed it three times, waited five seconds, and flashed three again. With no delay, three flashes answered from my left. He had waited in the tender close enough to know if anything went amiss.

With dead fingers, I tied the Niv's wrists and ankles with shoelaces I borrowed from one of his buddies. When I had secured him adequately, I rendered him unconscious with a nasty little baton I found on one of them. I pulled number four Niv out of the water and up onto the beach beside his friends. With an armload of guns and knives, I ran to the trenches and cut Rainy free.

"Here's a knife, Rainy. Cut the others loose."

At least four more Nivs might show up any second. If we hoped to survive, we should exit the beach before that wave of invaders arrived. We needed one of those kayaks, but the one nearest me had died from too many shell holes. I searched for the other one and found it—headed toward Hawaii. I pushed the half-sunk kayak out from shore so it could rest on the ocean bottom and not warn any new group of Nivs. I took one more look out over the water to remember the position of our kayak, grabbed my clothes, and headed to where Rainy knelt over Tia. She had cut her free and was trying to pull her out of the sand.

Blood trickled steadily from wounds on my leg and shoulder, but I couldn't take time to fuss with them. We needed that boat.

"Rainy, as soon as you cut them free, all of you must get to your feet and move no matter how killing the pain. You'll for sure die if you stay on that cold sand. More Nivs should arrive soon, and I have to bring back that kayak out there."

Rainy took the flashlight from me and blinded me with it for a minute.

"You're blue and shivering, and you're bleeding in three places. You can't go after the kayak."

My mind wanted to say, "Yes, Mommy, I'll stay under the covers and sleep like a good boy," but I shook off the vision, if not the lethargy.

"I thought they only hit me in two places," was the next best answer I could summon from the depths of my numb brain.

Rainy took hold of me and drew me to her. She held me close and kissed me fully. Those were the coldest arms and the coldest lips I had ever felt. She was icier than I was. It woke me to my duty.

"I'll soak the wounds in salt water. That always helps," I said and pulled away from her.

"You can't swim out there. You'll attract every shark within miles."

Did she have to say that? That thought had sloshed around in my half-frozen mind ever since I saw the escaped kayak. At that moment, I knew my friend had been all wrong. Maybe I wouldn't have run naked into the street to save my baby, but I intended to run half-naked into numbingly cold water while my three bleeding wounds announced to every shark in the neighborhood, "Here comes dinner." I would swim to that tiny plastic stick bounding merrily across the open Pacific. I dove in without hesitation. Who dared imply males were inferior?

Chapter 16

Somewhere inside of me, heat still existed. My chest felt like a giant furnace working overtime. I could feel the heavy pound of my heart and could almost see the heat radiating out as a narrow shield, a buffer between the cold water and me. Without asking my permission, my body had taken all the energy left in it to help my heart pump blood to my chilly brain and limbs. At the rate it worked, I doubted it would last until I caught the kayak. When I glanced behind me to see how far from shore I had come, I saw four kayaks bearing down on our beach.

A quick calculation told me the Nivs would reach the beach long before I could reach that kayak and get back with it. They would also for sure make the beach before I could swim back, but I would still reach the beach quicker by swimming than by chasing after the kayak. A shark couldn't have caused me to swim any faster.

My half-dead mind searched for possibilities. Rainy couldn't see the invaders and wouldn't see them until they landed on the beach. She still knelt by the rocks. No doubt she had cut the others free. If only she didn't talk loud enough to draw the Niv's attention. Even as the thought came, I knew it didn't matter. It would only gain her a few seconds, and I would reach the beach minutes too late.

I had stashed the Niv's guns near her, but if she found and used them, she would immediately draw fire in her direction, and she wasn't experienced with firearms. I couldn't think straight, and I didn't look toward the beach again for a long minute. My entire body worked at covering distance, nothing more. Niv voices eventually drew my attention. They had paddled close enough to see the bodies on the beach but hadn't gotten far enough around to see Rainy and the others.

Maybe for a second or two they would think that those were our bodies and that their buddies had beat them to the job and gone on. With no cell phone reception on that part of the island, they would act on their earlier instructions. The first four had taken the prize, probably because they rowed two to a kayak while these four each had a one-person craft.

Rainy had heard them. The others were down and she was slinging sand back over them. She tried to run to where my clothes lay and fell flat. Her limbs weren't ready for that kind of movement. All at once I understood what she was up to—she was moving my clothes and the weapons out of sight. I tried for more speed but instead ended up with nothing. Both my arms quit on me and refused to make another stroke, but my legs had enough life left in them to send me gliding toward shore. In some ways that was good because I had come much too close for violent movement.

Rainy lay prone against the furthest point of the rock wall. My gray pants covered her and blended her into the dark rocks as well as the sand would have done. I knew she had all those guns and knives with her. I also knew that she chose that furthest most point so she could get the guns to me when I returned. What she didn't know was that I had lost the battle with cold and fatigue. I tried to dogpaddle and felt like a jellyfish at the mercy of waves and current.

The Nivs beached their kayaks and didn't rush upon the bodies as I had expected. They moved cautiously, all their attention riveted on the four still forms lying there in the starlight. Those powerful flashlights should have told them that something had gone wrong.

When my knees scraped bottom, I discovered that I couldn't carry my own weight. I struggled forward onto the rough, gravelly beach, no longer kneeling but lying flat. Everything in me and on me had given out. I couldn't will one more iota of effort from my body. As I lay there helplessly, I watched the rock wall move closer to me. I closed my eyes hard and opened them again. Rainy, with my pants on top of her, slithered across the sand toward me.

From somewhere I found strength to pull myself to my knees.

She pressed a hard, cold object into my fingers, and I closed my hand around it. I knew what it was, but I couldn't hold it steady. It did this weird, foot-wide circular motion, and I couldn't find the trigger.

Rainy snatched it from my hands and shoved me face down onto the hard beach. It felt so good to lie flat. I turned my head sideways and tried to find her.

I felt weight on top of me and heard Rainy whisper in my ear, "Don't move. Your pants are covering us. I have the gun."

"I couldn't find the trigger," I said stupidly.

"You held the barrel. Be quiet. I think one of the Niv's regained consciousness."

"Probably the live one . . ."

"Ssh!"

"They'll see us," I half whispered, half croaked, but I couldn't move with her added weight.

She touched her cold fingers to my lips. We were so close I could hear them.

"Untie me. Get me . . . out of here. . . . They took our kayaks. They've gone for the police."

Panic ensued. They cut his ropes and helped him down the beach.

"Ride with Aaron. He weighs the least."

I lay there in dumb amazement. They never once turned a flashlight in our direction. They never once looked our way. If they had bothered to look, they would have seen that long, dark rock stretching out on the beach that hadn't been there earlier. When they were out of sight, the weight left my back and tugged at me.

"Warren, move up the beach a few feet. You're too exposed. They might come back. There could be more on the way."

It sounded like good advice, but I couldn't move. I tried to go to sleep, but she and Tim joined forces and pulled on my arms. I smiled at them but they couldn't move me. Finally they dragged me sideways to the incoming waves and rolled me over, and then over again. I couldn't decide if I felt more comfortable on my back or on my face. They never asked my opinion. Finally, I offered it.

"M-may I . . . sleep? For j-just a moment?"

"He's wounded in three places, Tim, and he's lost a lot of

blood. He was swimming after the kayak when the Nivs came."

"Fast. Swim f-fast," I added.

"Hush," someone said. That was all the recognition I got.

She draped my pants and shirt over me. They were wet, but they helped a little.

"Shouldn't we give him a gun?" I heard Tim ask.

"He'd shoot himself. Let him rest while we dig the others out."

Sound faded for a blissful interval, but it didn't last.

"I know you've only had ten minutes, Warren, but see if you can move at all. We want to set up camp about twenty feet further in. It's more protected and we can dig in like we did here and be warmer."

"But I already dug trenches."

I sounded amazingly similar to a whiny baby.

"We'll dig new ones. You can rest and watch. But I need you to crawl up the beach a few feet so we can get out of this wind and tend your wounds."

She was humoring me now. I wiggled one finger of my sandy hands. Evidently that wasn't enough effort to satisfy her.

"Crawl, Warren. Please."

"I'm on my back," I said helplessly and wished they would let me alone so I could sleep.

I felt someone shove me over onto my face. She and Tim both pulled at me again, but it would take more than their wimpy efforts to move a dead weight of my size. Not even a taser could budge me now.

"Warren, you have to try. . . . I-I think they're c-coming back . . . Do you hear voices?"

"I hear more than voices. They're coming like a flood. Let's get out of here . . ." Tim answered her sharply.

With my forearms in the sand, I pushed myself to my knees and crawled.

"Get me a gun," I croaked and made it to my feet, though wobbly.

"We've already played 'hide-and-seek.' Let's try 'king-of-the-mountain,'' came Grady's voice softly over to me.

"You try to climb these rock . . ."

"That's not the next line, Warren. The actor says, 'There's no place to stand,'" Rainy reprimanded.

"Have you noticed there's no place to fall?" Grady continued dramatically.

"Now you're supposed to say, 'Okay, I'll . . ."

"Stand. . . . Okay, I'll stand," I finished, playing their cruel but effective little game.

I had been duped, but even my fuzzy, frozen brain remembered that line from their movie. I wanted to murder all of them. Instead I laughed until I fell over—and then laughed some more.

When I finally made it to my knees again, I saw that both Tia and Grady sat with their backs against the rock wall and their eyes wide open. Thankfulness rolled over me. I struggled over to them immediately.

"How are you? Can you move your limbs, your fingers and toes?"

"Barely, but everything works," Tia answered in a weak but happy voice. "I think we suffered more from bad air than from hypothermia. Whenever he checked on us, he shot more gas into the bilge. I dreaded that gas more than the cold or the darkness or the pain."

"Tia's and Grady's heads were lowest," Tim added. "The gas probably settled more around them."

"I'm sorry I didn't get the kayak. That new group showed up too soon. I feared they'd catch you unprepared, and I didn't dare shout to you. I turned around and tried to swim back, but I didn't have enough fuel left in me to beat them to the beach."

"You probably ran out of blood, not fuel," Rainy corrected.

"I shouldn't have risked swimming after it. I knew that more Nivs could show up."

"I'm glad you swam out there. One more lump hidden under the sand, especially one of your size, would certainly have given away our hideout. God sent you exactly where He wanted you, and you weren't even eaten by a shark."

"I admit it was a g-good plan on God's part. But why didn't He bother to tell me I could slow down?"

"Maybe He saw the sharks directly behind you. Or maybe he wanted you to be so tired you'd stay put here until help arrived."

"We have to stay put since we have no boat. Have you picked your spot for a trench?"

"Right here. It's the least windy place. We'll dig down, and everyone can try to sleep a few minutes."

"Don't bury us again," Tia wailed in a tiny breathless voice. "I've been eating, drinking, and breathing darkness. I want to sit up and wait for morning. I want to see the light again."

"Me too," Grady seconded. "I don't ever want to lie down again. Can't we dig down enough to get a low wall of sand in front of us and sit up with our backs to the rock wall? This cliff feels warmer than the air. If anyone came, we could duck down. We have guns now."

That sounded like a good idea to me, and it cheered me to hear both Tia and Grady take an interest in life again, but I had to consider their physical condition too. Their recovery depended on getting them warm and cared for right away. Almost I would have welcomed the Nivs' return—just to get hold of some kayaks.

"We'll all dig. Everyone needs to get their circulation going no matter how tired they are."

"Everyone but you, Warren. You have bullets and bullet holes in you, and you've lost blood. You lie still, and we'll dig the trench," Rainy insisted. "Tim, would you please check those three corpses over there and see if they have any clothes we can use that aren't blood soaked? I also need bandages for Warren. He'd probably like to put his clothes back on, but he needs his wounds tended first.

Tim showed his weakness when he crawled slowly down the beach to the bodies. Tia and Grady fell asleep, slumped against each other and the wall. Rainy scraped a football-sized dent in the hard packed sand and studied it half asleep. I meant to tell her to forget the trench, but before I could speak, I dozed too.

Tim woke us when he came back with an armload of clothes and a candy bar. Rainy's hole had grown to the size of two footballs. She took one of the tee shirts from Tim and cut it into bandages with the knife I had given her.

"The one in your shoulder went clear through, but a doctor

will have to remove the one in your thigh. You got another hole in your side, just an inch away from the last one I bandaged. It went all the way through too. I'll tie them as best I can. I think you're out of blood."

"Then it would be safe for me to swim in shark infested waters now. Shouldn't I swim out and see if the kayak's anywhere in sight? Ouch, not so tight. My blood may be gone, but I still feel pain."

"I'm sorry. It's difficult to work by flashlight. Better slip back into your clothes. Sorry they're still wet, but maybe the wind will dry them. I don't believe you have any body warmth left to do the job."

It took most of the energy I possessed to dress in those wet clothes. They felt colder than my skin.

"I'll take one more look before we get comfortable," I volunteered and wondered if I would ever be comfortable again.

Like a drunkard, I struggled down to the water's edge. There was no sound of voice or paddle, no sign of any boat on the horizon, and no light but the stars. It could have been a desert island in the middle of the sea in view of its lonesomeness at that minute. I studied in every direction for sign of the runaway kayak and thankfully it didn't appear.

The tide had gone out a ways, and the ruptured kayak sat within reach, sunk but with enough of an air pocket to keep a small portion on top of the water. I waded in to see if it contained anything useful. I found its rope and pulled it a few feet further ashore with the help of the small waves washing in. The water poured out of its gaping holes, and I found two personal size bottles of drinking water in the bottom. Those were probably the most valuable commodities I could have found, and I wobbled back to divide the spoils.

I refused any for myself and watched satisfied as they emptied the bottles. Tim divided the candy bar into five pieces, and we sat shoulder to shoulder and tried to find warmth. Tia, Rainy, and Grady had dressed in the few pieces of clothes Tim had taken from the Niv's. Everyone acted lighter except Rainy. She wore a distant look.

"We won't bother with the trench, Rainy. They may not come back. If they do, I'll have the advantage of surprise, plus plenty of weapons. Everyone should lie flat on the ground if that happens."

She nodded, but didn't seem relieved, so I tried again.

"I don't intend to die from these wounds and leave you all to be murdered."

Obviously that wasn't her concern because it was as if she hadn't heard me. She might as well have said, "Go ahead and die. See if I care." I couldn't think of anything else that might trouble her. If they lived and I lived, what else could matter?

"You hadn't returned from the SAG office when Tug got us, Warren. You don't know the whole story. We signed out early that afternoon but couldn't leave because they hadn't wrapped Linda yet—the girl who offered to keep Rainy's cat for a few days. We stood there with all our bags, and Rainy had the cat in one of them."

Tia's voice had almost become inaudible. That had been a long speech for someone in her condition.

"Rest, Tia. I'll explain it," Tim offered. "We'd only stood there a few minutes when Tug came over and insisted we come see his boat. We tried to get out of it, but right then Linda called over to us that she'd be another fifteen or twenty minutes. That ruined our only excuse, and it seemed so important to Tug. We couldn't hurt his feelings again.

"We had our bags with us when we went to his boat. He led us down to his galley and fixed us all a drink. We felt strange right away. All at once, the galley door closed and he gassed us. I don't know what chemical he used, but we couldn't do anything to defend ourselves. Tug wore a diving mask and tank, so it didn't bother him. He tied us, crammed us into the bottom of the boat, and squeezed our totes in on top of us . . . even the cat one. I think that was the first one he put in. He didn't know it contained a cat. He closed the hatch down on us and everything became dark. We couldn't breathe, we couldn't see.

"We heard the engine start. It must have been half an hour or more before he stopped the boat. He came back, took out all our bags, and said he would dump them in the ocean because we wouldn't need them anymore. He'd left the hatch open, and I saw him tie them together with a weight attached. He closed the hatch on us, and we never saw the bags again."

Grady finally came alive to the conversation.

"Rainy, I told you the cat climbed out of the bag. He got

free in there. He sniffed my face once. You know you always leave it unzipped a ways so he'll have an opening for air. My head was closest to his bag. I know that I was loony most of the time, but I'm sure that wasn't a dream."

Rainy showed a slight glimmer of hope.

"I thought you said that to make me feel better. But why didn't the cat come to us? He would have come to me at least to get warm if he was still there—if he was alive. We were in there a long time."

"Maybe he found a place with better air. You know how Tug shot gas in on us again before he closed the hatch. Maybe the cat found a place to get away from it. I didn't see him ever climb back into the bag. We've all seen him do that, but only when you leave the top totally open. You only left a small opening—easier for him to get out than to get back in. I'm just saying that he could be hiding in the bilge. I don't know if he's still alive. The gas could have hurt him worse than it hurt us since he's so much smaller."

"I'd rather he died from gas than from drowning in that bag. Thank you, Grady. You were so spaced out that I didn't think you even realized what you'd said. After that, Tug came and taped our mouths, and I couldn't ask you anything more. If the cat's still in there, I hope Tug doesn't open the bilge and find him. . . . He-he could have opened a hatch further up and found him and never told us."

"Now you're inventing trouble. If God sent me out in that freezing water to keep us all from getting shot, then He knows where your cat is, right?"

For once in my life, I must have said something right. Rainy became cheerful, and when Rainy was cheerful, we all were—except I fell asleep and didn't get to enjoy it.

When I awoke, everyone but Rainy had fallen sound asleep curled in tight balls. She had fallen asleep with her head against my shoulder. I touched her hand and found it slightly warmer. The damp ground had chilled me to the bone, and a sick dizziness descended on me with no warning. All three of my wounds throbbed simultaneously, and I knew I wouldn't sleep again that night.

I rechecked the loads in the four guns I had collected. My

cold, fumbling fingers worked slowly and inexpertly. With two pieces stuffed under my belt and two on my lap, I tried to settle back. They afforded a genuine feeling of safety, a wall between us and the enemy—a wall that I could build in a hurry. I tried to move my hands and fingers to warm them so they would work efficiently when the time came—if the time came.

The only warm spot on me was where Rainy leaned close against my side. I needed to move but didn't want to disturb her rest. I breathed in the fragrance of her hair mingled with the fresh scent of salt air and found it difficult to believe that she lay here safe beside me. Only hours ago I was a desperate, wild man who thought he had lost her forever. I didn't know where to look or what to do. Now, thankfulness rolled over me so completely I forgot the throb of my wounds for a minute and sat there in awe, wondering what the future might hold. When this ended, would I have to leave this fragrance behind and go my lonely way? A short while ago morning had seemed too far off. Now it seemed too close.

Without warning, Rainy leaned close to me and looked into my face. In the moonlight her eyes gleamed like dark green fire.

"Are you in much pain?" she asked gently.

I drew a long deep breath, afraid to speak, afraid she would hear the hunger in my voice. I wanted to taste another of her cold kisses. The last one washed away in an ocean of saltwater. Now I wanted one to keep for my own. The silence grew more painful than my wounds. I saw tremulous lips only inches away from mine as she examined the hole in my shoulder. She was wonderfully tender when all I wanted was passion.

"I'm sorry you're suffering. I wish I could help."

And then she did. Her lips pressed gently to mine, and I couldn't keep from crushing her against me. She was alive—so alive. I hadn't failed her after all. I held this wonderful girl in my arms. She showed me her passion now, and in her passion she forgot to be tender. Her weight came against the wound in my thigh, and I suppressed a groan, holding my breath against the pain. We kissed again, and I forgot the pain, the cold, and the danger.

When she finally pulled away, she laughed and helped me retrieve the guns that had slid from my lap.

"And two more in your belt? Four guns, Warren? Aren't you acting a trifle stingy? Do you intend to defend us all by yourself?"

"That's my job. I can do that."

When she continued to look at me, my smugness wilted. Being the suave, romantic, affectionate male that I was, I handed her one of the guns.

"A token of my affection, Rainy. It goes on the first finger, right hand. If I fail you, I hope it doesn't."

That ended my lovey-dovey talk. I wanted to get to the real stuff. I needed to hold her in my arms again and realize that I hadn't been too late. I put my hand over hers on the gun, and she shivered.

"I'm glad to know you need me for something."

"What?" I asked, and my voice sounded almost harsh.

"You need me to hold your cold-as-ice hand."

"The coldness runs all over me. I'm . . . whoa . . . a boat, Rainy."

"T-Tug's? . . . It's not his, is it?"

The boat cruised slowly and shined a light along the shore. The light stopped when it found the three bodies on the beach. Had Tug brought back more gang members? My intelligence told me Tug wouldn't let any of the gang see him. Maybe the gang members had confiscated a boat. It didn't look like a Coast Guard boat.

"Rainy, lie flat. I'll circle around. Don't use the gun unless they kill me and locate all of you. You're their protector if I fail."

I scooted on my belly around the small beach, following tight against the rock wall. If firing started, I would keep it away from Rainy's direction. A small tender made its way toward shore, and flashlight beams told me it brought at least two people. Another light on the main boat searched the surrounding cliff tops, probably on the lookout for possible ambushers. My frozen brain began to work. Neither the gang members nor Tug would likely come back. Tug would be acting the last scene of his drama, and the gang members thought we escaped in the two kayaks. They would fear the police and would run the other way.

Two men came up the beach, their lights aimed at the bodies. I had made the complete round and crouched at the water's edge where I could crawl up behind them. I could see the pieces in their hands and hear their voices.

"Dead—probably Nivs. Not exactly dressed for the weather."

The voice sounded too cop-like to be a gang member. I could almost have cried like a baby—but that wouldn't have been cop-like of me.

"I'm guessing Warren lived through this foray—otherwise someone would have carried off their dead, that is, if he left anyone alive to do the job.

"Warren," a loud voice bellowed and resounded off the rock walls.

"Quiet," I growled behind them. "People are trying to sleep over there."

The darkness couldn't hide their shock nor the bellower's identity. I recognized Wade Jennings immediately, even when he dressed civilian. Though his height fell a couple of inches shy of mine, his weight made up for the difference. He hadn't been subsisting on LA starvation fare.

"Rainy, it's all right. Put the gun down. Friends have come to call."

I got to my feet and started to walk up the beach to her but fell flat on my face in the sand. Guess I shouldn't have tried to stand upright. Wade turned his light on me.

"All battered and torn to pieces, I see. We brought a doctor—Lauri insisted. How many places?"

"Three, I think. Someone will have to dig a shell out of my leg, but those four over there need attention quick. They've been gassed, drugged, and tied in the bilge of a boat. They're hypothermic and need medical attention immediately—and they'd probably be thankful for some food and water. Get them to the boat first."

He didn't listen to me but dragged me onto the tender and headed to the main boat. I must have been weak to let him get away with that. The boat had pulled in closer to shore and we arrived in a minute. Three men waited to help.

"Don't waste time with me. You've got four patients coming," I said as I tried to help pull myself aboard and evidently lost consciousness again.

I awoke in one of the ship's berths. The doctor must have

tended my wounds while I lay passed out and must have given me something for pain because I felt decent. Lauri stood there along with Captain Nobel, who smiled down at me.

"We searched for you all evening. We took one of my uncle's smaller boats, one that wouldn't be recognized."

"How are the others?"

"Warm, comfortable, and probably asleep by now. The doctor says they'll all be fine once they get some rest and nourishment. We'll bring you a tray now. You've lost blood and need to build yourself back up—doctor's orders."

"Coffee—scalding coffee," I gasped and tried to sit upright. Immediately the lightheadedness came back and my head dropped like a rock onto the pillow.

"I'll bring a straw with it."

When he left, Lauri held a bottle of water close to my face and put its straw in my mouth.

"The doctor said to load you with liquid. He removed the shell in your leg, gave you a tetanus shot, and cleaned all your other wounds. We can take you to a hospital . . ."

"Lauri, you know I won't go to a hospital. . . . Could you get Wade down here so I can fill him in on everything? We can't go to the mainland yet. We have to meet someone."

"We've already learned quite a bit by following all your leads and talking to people who last saw you. Wayne told us who boated you to Catalina. I also took your advice and went to Al Ertsly for help. He brought a copy of the accident footage down to police headquarters and reviewed it with us. Tug was decidedly prominent, almost ludicrously prominent. His every rescue attempt brought him directly in front of the camera. The police department's gang division located Armind and brought him in. He cooperated nicely when they told him that his supplier had double-crossed him and intended worse. . . . I got the impression you'd planted that seed in his mind."

"A spur-of-the-minute idea for a tight situation—I didn't realize it would accomplish anything."

"It helped considerably. Later, when Tug was still in cell phone range, he called Armind to arrange a contraband pick-up and a payoff for services rendered. Armind had to take the call in the police station, and Wade said Armind enjoyed leading Tug on to make incriminating statements. So if we don't get Tug tonight, they'll get him when he rendezvous with Armind."

"Tug plans to culminate his dealings with the gang at the rendezvous."

Wade and Capt. Nobel had walked in on the tail end of our conversation. The captain carried a tray of food. He and Wade helped prop me up so I could eat.

"We found Tug's boat a few minutes before we found you—no one on board and the tender was gone. We have no idea where to find him."

"How long does it take to swim from Catalina to the mainland," I asked.

The glance they passed back and forth at each other said that they must humor my lunacy. After all, I had lost a lot of blood.

"Not many people swim the channel. It's a rough undertaking," Capt. Nobel explained as he helped me hold the coffee cup. "I think good swimmers have done it in ten or eleven hours, but usually it takes much longer. The water's colder this time of year—too cold for that. Why would he swim if he has the tender?"

"For the same reason he blew up the yacht—to appear heroic and get back in the limelight, to be a star again. He won't swim all that distance. What is it, about twenty miles? He was dressed in a wet suit when he said goodbye to us. He'll stay in his tender, close by the mainland, until enough time has elapsed for someone to swim that distance. Then he'll send off the boat, or sink it, and be found swimming in the cold water. If I've figured correctly, Tug, the hero, should show up in the water about daylight."

"Most people who attempt the swim to Catalina do it sans wet suit. It's traditional. He won't be much of a hero if he wears a suit."

"He'll chuck that too before he's rescued. It wouldn't fit well with the story he plans to tell the police and press when they fish him from the water."

Like a good detective, Lauri got out her notebook so she could fill in all the minute details. I didn't mind because they kept the coffee and food coming, and for once I knew a smidgeon more than Lauri. However, she didn't have all those holes in her.

I enjoyed watching the shock on their faces at the audacity and cruelty of this man. Even for a cop, the situation was bizarre and extraordinary. At some point in our discussion, I must have fallen asleep again, but the next time I awoke I felt extraordinarily human. Someone had laid out a fresh, white, tee shirt for me, a couple of sizes too small but a wonderful improvement over what I had been wearing. My pants looked disgraceful, but I pulled them on and headed for the galley and a cup of coffee. Though still dark out, dawn was near. I found Wade there, drinking a cup of coffee.

"Shouldn't we take the tender and look for Tug," I suggested, but Wade only laughed.

"And miss the fun of possibly being the boat that rescues him? Relax, Warren. This will be too good to miss. You intrigued us with the trailer, now we all want to see the flick. Everyone on board has read Lauri's report. Tug won't be armed. He'll be cold and wet and miserable. We shared our information with the LAPD, so they'll watch the shore and all boats that come in—and warn any boats that go out. Maybe we won't be the lucky ones, but right now we sit in the main route across the channel and there are no other boats around. We're a big, important looking boat, we've got fishing rods set, and all our lights are on. How could he resist?"

"But what if he accidentally came upon those guys in their Kayak? He's smart enough to figure things out or at least become wary."

"Oh, that news came in shortly after you fell asleep. The Coast Guard rescued five men in kayaks due south of Catalina—and put them in custody. They were afraid to go back to Avalon, thought you'd warned the police, so they tried to row to Long Beach, got lost, got scared to death, and got caught."

"Then there's absolutely no way Tug will know his plan fell through?"

"None that I know of.

"I suppose I'll have to stay out of sight for a while, along with anyone on board he'd recognize. Wish I could see the fun. Did you bring a movie camera? He'll expect a big fuss, you know. If more than one boat was available for rescue, he'd choose the larger one—one that can contact shore and bring the press to the docks in time for his landing. I imagine he's already spotted his rescue boat by this time. He'll anchor his tender nearby it and wait for the right moment."

"We're counting on that. I need to be on deck now. It shouldn't be long."

Rainy came in as he left.

"How did I know I'd find you here?"

"We have to stay out of sight, Rainy, until they catch Tug."

"They already told us that. The doctor is checking on the others now. He finished with me so I slipped away. . . . Wish someone had given me a fresh shirt to wear. You look like . . . like you did that night on the beach in Long Beach after we escaped the gang."

"That seems ages ago. I don't remember how I looked that night."

"At first you looked fierce—unapproachable. I wondered where all the burning hatred and violence came from. It didn't take long to discover that you just liked breaking things and using your body—and now and then your mind. I began to see the real you, the good in you, and . . ."

The cook interrupted her speech and brought us plates of eggs and toast. They tasted better than anything I had eaten recently, but I would have given them up to hear more praise from Rainy. She must have been hungry because she didn't say another word after he set that food in front of her. She reminded me of me, and for once she outstripped me in the eating department.

All at once Lauri busted in on us full of excitement.

"They've spotted him—just like we figured. No wet suit and swimming fast—not like someone who endured cold water for ten hours."

"He's a fantastic actor. When he comes aboard, I guarantee he will exemplify heroism and exhaustion to the extreme."

"The captain wanted to start the engine and take off, pretend we didn't see him and make him stay in the water for a while, but Wade didn't want to take a chance of losing him. It would have been what he deserved though."

The tone of her voice reminded me that Tug wasn't just our assailant, he was Bob's murderer. Lauri had suffered the great loss.

"Come with me, quick. I found a place where we can watch behind cover. They won't let me go out there either since He might have spotted me on set."

Rainy and I hurried after her and crowded around a small window, open far enough for us to hear any conversation. Wade sat in one fishing chair and a man in overalls occupied the other one. They both looked intent on their fishing. The doctor sat in a deck chair with a cup of coffee and obviously enjoyed this unique break from his every-day medical schedule.

"I hope Wade is up to the acting challenge facing him. I could have given him some good pointers now that I'm union and have experience."

That got Rainy and Lauri's attention. They looked at me in astonishment for a few seconds before they laughed.

"Will Wade have to read him his rights before he talks?" Lauri asked. "That would ruin our chance to hear his outlandish story."

"I told Wade not to worry about that. The hatch was open when he told us everything you have on your report. Five witnesses heard his confession. We don't need anything more. We just want to watch him hang himself a second time. Wade said someone has a small video camera with them, so they'll probably set that. It won't matter if it's admissible in court. We have everything we need plus Armind's testimony as a bonus."

We felt the tension in the air when the drama commenced. Both Wade and the overall man stood and looked down at the water.

"Hey . . . young fellow," the overall man hollered, "don't mean to spoil your fun, but we'd appreciate it if you'd swim somewhere else. We're trying to fish and you're gonna scare them all away."

That ruined Wade for all practical purposes. He turned away quick and ducked out of sight of the swimmer. His body shook enough to rock the boat and his face turned bright red from trying to stifle his laughter. Rainy fell victim to the same state and laughed until the tears ran down.

The overall man nonchalantly turned away and walked to his chair, but not without calling out, "We got lines set out there. Be careful. . . . What's that? . . . Come aboard? Well, I don't want to be inhospitable, but it's not my boat. You want me to go ask the captain?"

He turned to address a question to Wade, but Wade kneeled on the floor again shaking uncontrollably. The doctor had lost it now too and was ready to bolt from his deck chair. Tug must have grown desperately cold.

"I'm coming aboard. Get the captain," he shouted loud enough for us to hear him.

A pale, thin man came out. He wore Capt. Nobel's hat, but it was three sizes too big. He stared coldly at Tug and didn't say anything. The man in overalls stepped forward.

"Found this fellow swimming around the boat. I warned him it wasn't a safe place for those kinds of shenanigans."

"I . . . swam all night . . . about dead. My boat . . . stolen. They tried to murder me. I need . . . the Coast Guard or the police."

He staggered and dropped to the deck as if he were about to faint. I had to applaud his efforts. He had managed to get onboard and get back into character in spite of Mr. Overalls. Wade motioned me to come out. They weren't going to let him tell his story. I was glad. I had heard and seen enough of him.

Wade yanked him to his feet and cuffed him before he realized what had happened, but that didn't subdue this man. With a frantic glance around him, he jerked away from Wade and bounded for the rail. I took a flying leap toward him, but evidently Mr. Overalls ran to intercept him at the same time. It was obvious Overalls didn't expect me to soar through the air between him and Tug. He thrust forward some kind of taser that zapped me but missed the intended victim. I don't know how many volts of electric passed through me, but when I hit Tug, my weight, not my strength, took him down.

Wade arrived instantly and secured a struggling hostile Tug while I still vibrated on the deck.

"I'm sure sorry. Didn't see you coming. I'd been saving that charge for him."

"It's a-a-all right," I assured him as I stumbled to my feet and gave a wide berth to the object he still gripped in his hand.

Just as I reached for Tug's other arm, Mr. Overall's jabbed the contraption into Tug's side.

"This one's for you. Don't want your feelings to be hurt, Mr.

Shark."

That time it got all three of us. Wade recovered first and told him to put it away before he killed everyone.

"I'm awful sorry. Guess I'm out of my head. I forgot it would get all of you. Honest, I'd rather it had gotten me than you boys. Next time I'll . . ."

"No next time," Wade said. "Put it away."

"Let him ride in the bilge," Overalls said, with more aggression than I would have expected from a man of his mild appearance. "Or maybe we could tie him on behind the boat."

We hurried Tug away and made certain he had no opportunities for further escape attempts.

"I guess everyone on board has read Lauri's report, haven't they?"

"Everyone," Wade assured me and smiled broadly.

Rainy rushed into the room and grabbed hold of me.

"I saw it all. Are you all right? I'm so sorry."

"Not your fault." I didn't tell her that I would gladly stand electrocution a few more times to get her to look at me like that. "It was that silly old geezer Wade brought to help him. I don't trust the man. Did you see his eyes? He's liable to sneak in where we're holding Tug and shoot him or something."

"Before someone kills you accidentally or otherwise, Warren, there's something you need to know."

Wade ducked discreetly out of the room, and we were alone. Here it comes, I thought. She is going to preach to me again. Of course, there is the possibility she intends to tell me she is madly in love with me—always has been.

"Yes, Rainy," I said dubiously but with a smidgeon of excitement and hope. "What should I know?"

"That geezer who zapped you is my father."

"The . . . the farmer? From Ohio?"

"Yes, Warren. He feels really bad about it. He wanted me to tell you."

"He carries a taser around with him?"

"It's a cattle prod. I knew he had it, but I didn't think he'd use it. He told me last night he'd brought it with him because he wouldn't go somewhere like LA unarmed! Someone gave it to him for Christmas a few years ago, but he said he never had the heart to use it on a dumb animal. At least he finally got to use it."

She laughed then, right in front of me. When she saw I wasn't laughing, she laughed even harder. My acting had gotten better. I stood there sober faced and offended. Finally, she kissed me. That was all I waited for, and darn fool that I was, I laughed right in the middle of it and couldn't stop—but I had enough sense to hold onto her so she couldn't escape.

"Rainy," I finally said when I got hold of myself, "I could get detective work in LA."

"Yes, Lauri told me she intended to keep the business going, possibly in LA as well as Chicago. She's made some good contacts here. . . . You know, I'm actually interested in the production end of the film business. I'd like to produce my own independent films. That's what I've aimed toward all along, and I can do that anywhere. Even Chicago might be an interesting location for a film sometime."

When I tried for another kiss, she held me back heartlessly.

"That leaves just two major concerns yet to work out."

"I'm tired of problems. Isn't the job finished? I'm ready for a vacation."

"Dad's kind of old fashioned, and I'm their only child. I know it seems strange, but it would mean a lot to him."

"What?"

"For you to tell him your intentions. . . . Ask his permission to date his daughter. He's right out there on deck waiting to apologize to you. This would be an excellent time and . . ."

I peeked out, and he most certainly stood there in a waiting posture. He also still held the taser in his hand.

"Rainy, he brought his taser. Haven't I been hurt enough?"

"It's just a cattle prod. You'll do fine."

I walked straight-backed out on deck to my execution. It wasn't about the taser. I'd gladly shoot myself with it to get out of telling him I wanted to be Rainy's boyfriend! Boyfriend! Now that sounded good.

"Did Rainy tell you I wanted to apologize?" He looked right at me and punctuated his words with the taser.

"Yes, but that's not necessary. I understand."

"You must have a daughter too. Believe me, I could have shot him, cut him into little pieces for fish bait, and not batted an eye."

I grew less confident by the minute.

"Sure, any father would feel that way about his daughter. I'd have done worse probably. We understand each other."

"We're friends then. Let's shake on it. . . . I want Rainy to see that I've apologized, in case she's watching."

"It would be a good idea for you to lose that prod thingy before we get to port," I recommended after we shook hands. "We don't want Tug to claim inhumane treatment."

He immediately walked over to the side of the boat and dropped it over. While his back was turned, I gave a thumbs-up to the window where I knew Rainy waited. I never expected her to rush out and throw her arms around my neck. When I turned to explain the situation to the old farmer, she sealed my lips with a kiss. This time I didn't laugh. At least the taser was gone. Somewhere in the middle of bliss, I heard Overalls say:

"No daughter, then. . . . I should have guessed."

Rainy heard him too and tried to pull away, but I held on for dear life. When she finally squirmed loose, I had enough forethought to change the subject.

"One major problem taken care of, Rainy—what was the other?"

Immediately her face clouded.

"My cat. I know it's too much to hope, but I want to check Tug's bilge. Is his boat still out there?"

"The Coast Guard is bringing it in. I'll tell Captain Nobel to radio them and ask them to leave all the hatches closed until we get there."

Rainy's dad still stood there with a funny expression on his face. At least the heat was temporarily off me.

"Dad, you didn't wear overalls on the plane, did you?"

"Honest, Rainy, I dolled up—new, sporty stuff. I'll show you them when we get to our hotel room. You know your mother wouldn't let me get away with overalls, but I couldn't wear those other clothes on board the boat or I wouldn't have looked like a fisherman.

I stuffed these clothes in my bag after your mom finished packing it."

"You don't look like a fisherman, Dad. Anglers out here don't wear overalls, but that's okay. It worked."

Before Rainy could reprimand either of us again, Lauri came on deck with Tim, Tia, and the pale man who had pretended to be the captain. No one had told me he was Tim and Tia's dad. Evidently Lauri had put together a regular family reunion.

"Wait till we dock, Warren, and you'll see how busy I've been. When you took off for Catalina, I called all the relatives and told them the whole story. I also notified the LA and Chicago police. The extras and the press would have been next if you didn't find the killer. Even if we couldn't prove anything, I figured there'd be safety in the sheer number of people who knew about it. The man in the recording wouldn't dare try to kill anyone else. Also, if the story had already become public, there would be no need to kill any of you. Their families agreed totally. It was the only idea we could come up with to keep everyone safe in case you failed."

"Smart move, Lauri. You're a good detective. You'd make a good cop."

Some of the shadow had lifted from Lauri's eyes. The investigative work meant as much to her as it did to me, and her deep involvement in this case had helped her as well as us. Perhaps she would find love again, like I had. I saw something in Wade's eyes that I knew Lauri hadn't noticed. Maybe it wouldn't take her nine years like it did me, or maybe it would always be Bob for her.

The rest of Lauri's party waited at the docks—one big family get-together. Tim and Tia's mother and a cute younger sister who looked like Tia stood there. Rainy's mother talked with Grady's aunt. Lauri had located her and flew her in from Texas. With everyone's lightened mood, Lauri plotted a memorable ending for each person's trip. The production still had scenes to shoot by the docks, and Lauri intended to let all of her party work as extras. Some liked the idea more than others did.

"You'll have to experience this at least once," Lauri announced. "I know the PA and the director. They'll make it possible. It's something you can tell your grandchildren."

"I don't have any grandchildren," Rainy's dad complained, but his wife gave him a not-so-subtle kick in the shin.

"Tell the cows then. We're going to do this," she told him bluntly. She made me think of Rainy, strong and stubborn—pretty, too.

That settled him, and he followed begrudgingly along with the rest. Rainy hung back on the outskirts of the set with Wade and me. I knew she only waited for news that they had brought in Tug's boat.

The whole story quickly made the rounds of the movie set. Lauri and her group created quite a stir on set as they stood around and watched the making of a movie. Tia's little sister sat with the PA, and he appeared quite smitten—again.

Finally, the call came letting us know they had docked Tug's boat back in its old space. A police officer at the pier unlocked the gate for us, and Rainy hurried on ahead. She rushed to board the boat but could go no further. Emotion had gotten the best of her.

"Warren, you'll have to do it for me. I-I c-can't."

Tears streamed down her cheeks. It was the most terrible minute of my life—and all because of a gaunt, battle-scarred cat that no one wanted except Rainy. I understood Rainy's state because I felt it too. He had gone through hell with us and never complained once. Gingerly I opened the hatch an inch. If the cat had died in there, I would smell it—even if it hadn't been dead long. I knew the scent of death. If the slightest odor reached me, I would send Rainy away while I got it. I leaned close to the crack and breathed deeply, staring into the darkness. A second or two passed before I realized it wasn't darkness I stared at but one large green eye pressed to the narrow opening. I yanked the hatch open and lifted him out. Rainy's shriek of joy echoed in my own heart.

She gasped and ran to take him from me. This time I didn't care how close she hugged him. I knew my time would come.

Grady showed up to share the moment and distract my attention. That helped. I would have drowned myself, instantly, if I had cried in public. Grady had something on his mind, but I felt contrary and didn't help him out.

"I've thought a lot about this police angle and . . ."

"Yeah."

"I-I really like the idea—the uniform and everything. . . . And there's more money in it—a lot more than I get."

"Yeah."

"Do you think you could help me? I know you're retired, but I thought you'd still have certain privileges. I'd want LA, not Chicago. There's more opportunity."

Now he spoke my language. He had shown signs of awakening just in the short time I had known him. Maybe the star-struck kid had found himself. He had always exhibited potential.

"Both LA and Chicago offer plenty of opportunities," I explained, warming to the conversation. "Like you say, the pay beats what you're doing. I can get you started if you're sure that's what you want. I guess you know by now how dangerous it can become."

Grady looked at me aghast for a full minute.

"N-no. N-not that. I mean, c-can you help me get a uniform—a complete regulation LA cop uniform and whatever goes with it? The extras with uniforms get great bookings, and they're paid a higher rate. It might even land me a day player roll somewhere along the way. And . . . and it's not just that. . . . I've seen how the girls look at the extras in cop uniforms."

THE END

Jean James was active in many outdoor pursuits before becoming a full-time writer. She collected live mammals and reptiles for international distribution, collected live venomous snakes for antivenom production, and was involved in sundry wilderness construction projects. She also worked as a press agent, a songwriter, and was the captain of a small, leaky cabin cruiser. She is the mother of six children, the youngest being her co-writer on this book—Mary James.

jamesauthors.com

Mary James began life as a musical prodigy—could read music before she could read words and wrote original songs at age five. By age seven, she was proficient on the guitar, banjo, and violin, and entertained audiences across the US with her vocal and instrumental skills. Since that time her life has been one long road show interspersed with TV, radio, and film work. Today this eleven-instrument-wielding musician is not only known internationally for her lightning-fast fingers and unmistakable vocals but is also an award-winning songwriter and book author.

meanmary.com